The Visitors

The Visitors
NATHANIEL BENCHLEY

McGRAW-HILL BOOK COMPANY

New York   Toronto   London

For
Peggy Stuart Coolidge
who knows a visitor
when she sees one

Note

This is a work of fiction, and the people in it are fictitious. The ghosts are real.

N.B.

M. V. *Nibble*
Harbor House Dock
Nantucket, Mass.
September, 1964

One.

The old Twitchell house was built in 1850, by a retired sea captain named Ebenezer Twitchell. Several families with different names have owned it since, but it is known as the Twitchell house because nobody has stayed in it long enough to have their names associated with it. In New England, you have to live in a house at least fifteen years before it stops being called by the name of the previous owner. Like most sea captains, Ebenezer Twitchell disliked the sea but couldn't be very far from it, so he put his house on the rim of a cliff overlooking a broad stretch of the Atlantic. Winter storms send up sheets of spray that have encrusted the house and turned it a soft, silvery gray, and even on quiet summer evenings the sound of the sea is always present. The house is as much a part of the sea as though it were a ship afloat. It is also generally conceded to be haunted.

On a cold, gusty day in April, when the surf boomed hollowly against the cliffs and the wind carried the smell of rain, an automobile wound its way up the road from the nearby village. As it approached the house the driver glanced at the couple with him, and hesitated a moment before speaking. The woman was good-looking in an unostentatious way, although her clothes very clearly said she came from the city, and the odds were she had never heard the stories about the house. "I tell you, Mrs. Powell," the driver said at last, "this house ain't been lived in for a few years, so it's likely to be a mite dusty. I wouldn't be showing it to you, only it's the last one I got. You seen all the others."

"Well, let's look at it, anyway," said Kathryn Powell. "It must have a beautiful view in the summer."

"What's the price on it?" asked Stephen, her husband. He was in his mid-forties, and had the pale, slightly haggard look of a man who is slowly losing the fight against city existence.

The real estate agent cleared his throat. "I'll have to find out," he said. "Last time, the people didn't stay the whole summer. And like I said, it'll need some work, so that'll come into account."

Powell settled back and looked dismally out the window, and the agent knew it would take some high-pressure selling before he would agree to a deal. But it was this house or nothing, and the commission if he could rent it would be very welcome. And the commission if he could *sell* it—well, he wouldn't let himself think about that.

As a rule, retired sea captains relieved their boredom by doing ornamental work on their houses, and Ebenezer Twitchell was no exception. The shingles had been notched and then set in a diamond pattern, giving an effect of almost Byzantine confusion, and the wide porch that surrounded the house was trimmed with wooden scrollwork that would have gladdened the heart of a scrimshaw artist. The gables above the second-floor windows came up to peaks like minarets, and the windows themselves, although boarded over, could be seen to have been decorated with scrollwork. The northeast corner rose in the form of a square tower with a crenellated top, and the entire house was surmounted by a cupola, in which one unboarded window stared like a blind eye out to sea. The house was silent, cold, and slimy.

The agent stopped the car, and reached for his bundle of keys. "Of course, it'll look different once it's opened up," he said tentatively. "You ain't seeing it on what you might call the best of circumstances."

"But think of the view!" Kathryn exclaimed, as she got out of the car and looked at the sea. "The view alone would make it worth having!"

"That's the way I look at it," said the agent, as he started up the steps.

Powell got slowly out of the car, and, ignoring the view, examined the house. It's so bad it's almost funny, he thought. It might conceivably be fun to spend the summer in a house as horrible as this—provided, of course, the beds are all right. The only thing I've got to be careful of is my bed; Gerlock said if my back popped once more he'd have to do a fusion, and I'm damned if I want to go through *that*. Powell closed the car door carefully, and followed his wife and the agent up the porch steps.

The house had a musty, dank smell like that in the others they'd looked at, but as he glanced around in the semi-darkness at the sheeted furniture and rolled-up rugs, he felt as though a cold wind were blowing on him. He rubbed his neck and shivered, and the feeling subsided. I'll be glad when we get out of here, he thought. What I need is a good, stiff glass of Scotch to warm me up. I wish to God I'd start feeling better again. I guess maybe it's my back, but it's certainly taking its own time. I'll have to ask Gerlock about it when I see him. A bad back shouldn't be giving me flashes like this.

He followed Kathryn and the agent through the downstairs rooms, while she peeked under furniture covers and took inventory of the items in the kitchen, and then they went to the second floor for a tour of the bedrooms. The agent used a flashlight, and Powell had the sensation of being in an Egyptian tomb, with the bobbing light illuminating brief patches of wall or floor or furniture as though reading ancient hiero-glyphs. In some places the wallpaper was peeling, and in others time-browned pictures hung askew and winked back the light from their glass, and in one corner was a dead bird, dry and dusty and ruffled. Powell pushed one folded mattress, and felt the crackling of straw beneath the cover. His neck felt cold again, and he rubbed it hard.

"Let's get out of here," he said.

Kathryn was surprised. "Why?" she said. "Don't you like it?"

"The beds are no good."

"The beds won't be no problem," said the agent, quickly. "We'll fix them up good."

"And anyway you've got your bed-board," Kathryn said. "Dr. Gerlock said that would help no matter where you slept." To the agent she said, "Mr. Powell has a bad back, and the doctor has told him to rest it as much as possible."

The agent nodded wisely, as though everything had been suddenly revealed. "This place gets real pretty when the sun's out," he said. "People come up here from all over, just to look at the view. Come to think of it," he added, almost as an afterthought, "if you was to rent this, the rent'd automatically apply against the sale price if you want to buy it." He paused, cleared his throat, and said, "Just thought you'd like to know."

"Thanks," said Powell shortly.

Something in his voice made Kathryn say, "Do you feel all right?"

"Now that you mention it, no. I keep getting chills."

"Then let's get you a drink. I thought you sounded funny."

"I'm all right. It's just that the back of my neck is cold."

She took him by the arm. "Come on," she said. "We shouldn't have brought you out today, anyway. You haven't recovered from the last bout."

"I just remembered," the agent said, as he shone the light

on the stairs for them. "Last time the place was rented it went for eighteen hundred, but I think you could probably get it for a thousand for the season. That's five hundred less than any of the others you seen.

Kathryn stopped. "Are you sure?" she asked. "Can we call that official?"

"Just about. I'd have to double-check, but I seem to remember someone saying something about a thousand if—uh—someone offered."

"Who owns the house, anyway?" Powell asked, as they emerged into the windy and welcome daylight.

The agent pulled the door shut, struggled briefly with the rusty lock, then put the keys in his pocket. "Right now the bank owns it," he said. "They'd probably give you a good price if you was to buy it."

"We'll cross that bridge when we come to it," said Kathryn. She breathed a deep lungful of sea air, smiled, and said, "This must be absolute heaven in the summer." Then she looked at her husband. "What do you think?" she asked. "If we can get it for a thousand, should we take it?"

Powell hesitated. He felt better now that he was out-of-doors, and the chills were gone. Still, there was something that made him uneasy, and he wished he could put it into words. "I don't know," he said. "Maybe we ought to look around some more."

"You won't find a bargain like this anywhere *I* know of," the agent said. "Most rents are going up this year, not down."

"With your bed-board and a new mattress you'd have no trouble sleeping," Kathryn said. "Stevie could have a room of his own, and we'd still be able to have week-end guests."

"Fifteen hundred's the lowest you'll get anywhere else," said the agent. "And that's for not half the rooms, not to mention the view."

"You *know* you're supposed to take it easy this summer. Where else could you relax the way you could here?"

"Got a TV rental place in town, too. They'll deliver a set right up here, and you won't have to get out of your chair from one day to the next."

"What is it you don't like about it? I wish I understood."

Powell sighed. "Nothing, I guess," he said.

"Then is it settled?"

"I guess so."

The agent jangled the keys in his pocket. "I got a bottle of whisky down at the office," he said. "Why don't we go through the formalities there?"

A half hour later the agent, whose name was Ed Lasker, stared at the fifty-dollar deposit check in his hand and smiled. He was undecided whether to bank it right now or keep it around for a day or so, as proof he'd actually rented the Twitchell house. Nobody would believe him without proof, but since the check didn't state what it was for it wouldn't be too convincing. He wished he'd asked Powell to specify when he wrote it out, but Powell had been so reluctant that he'd decided not to press his luck, and took the check as it was. Even if Powell backed out now, fifty dollars was fifty dollars, and Lasker concluded that the best thing was to get it to the bank right away, in case Powell should think of stopping payment. Then an idea came to him, and in the lower left-hand corner, just above the gibberish of the code number, he wrote: "Deposit against season's rent on Twitchell house." The fact that it was in his handwriting was in no way illegal, and it would serve at least to convince the people at the bank. And they, he knew, would pass the word around better than he could. Anyone who wanted his business affairs kept secret had two banks, the local one for everyday use and an out-of-town bank for whatever he didn't want to be common knowledge. He endorsed the check, took it to the bank and deposited it, and then went out for lunch. He had two ryes before lunch, as celebration.

The ryes, plus the shot he had had with the Powells, made him sleepy, and after lunch he returned to his office for a nap. He had slept for perhaps an hour when the bell atop his door tinkled, and he woke up to see the lean, gangling form of Doc Mellish, the local veterinarian. Doc Mellish was a building contractor as well as a vet, and he and Lasker often exchanged information for their mutual benefit. It was surprising how many areas were covered by their common interests.

"Hi there, Doc," Lasker said, tilting his chair forward and taking his feet off the desk. "What can I do for you?"

"Nothing," said Doc. He hooked the rung of a chair with his foot, pulled it out, and sat down. "Just passing by, and thought I'd drop in."

Lasker produced a crumpled pack of cigarettes, offered one to Doc, who took it, and they both lit up. There was a short silence. "What's new?" Lasker said, at last.

"Not much."

"Well, things should pick up in a month or so."

"Better had. Can't make a living worming dogs."

"I heard someone's going to take the old Gossett farm and make it into a riding stable. You hear that?"

"I heard, but I'll believe it when I see the horses. There ain't that kind of money around here." He paused, then added, "Least *I* ain't seen none."

"Me neither."

There was another silence, and then Doc said, "How're things with you?"

"So-so," replied Lasker, eyeing the end of his cigarette. "It's a little early yet."

"Yeah, I guess it's early all over."

"Take May, now. All of a sudden in May everybody wants a house, and May through July I'm busier'n a bitch with one tit. If I could spread that work over a year, I'd have no complaints."

"Hear you rented the old Twitchell house."

Lasker smiled to himself. He'd known it was coming, and almost hoped that Doc would fence around a little longer before getting to the point. "The lease ain't signed yet," he said.

"A man puts down a deposit, that's a pretty good sign he's going to rent."

"I'm waiting till I see his name on it."

"How long's the place been empty?"

Lasker looked at the ceiling. "I don't quite recall," he said. "It's been a while."

"Who're you going to get to open it?"

"Hadn't give it a thought. Like I said, I'm waiting to see the lease."

"It ain't going to be easy. Lot of people wouldn't go within a mile of that house."

"I know."

"Last people lived there had a cat. I recall they brought that cat to me one night, and if ever I seen shrieking hysterics in an animal it was that cat. Christ, I couldn't do *nothing* to calm it down. Finally got a phenobarb into it, and that helped a little. But soon's they took it back it ran away, and I don't think they ever found it."

"I remember. They left a while later. They'd paid the full rent, though, so it didn't make no odds."

"You better collect your rent in advance this time, too, or you may get stuck for the last half."

Lasker looked out the window, and thought a moment. "That might not be a bad idea," he said.

Doc stood up. "If you need any help with the house let me know," he said. "I got a couple of guys in my crew who ain't afraid of nothing."

"Thanks," said Lasker. "I'll let you know."

Two.

Stephen Powell's life had been full of near misses. In college he missed his athletic letter by breaking his ankle the day before the letter game, and missed graduating *cum laude* by unknowingly offending the man who read his honors thesis; in the Second World War, he missed promotion to lieutenant commander by three days' date of rank, and missed being among the first to return by exactly two points; and in his business, which was magazine editing, he missed being appointed Managing Editor and had to be content with the vague and noncommittal title of Assistant to the Editor. He had started off with great promise and considerable talent and almost unlimited energy, but his shafts had never quite hit the mark or were blunted by forces beyond his control. Gradually his energy subsided, and when it was suggested he take a leave of absence over the summer "to get his back in shape," he acquiesced with the knowledge that the job might not be there in the fall. He offered to do some long-range editing if they'd send the material to him, and the Managing Editor said that was a great idea and he'd see what could be done. So far, nothing had arrived. If it had not been for the fact that Kathryn had once inherited money from an aunt the immediate future would have been, to say the least, uncertain. As it was, Powell knew that his family would be fed and housed, and he seemed remarkably cheerful, but there were nights when he lay awake in an anguish of self-recrimination, unable to find out what he was doing wrong. His back didn't hurt him as much as his conscience.

Now, warmed by the drink in Ed Lasker's office, he sat beside Kathryn as she drove their car back to the city, and felt almost cheerful about the prospects for the summer. He glanced at her out of the corner of his eye, and thought how lucky he was to have an understanding wife—one who had, over the years, put up with his various defeats in a calm and sympathetic way. And not only was she understanding, she was also extremely handsome. Her profile was clean and Grecian, and her dark, unswept hair was almost always neat. Although his experience was limited, he felt that she looked better in the morning than any other woman he knew. All in all, he reflected, his luck in being married to Kathryn went a long way toward atoning for his lack of luck in other areas.

"I'm sorry I got so noodgy about that house," he said. "I guess it was just damp in there, or something."

"I shouldn't have taken you out," she replied. "It was my fault."

"I'm all *right*," Powell said. "There's nothing the matter with me." He paused, then said, "I wonder about getting a boat, to use in the cove. There seemed to be some kind of dock arrangement there."

"Would that be good for your back?"

"Well, I'd like to have *something* to do. Just sitting around all summer isn't going to be the most stimulating thing in the world."

Kathryn was momentarily quiet. "I hope I haven't dodged you into anything," she said at last.

"What do you mean?"

"Well"—she paused, searching for the tactful way to say it —"I. mean, I don't want to spoil your summer completely, what with your back, and your, well—"

"You mean my job."

"Yes."

"I'll tell you something. If I never go back to that job, it'll be fine with me. I'm sick of being assistant to a man who's scared of the advertisers, and I'd like nothing better than just to walk out and tell them all to go to hell."

"Where would you go?"

"I haven't the faintest idea, but I'm going to look around·"

"I'm sure Uncle George would—"

"And I don't want a job with the family, thank you just the same. If I do anything it's going to be on my own, and my own terms."

"That's fine," Kathryn said. "I think that's just wonderful."

"I know what I'd *like* to do," Powell said, with a faint smile.

"What?"

"I'd like to charter a sixty-foot yawl and take you down to the Caribbean, or the South Seas. I'd like to get you, as the song goes, on a slow boat to China."

"I'm right here. You've got me."

"It's different right here. Just for a change, I'd like to see you in another context."

"This house will be another context. You never have seen me in a thing like that before."

"It's a poor substitute for a sixty-foot yawl."

"What's sixty feet got to do with it? Wouldn't fifty-eight be as good?"

"Almost. I'd like room to chase you around in."

She smiled. "I keep telling you, remember your back."

He said something short and sharp about his back.

"Listen," she said. "Just for now, let's pretend the house is a sixty-foot yawl. Maybe someday we'll have one, but until then some sort of substitute will have to do. If you tried hard enough, couldn't you pretend this was it?"

He was quiet for a long time, and then he said, "I suppose so, but every now and then I think I've done enough pretending. I'd like to get my kicks out of reality, just for the novelty of it."

"You will," she said gently. "Believe me, someday you will."

When they got home their son Stevie, who was fifteen, was lying in a chair in front of the television set, alternately sucking on a soft drink and eating from a pile of crackers in his lap. He didn't look up as they came in, and Powell glanced at him briefly and went to the bar and made a drink. He was never sure just what Stevie was thinking, but he had the feeling that everything he said to him sounded pompous, and that Stevie thought he was a bore. He needed a drink to loosen him up before talking to his son. Kathryn, on the other hand, had no such fears; her conversation with Stevie was direct and to the point.

"Have you done your homework?" she asked, as she put her coat in the closet.

Stevie nodded, and sucked loudly on the soft drink.

"Yes, Mother," said Kathryn.

"'S'm," replied Stevie.

"Well, we've taken a house for the summer," Kathryn said. "It's a big one, and it has a beautiful view."

"Swingin'," said Stevie. "Where is it?"

Kathryn told him, and quickly added, "But it's right by the sea, and there'll be plenty of room for you to have friends come and visit. I know you'll love it."

Stevie swung around with a look of pop-eyed outrage, and for the first time looked directly at his mother. "Holy potato!" he said. "That's a dump! Nobody goes *there!*"

"Well, we're going," said Kathryn. "And you're going to like it. There's a cove where you can go boating, and I'm sure there will be plenty of other people your age. It's a very picturesque house, with a long history behind it."

"History schmistory!" wailed Stevie. "What am I going to *do* with myself? That place is Devil's Island! The Black Hole of Calcutta. Only creeps and spastics and the walking dead go there!"

"You've never been there, or you wouldn't talk like that. It has one of the most beautiful views on the whole coast."

"So what can you do with a view? Can you put it on a piece of bread? Can you drink it? Can you play tennis with it? What good is it?"

"Stevie, I'm not going to argue any more. We've taken the house, and that's that." Kathryn emphasized her point by leaving the room and going into the kitchen.

"And will you please quit calling me *Stevie?*" her son called after her. "My name is Steve, how many times do I have to keep telling you?"

"Stephen, that's no way to talk to your mother," Powell put in, and immediately wished he'd kept quiet. Stevie threw him a look of scorn, and turned back to the television set. "You can have friends down," Powell went on, trying to sound reasonable and as a result sounding plaintive. "There's plenty of room, and—and there's no reason you can't have a good time."

"I don't know anybody I could ask," Stevie replied, glaring at the television. "Any of my friends would spit in my eye if I asked them to come there."

"Then you need a new group of friends," said Powell. "Or, just possibly, you need to get a job for the summer."

Stevie glanced at his father. "Doing what?" he said. "Plucking seagulls?"

"We can find something. Don't worry about that."

Stevie lapsed into sullen silence, and Powell joined Kathryn in the kitchen. "I had a talk with him," he said. "I think he'll be all right."

Three days later the lease arrived. Powell opened it, and was about to sign it when something caught his eye, and he stopped and studied it. Then he put the pen down and hunted for the slip with Ed Lasker's number. He found it, and put through the call. When Lasker answered, he said, "Mr. Lasker, this is Stephen Powell. I've got a question about the lease that maybe you can answer."

There was a pause, and then Lasker said, "Sure thing. What's on your mind?"

"It specifies that I pay all the money on signing. Isn't that unusual?"

There was another pause, and the sound of Lasker clearing his throat. "Well, it's like this," he said at last. "One way of looking at it, I suppose you might call it unusual, but looking at it another way, it makes sense. Now, if it's going to put you to any trouble, I can ask and maybe get it changed. But seeing as how they've already come down so far on the price—"

"It's not the money I'm thinking of," Powell interrupted. "I just want to know why it's set up that way."

"Well, I'll tell you," Lasker replied in a confidential tone. "You seen that house, and you know well's I do there's a lot to be done before you folks move in. That mattress, the one you didn't like, that's got to be replaced, and probably a couple of others, too. We've got to hire people to open the house, clean it, and do some repairs here and there, and all that's going to cost money. If you was getting it at the regular rate, then your first payment would take care of it, but seeing as how you're getting it almost half price, they figured it was fair you pay the whole thing at once, so's they can pay to get it in shape."

"You mean the bank hasn't the funds to do it on its own?"

"Oh, they got plenty of funds. More'n they know what to do with. It's just a matter of equity, you might say."

Powell thought this over for a minute. "I see," he said. "Well, then—"

"Like I said, if it's going to be hard for you I can maybe get them to change it, but—"

"No, that's all right. I'd just never seen a lease like this before."

Lasker laughed. "Well, you never seen a house like this before, either."

"No," said Powell, laughing politely. "I certainly haven't."

"And remember what I said, too. If you want to buy, this rent'll go into the sale price, so you'll be making a saving there."

"That's nice to know, but I don't imagine we'll be buying right now."

"Sure. Just thought I'd remind you." Lasker hesitated, then said, "Well, I guess that takes care of everything. Oh—do you folks keep a dog, or a cat, or anything like that?"

"No. Why?"

"No reason. Last tenants had a cat, and I just wondered. Some cats don't take to the seashore—the salt gets in their paws, or something."

"Well, that's one worry we don't have."

"Fine. Fine. Well, nice talking to you, Mr. Powell. Soon's I get the lease we'll start to work."

Powell hung up and looked at the telephone for several moments, then picked up his pen and slowly signed his name to the lease. Then he rubbed the back of his neck, stood up, and went and made himself a drink.

Three.

To open the Twitchell house, it was necessary to get two of Doc Mellish's workmen and a full-time cleaning woman. The cleaning woman, whose name was Gloria Tritt, refused flatly to enter the house until the windows were unboarded; she further stipulated that she would work only during daylight hours, and then only if the men were present. She also demanded a week's wages in advance. Lasker gave her the money and tried to set her fears at rest, but his heart wasn't in it because he knew he could never convince her.

"There's nothing the matter with that house," he said, as he handed her the money. "You've just been listening to a lot of talk."

Gloria was a short, wiry woman, with gray hair and a pageboy bob. She looked something like a weatherbeaten jockey, dressed in an old seaman's foul-weather jacket and a soiled tweed skirt. She licked her thumb and counted the bills, then looked at Lasker. "Oh, sure," she said. "Then how come Milly Stemhouse went crazy there?"

"Milly Stemhouse was crazy the day she was born."

"Not crazy like she was after she worked in *that* house. And how come Jeb Hartwick up and died right on the front steps?"

"You know as well as I—his horse reared, and threw him."

"Sure. A horse that could hardly stand on four legs, let alone two. Something made that horse rear, and it wasn't nothing human. I'll tell you something"—Gloria reached into the front of her jacket, and from around her reedy neck produced a chain that jangled with charms, medallions, and crucifixes, and she waved the string of hardware at Lasker— "I'm going up there prepared, but by God if I see anything, or something happens, I'm getting the hell off that property so fast you won't see me for dust. I wouldn't of took the job if I didn't have a husband to support, and if it means I got to mess around with ghosts then he's going to go hungry. I'll mess around with lots of things, but not ghosts."

"All right, Gloria," Lasker said placatingly. "I'll tell the ghosts to stay away while you're there."

Gloria glared at him, and stuffed the necklace back into her clothing. "Some funny," she said, and left.

When she got outside she looked at the town clock, and saw there were still two hours to lunch. The contractor's men wouldn't have the shutters off the windows yet, and she wasn't going in the house until they did, so she figured she had some time to kill. Fingering the bills in her pocket, she strolled across the street to a small bar and grill, known technically as the Heart's Ease Café but locally as Mother's. Nobody knew how it got the name, because the owner and bartender was a burly citizen named Antonio Gianbattista, but it gave his patrons mild pleasure to call him Mother, and one or two of them were even able to tell their wives they had gone to Mother's after work, thus creating the impression they were dutiful sons. The deception seldom lasted long, but it was worth it while it did. Gloria nodded a greeting to two men who were sitting at the bar, then took a stool farther along. "Gimme a Carstairs," she said to the proprietor. "Neat."

"You gotta take a table," he replied. "I can't serve no ladies at the bar."

"Come off it, Mother," Gloria snapped. "I ain't in no mood for talk. I gotta go open the Twitchell house, and I need a boost."

"*Santa Maria*," said Mother, reaching for a bottle. "I heard they rented that house, but I didn't believe it."

"Well, they did," said Gloria, her hand held out for the shot glass. "And I'm the one that's gotta put it in shape." She took the brimming glass, put it to her lips, and threw back her head. Her eyes watered slightly, and she coughed, then reached in her pocket and produced a bill. "Let's have one more," she said.

"I wonder who they got to take it," Mother said, refilling Gloria's glass. "It musta been some foreigners."

"Well, they won't stay long," said Gloria. She drank half of the new drink, then set the glass down.

One of the men at the bar turned to her and said, "You remember the time they found a stiff in the cove by that house? They tell me he still haunts the place—goes up a secret passage, or something."

"Damn it, I didn't remember till you told me," Gloria replied angrily. "I'd forgot about that one." Her eyes got a frantic look, and she said, "I wish I'd never took this job." Then she finished the drink, and slid the glass across the bar. "I guess I'd better have one more," she said. "I'd forgot about that stiff in the cove."

The two workmen from Doc Mellish's crew finished taking off the shutters and then, seeing it was ten minutes to twelve, decided to relax and have lunch before going on with their work. They took their lunchboxes around to the sunny side of the house and sat on the steps, which were rotting and splintered but had not been included on the repair list. The taller of the two, a gangling youth named Fess Dorple, bit into a bulging salami sandwich and then, talking through and around the food, said, "I don't see nothing so scary about this house. It's just in lousy shape, that's all."

His partner was about twenty years older than he, and was short and grizzled. His given name was Arthur Warren, but because of a now-forgotten escapade in his youth he was nick-named Rabbit, and nobody called him anything else. He surveyed the contents of his lunchbox, picked out a banana-and-liverwurst sandwich and bit off one end, then said, "There was a time when I wouldn't of come near it, but that was when I believed everything people told me. Then I found out what liars people are, and I decided to see for myself. Haven't had no trouble since." He chewed his sandwich and stared down the road, where an ancient Chevrolet coupe was shivering and lurching its way toward the house. "Well, what do you know if it ain't Gloria," he said. "Drives like she's got a real good bun on, too."

They watched in silence as the car maneuvered the last turn, and then it plunged into the driveway and came to a slightly off-kilter stop. Gloria got out, and looked owlishly at the two men. "You been inside yet?" she asked.

"Nope," replied Warren. "We just been taking off the shutters."

"Well, I ain't going in till one of you goes first," Gloria announced. "I'll be damn if I go in that place alone."

"That's your choice," said Warren. "If you want to stand around till one o'clock, then I'll go in with you. But I ain't moving off this porch till then, because this is my lunch hour and I don't do nothing for nobody in my lunch hour."

"Rabbit Warren, you're chicken," said Gloria. "That's what your name should be, Chicken Warren." She swayed slightly, and caught herself on the fender.

"That's as it may be," Warren replied. "But I ain't anything except having lunch until one o'clock."

"Chicken, chicken, chicken," said Gloria. "All right, then,

I'll show you who's afraid." She squared her shoulders, took a deep breath, and marched up the steps to the front door. It was locked, and she tugged at it twice, kicked it, then turned around, went down the steps, and headed for her car.

"Where you going?" Warren asked.

"Home," said Gloria. "I can't be expected to clean the house when the goddam door's locked." She got into her car, and slammed the door.

"I got the keys here," said Warren, producing a bunch from the pocket of his overalls. "It's locked because we ain't been inside yet."

Reluctantly, Gloria came back, took the keys, and opened the front door. She went inside, and the two men could hear her banging noisily around on the first floor. They smiled at each other, and went back to their lunch. From time to time the sound of scraping furniture and muffled cursing came from inside, and then a scream split the air, followed by another. The men jumped up, their neck hairs prickling, and ran into the house. As they reached the stairs Gloria came hurtling down, wide-eyed and gasping, and Warren caught her and spun her around.

"What's the matter?" he asked. "What's got into you?"

"There's a bird up there!" she cried. "A dead bird!"

"So what? Did it bite you?"

"It's bad luck! A bird in the house is bad luck! Let go of me, and let me outa here!"

"Oh, for God's sake, Gloria, shut up," said Warren. To Dorple he said, "Go get that bird, and throw it the hell outa there." Then he turned back to Gloria, and forced her into a chair. "Listen here, you silly bitch," he said. "You got yourself a snootful because you decided this place was haunted, and you're looking for anything that won't make you a liar. So I'm going to take you through this whole house, from the top right down to the cellar, and I'm going to show you that it ain't no more haunted than Baxley's pizza parlor. Now get off your butt and let's get going. And remember, I'm doing this in my lunch hour, so don't give me no trouble."

They started at the cupola, which contained one reed-bottomed rocking chair and a dusty table. Through the window they could see a shining expanse of sea, with the surf breaking on the rocks far below and the shore curving around to a point that was blurred by wisps of fog. The view had a calming effect on Gloria, and she was somewhat more sober than when she arrived. Warren could see she was trying to find some way to excuse her hysterics, but was having a hard time. There was an empty attic below the cupola, and the next floor consisted of bedrooms, and two bathrooms. The mattresses had been taken from the beds and folded over the footboards, where they hung like monstrous pieces of bread, broken in the middle. On their undersides were circles of rust from the bedsprings, and larger, less definable stains that gave them a mottled and moulding appearance. The toilets were rust-stained and empty, and the mechanism in their tanks looked as though it had been dumped there from a great height. It was hard to imagine that the beds had ever been made, or that there had been running water, or that anyone had lived there. The whole place hung in mute suspension, like a Dali painting but colder, and more lifeless.

On the ground floor was the living room, a small study, the dining room, kitchen, and maid's room and bath. The living room had been furnished in what could only be described as haphazard Gothic. There was a large oak table, with scroll-work on its bulging legs and a faded red velvet runner on top; there was a wrought-iron lamp with a beaded fringe shade and a long shaft, up which climbed frogs and salamanders; there was a Morris chair and several varieties of rockers; and in one corner stood a near-life-size ebony statue of a woman, shrouded in plastic and with one black hand protruding in a supplicating gesture. Between the living room and the study was a stained-glass window, which threw orange and red and blue lights on the opposite wall, and the study itself was a jumble of books and chairs and crackling, rolled-up charts. The maid's room and bath were like any maid's room and bath anywhere—small, and gritty, and airless. The kitchen was the only room that seemed to have had any attention; it contained a modern gas range and a fairly modern refrigerator, and the dishes and kitchenware seemed in reasonably good shape.

By the time they had completed the tour Gloria was almost bored, and when Warren opened the door from the kitchen that led to the cellar, she said, "Never mind. I never thought the place was haunted, anyway. I just thought the floors might give way."

"No, by God, I said I'd take you—" Warren began, and then he stopped. A mass of dank air enveloped him, and he peered down into the darkness and tried to see a light switch. He couldn't find one, and he hesitated a moment, wondering what to do.

"Close that door!" snapped Gloria. "I'm freezing to death."

Warren closed the door and latched it tightly, and shrugged. "There's nothing down there, anyway," he said, and turned away.

Gloria spent the afternoon cleaning the upper floor and the cupola, while the men patched and reshingled a leaky spot in the roof. They had to put new flashing around the chimney, and all but rebuild the place that had leaked, and by the time they were through it was almost four o'clock. Warren looked at his watch, and then at Dorple. "Looks to me like quitting time," he said. "There's nothing more we can do today."

"You know it," said Dorple, and eased his way toward the ladder.

They retracted the ladder, put away their tools, then loaded everything into their pickup truck, and left. Gloria was in one of the bedrooms, trying to get the dirt, mothballs, and mouse droppings out from behind a dresser, when she heard them go. She ran to a window and called, but there was only the echo of her voice and the sight of the truck disappearing down the road, and after a moment she turned back to the dresser. I'll just finish this room, she thought, and then I'll go, too. Damn them, anyway. I told them not to leave me. Well, it's still daylight, and there's— She stopped, and her skin felt cold. The hell with this, she said to herself. I'm getting out right now. If they left it must be quitting time, and there's no point staying any longer'n I have to.

She dropped her broom and hurried downstairs, and without looking to the right or left went straight through the living room and out, slamming the door behind her. If she had looked in the kitchen, she would have seen that the cellar door was wide open.

Four.

The Powells moved in the first week in June, after Stevie's school was out. It was a bright, sunny day, but the wind off the sea still had a bite to it, and the surface of the water was speckled with whitecaps. As they approached the house Kathryn became rhapsodic about the view, and pointed out to Stevie the various boating and swimming possibilities, but Stevie remained glumly unimpressed. His only comment when he first saw the house was "Holy cow," and then he resumed the silence he had maintained throughout the trip. As far as he was concerned, the summer would be a total loss except for one thing: he would have his sixteenth birthday in August, and would be able to get a driver's license. Nothing his parents could do would stop him from being sixteen, and after that he'd be free. He had even put away some money toward a car, to avoid the necessity of asking them for theirs. But, although he had resigned himself to a hideous summer and was determined to make the best of it, he didn't for a moment want his parents to think he was anything except miserable. He'd show them what agony he was going through by being tight-lipped and silent, like a man bearing up under the torture of the Inquisition. He had studied the Inquisition in school, and had privately thought that those who broke under the torture were chicken, and deserved no sympathy. He felt that he, having suffered more than anyone realized, was inured to pain and would be able to stand the rack or the fire with comparative calm. He saw himself as a man of great calm, with nerves of steel.

As they went into the house with their first load of baggage, Powell saw how much had been accomplished. Nobody would ever be able to call it attractive, but Ed Lasker had been right in that sunlight made a big difference, and with the cloths off the furniture and the rugs on the floors it looked like a place that could be lived in for one summer, provided you had a sense of humor. There was a new mattress on the double bed, and Powell established that this room would be his and Kathryn's. It overlooked the sea, and was clearly intended to be the master bedroom. Stevie, who had brought in his portable phonograph and left it in the living room, came into the bedroom while Powell was transferring clothes from a suitcase into a dresser.

"Which one of these cells is mine?" Stevie asked tonelessly.

"Whichever you want," said Powell.

Stevie considered this. "I'll take the one downstairs," he said.

"You mean the maid's room? That's the worst of the lot."

Stevie shrugged. "At least it's got privacy," he said. "And my own can."

"Suit yourself," said Powell, and resumed unpacking.

"I didn't see any TV," said Stevie. "I suppose its broken."

"There isn't any," Powell replied, without looking up.

"*Isn't* any? Is that a joke?"

"No. If you want to look at television, you can rent a set in town. And with your own money. I don't intend to have it."

"Well, h-o-l-y cow. Now I've heard everything."

"Then listen to one more thing. You can have a perfectly

good time without television, and if you'll just make up your mind to it you can enjoy yourself all summer on your own. It's completely up to you."

"Boy, what a drag!" Stevie turned and stamped down the stairs, and Powell heard him slamming his belongings into the maid's room.

Kathryn came upstairs with a suitcase and a makeup kit, and set them down. "What's the matter with him?" she asked.

"Nothing that hasn't been the matter for a long time. He thinks the world is run for him."

"That's no excuse for bad manners. I'm going to have a talk with him later."

"My advice is to leave him alone."

From downstairs came the crash of something being thrown against the wall, and Kathryn said, "*That* does it," and turned and walked swiftly from the room. She went down and through the kitchen to Stevie's room, which was littered with assorted clothes, bags, and phonograph records, but Stevie wasn't there, and as she looked back into the kitchen she saw on the floor a porcelain beer mug with the handle broken off. There was a mark on the wall above it, where it had hit. She went into the kitchen, and through the window saw Stevie, standing on the lawn. She opened the kitchen door and called, and he turned around.

"Now what?" he said.

"Come in here," said Kathryn. "This instant."

Stevie sighed and ambled into the kitchen, and Kathryn pointed to the broken mug on the floor. His eyes widened, and he said, "Hey. How did that happen?"

"I'll give you three guesses. First, pick up the pieces, and then clean the floor and the wall."

"But, Ma, I didn't do it! It's my souvenir from Asbury Park!"

"I don't care what it is. It's time you learned to control your temper, and you're going to start right now."

"But I didn't *do* it. I was out on the lawn—you saw me! How could I throw the beer mug if I was out there?"

"I assume you threw it, and then went outside. Now pick it up."

Stevie kneeled down and gathered up the fragments. "Boy oh boy oh boy," he said. "This is going to be a great summer, I can see that. A real swingin' fiesta."

"It's going to be a great deal worse if you don't control your temper."

Stevie straightened up and looked at Kathryn, and his eyes were moist. "Ma, I swear, I didn't throw that beer mug," he said. "I was out on the lawn for the last five minutes."

"Then who did? Your father and I were upstairs."

"I don't know, but I know it wasn't me."

Kathryn hesitated. Whatever Stevie's shortcomings, lying wasn't one of them, and he was so sincere she hesitated to punish him. "All right," she said lamely. "This time we'll overlook it. But you were rude to your father, and your whole attitude has been truculent. It's time you tried to cooperate, and be a little pleasanter."

"What's truculent?"

"Arrogant, overbearing, surly." Kathryn could almost see a veil closing behind Stevie's eyes, and she knew any further words from her would bounce off him like rice thrown at a wall.

"Yes'm," he said.

"Now, go straighten up your room. It looks like a pigsty, and you might at least *start* the summer with everything in its place."

Stevie turned without a word and went into his room, and Kathryn went slowly upstairs. Powell was snapping closed an empty suitcase as she came in.

"How'd you make out?" he asked.

She thought a moment before answering. "I don't know," she said. "He swears he didn't do it."

"Can he suggest who did?"

She shook her head. "I guess he *must* have done it," she said. "But for some reason I couldn't—" There was another crash downstairs, and Stevie shouted "Hey!" and Powell and his wife ran out of the room and down to the kitchen. Stevie was standing, pale and shaken, in the door to his room, and on the floor under the kitchen sink was a shattered water glass. Stevie pointed at it, and then at a shelf across the room.

"It flew!" he said. "It came off the shelf, and flew across the room!"

"Now, that I will *not* believe," said Kathryn. "I excused you once, but this is too much. You will go in your room and close the door, and you will stay there until suppertime. But first, clean up the glass."

"But I didn't *do* it!" Stevie protested "It flew off the shelf!"

"Stevie, stop that this instant," Kathryn replied. "Lying will get you nowhere. Do as I say."

Wearily, and again close to tears, Stevie squatted down and began to pick up the pieces of glass. Powell watched for a moment, then turned to Kathryn. "Remember that house on Long Island that had a poltergeist?" he said. "The one that was in the papers?"

"Yes, and I also remember they had a teen-age child," said Kathryn. "I think that explains a great deal."

Stevie went to his room, and closed the door softly.

Kathryn looked at Powell. "What else could I do?" she asked. "Especially since he stood there and lied to my face."

"I don't know," said Powell. "I'd like to look into that poltergeist business, though. I always meant to, but I never got around to it."

"Dearest, I think it's wonderful for you to have a hobby, but

I don't think we can explain Stevie's temper away by poltergeists, do you?"

"No, but I'd like to read up on it anyway. There must be a library around here someplace."

Kathryn laughed, and started back upstairs "All right," she said. "Let me know what you find out."

He went first to Ed Lasker's office, and Lasker rose hesitantly. "Everything all right?" he asked.

"Oh, yes," said Powell. "Everything's fine."

Lasker relaxed, and he smiled. "That's nice," he said. "I knew it would be."

"And thank you for the new mattresses."

"A pleasure. I hope you sleep good on 'em." Lasker paused a fraction of a second, then added, "I hope you sleep *real* good."

"Is there any reason we shouldn't?" Powell asked mildly.

"None I know of. No reason at all." Lasker said it too quickly, but Powell decided not to press the subject.

"I'll tell you why I came in," he said. "I wondered if there was a library of any sort nearby."

"Well, Fisk Poltice keeps a big line of paperbacks, but if you was to want anything serious you'd have to go to the Atheneum, in Cranton. They got most every kind of book there is."

The Cranton Atheneum was a white, neo-classical building, with four Doric columns in front. It was dim and cool inside, and Powell crossed the creaking floor to the librarian's desk on tiptoe, feeling that every noise he made would echo throughout the building. The librarian was an elderly lady, so small that she must have been sitting on cushions to see over the top of the desk. Her eyes were bright blue and sharp as those of a fieldmouse, and her face was deeply creased with smile lines. Under the desk Powell could see that her feet, which didn't touch the floor, were shod in faded blue sneakers. He leaned forward and down to speak to her.

"Do you have anything on poltergeists?" he whispered.

"My heavens, yes," she replied. "The supernatural shelf's the third from the bottom on that stack there."

Powell thanked her and went where she indicated, and saw there was an impressive collection. There were books on psychic research and psychic phenomena, there were long and heavy tomes on the occult and the supernatural, and there were what looked like more readable books, such as *Ghosts in American Houses* and *Ghosts in Irish Houses*, both by James Reynolds, and then, exactly what he wanted, *Ghosts and Poltergeists*, by Herbert Thurston, S.J. He opened to the title page and saw it had been edited by J. H. Crehan, S.J., and printed in 1954 by the Henry Regnery Company in Chicago, and on the last page of the front matter was the legend:

DE LICENTIA SVPERIORVM ORDINIS

NIHIL OBSTAT: EDVARDVS MAHONEY, S.T.D.
CENSOR DEPVTATVS

Well, this must certainly be the last word, he thought. With a group like that to back it up, there'll be no frippery here. He scanned the chapter headings, some of which were "Ghostly Visitants That Bite," "Ghosts That Tease," and "Poltergeists before the Law Courts," and without further ado he went to a table and sat down. He had not gone beyond page 2 before he found what he'd been looking for. Speaking of a publication by the late Sir William Barrett, F.R.S., Father Thurston had written:

> The points upon which he lays stress as characteristic of the poltergeist are the invisibility of the agents, the sporadic and temporary nature of the manifestations, and notably

their dependence upon the presence of some particular individual—usually a young person and often a child—who must be assumed to possess strange, if unconscious, mediumistic powers.

Powell read on at random, and in virtually every documented case of poltergeistery these characteristics were present. Rocks were thrown, furniture smashed, people pulled out of bed, and crockery sailed through the air, but nobody was badly hurt, and after a while the disturbances stopped. And there was always a young person in the family. Powell closed the book, and thought for a long while. Maybe that's what it is, he thought; if Stevie's telling the truth, then it means we have a poltergeist, and we can only hope it'll go away soon. But it's going to be all hell trying to convince Kathryn; she'll have no truck with this sort of business, and the blame will land on Stevie. Perhaps if he were to get a job, it would keep him away from the house, and then—well, we'll just have to see. Assume it won't last too long, and hope for the best.

He returned the book to the librarian. "Would you like a card?" she asked. "That way you'll be able to take the books home, and keep them longer."

Powell hesitated. "I might, at that," he said. "What do I have to do?"

The librarian produced a card and a pen. "Just fill that in. Give your home address as well as your—I assume you're the one who took the old Twitchell house, aren't you?"

Powell looked up from the card. "Yes," he said. "How did you know?"

The creases in her face arranged themselves into a smile. "I guessed."

Powell completed the card, and handed it to her. "I gather the house is—uh—well known around here," he said.

"Oh, my, yes. Everybody knows about the Twitchell house."

"What do they know?"

She smiled again. "It's hard to say. But it's got quite a history. It's more than a hundred years old, you know."

"Yes."

"A lot can happen in a hundred years. We have a life of Ebenezer Twitchell here, if you'd care to read it."

"Not right now, thanks. I have to be getting back."

"Well, any time, then Mr.—Powell. You're here for the summer?"

"Yes."

"I hope you enjoy it. And drop in often. We're open every day except Monday."

"Thank you. I will."

He drove slowly on the way back, trying to think of what to say to Kathryn. She was a materialist, who believed what she could see and no more, and her enjoyments came from the readily accessible pleasures. Her capacity for enjoyment was great, and she was usually warmhearted and outgoing, but when she ran against a problem that had no visible answer she tended to tighten up, and fall back on rules of thumb that most likely didn't apply. She was a descendant of pioneers, both agricultural and financial, and she had inherited their impatience with obstacles. For Kathryn, if a thing was worth doing it had damn well better be done, and done fast. He simply didn't know how to approach her on the present problem.

As he drove through town he saw a lighted sign saying Heart's Ease Café, with a neon beer advertisement in the window, and it occurred to him that a drink might help him relax for whatever lay ahead. He stopped the car at the curb, and went into the café. Two men were sitting at the far end of the bar, and Powell took a stool one away from them. The bartender came toward him, saying, "Yes, *sir*. What can I do for you?"

"A Scotch, please," said Powell. "Make it a double."

The bartender drew a glass of water and set it in front of him, then selected a bottle from the back bar and filled a double-size shot glass. "Down for the summer?" he asked.

"That's right," said Powell. "Just arrived today."

"Oh, yes," said the bartender. He turned away to replace the bottle, and said, "How'd you like the house?"

"You mean—" Powell began, and stopped.

"You took the old Twitchell house, didn't you?"

"That's right."

"Never been in it myself. Just wondered how you liked it."

"Well, it's a little early to say. We just moved in this afternoon."

The bartender nodded, and wiped the formica with his towel. "That's true, too," he said.

"Is it all right to ask why everyone's so interested in this house?" said Powell. "Everywhere I go, somebody says, 'So you're the one who took the Twitchell house.' Is there something wrong with it?"

"I wouldn't know. Like I said, I never been in it."

"Well, what have you heard?"

The bartender picked up a glass, blew on it, and polished it. "Nothing much," he said.

Down the bar, one of the two men slid off his stool and approached Powell. He was short and dirty and had a white stubble of beard, and he wore a long overcoat that was fastened with safety pins. "I tell you something, Mister," he said, in a voice that wheezed with every breath. "You take my advice and get outa that house right now. Just pack up your duds and skedaddle, and you'll thank me for it later."

"Shut up, Shorty," said the bartender. "Get back to your stool."

The man ignored the bartender, and brought his face close

to Powell's. He smelled of stale whisky, and his teeth were black and jagged. "You got a family?" he asked.

"Yes," Powell replied. "Why?"

"Where are they?"

"At the house, I assume."

"Shorty, I told you to shut up!" the bartender snapped. "Now, get back to your place before I lose my temper."

"You keep outa this, Mother," said the man. "I'm doing the man a favor." To Powell he went on, "If you want to see your family again, you get off that stool and get them outa that house before sundown, and don't come back. That's all I got to say." He glared at the bartender, and shuffled out onto the street.

"Don't pay him no mind," said the bartender. "He's drunk, and a little crazy. I didn't see how drunk he was before, or I wouldn't of served him."

"Is that what all this is about?" Powell asked. "Is it supposed to be haunted?"

"Hell, I don't know. Like I said, you hear all sorts of things. Any time a house is empty for a while, people start making up stories." He turned to the other man at the bar and said, "You worked up there, Rabbit. Did it seem haunted to you?"

Robert Warren shook his head. "Nope," he said. "Went through it from top to cellar—well, almost—and there wasn't nothing but a dead bird." He chuckled. "Scared the ass off Gloria, though."

"What did?" asked Powell. "The bird?"

Warren nodded, smiling. "She run across it when she was dusting."

The bartender turned to Powell. "You see?" he said. "The only person who's *been* there says it ain't haunted. It's only the ignorant bastards like Shorty who believe the stories." He looked at Powell's glass, which was empty, and said, "Here,

let me touch that up. On the house—this house, I mean."
He laughed.

"Thanks," said Powell, absent-mindedly. "Just one, and
then I'd better be going." He glanced at his watch and saw it
was long past the hour he had said he'd be away.

It was nearing sunset when he reached the house, and the
upper windows were squares of bright orange. Pale, lemon-
yellow light shone in the living-room windows, and the rest of
the house was dark, silhouetted against the slate-colored sky.
The drinks had made him slightly more confident, and as he
mounted the squeaky porch steps he could understand why
people should make up stories about the place, but he was in
no way concerned by them. The poltergeist—if such it was
—didn't worry him, and in his state of mild euphoria he even
felt he could convince Kathryn of its existence. Or at least of
the possibility of its existence; he himself was by no means sure,
but he wanted to give Stevie the benefit of the doubt.

Kathryn was arranging flowers in the living room when he
came in. The field behind the house was white with daisies,
and she had cut a few dozen and put them in vases. She
looked at him and smiled. "How was your afternoon?" she
asked.

"Very interesting," he replied, rubbing his hands together.
"V-e-e-ry interesting. Would you like a drink?"

"I'd love one."

"I'll get out the ice. Where's Stevie?"

"In his room. We haven't had supper yet."

Powell looked at his watch. "Don't you think he's been
there long enough? Normally, we'd be having supper about
now."

She continued to arrange the flowers. "Whatever you say,"
she replied.

He felt a draft as he went into the kitchen, and noticed that the cellar door was open. He closed it, and latched it tightly, then knocked on Stevie's door.

"What?" came Stevie's voice.

"General Quarters. All hands on deck." He opened the door, and saw Stevie lying on his bed in the semi-darkness, staring at the ceiling. "All prisoners are released," said Powell. "The brig is open."

Stevie continued to lie there, saying nothing.

"Are you all right?" Powell asked.

There was a pause, then Stevie said, "I guess that depends on what you mean by all right."

"I mean, you're not sick or anything."

"Nope."

"O.K. You're on your own. Supper won't be for a while yet." He got ice from the refrigerator, made drinks for Kathryn and himself, and took them into the living room. He gave one to her, then sat in the Morris chair. "Why don't you relax for a while?" he said.

She sat down tentatively, almost uneasily, and took a sip of her drink. From the back room came the tinny sounds of voice-and-guitar music from Stevie's phonograph. "Well," she said. "Tell me what you found out."

"I went to the library in Cranton, and I did some fascinating reading."

"Oh?"

"Yes. It seems that poltergeists have been known for centuries, and all over the world. Right down to the present, in fact. There are documents—"

"Good Lord, I forgot to take the chops out of the freezer," Kathryn said, standing up. "Go ahead—I can hear you. There are documents about what?"

"There are documents as to what poltergeists have done," Powell said, raising his voice as Kathryn disappeared into the kitchen. "There are some present-day documents that have been signed by reliable witnesses, and there seems to be no doubt that—"

"What do you want for a vegetable?" Kathryn called. "There's frozen spinach, peas, or beets."

"Spinach!" shouted Powell. "And the hell with it," he added more quietly.

In a few moments Kathryn was back. "I'm sorry," she said, sitting down. "Those chops are like rocks, and I completely forgot them. Now, what were you saying?"

"What I'm getting at is the fact that poltergeists are by no means old wives' tales. There's a book, written by one Jesuit and edited by another, that piles up an impressive list of evidence on the—"

"I thought Jesuits weren't supposed to believe in ghosts," put in Kathryn. "Except of course the obvious one."

"That's why this is so impressive. And he says he's not prepared to explain *why* they are, any more than he can convince a materialist of the possibility of miracles, but he says the evidence leaves him no choice but to believe that these phenomena can, and do, exist. And the most interesting thing to me was the matter of the mediums. In almost all—"

"Do you have a pencil?" Kathryn asked, standing up.

Powell reached in his pocket. "Do you want to hear what I'm saying, or don't you?" he asked, as he produced a pencil.

"Of course I do, dear. I just have to make a marketing list for tomorrow." She found a piece of paper on the table, and scribbled on it. "If I don't put something down the minute I think of it, I'll never remember it again." She sat down, and smiled. "Go on."

Powell took a deep breath. "The point of the whole thing is that in almost every case the medium—the person through whom the poltergeist gets into the house—is a young person, sometimes a child but sometimes also a teenager."

"I wonder why."

"I have no idea, but there it is. "

"Well, isn't that interesting. I thought we might have some people down for the week end following this one, after we're settled. Whom would you like to invite?"

"Damn it all, will you listen to what I'm saying?"

"I have been listening! What do you want me to do— have it tattooed on me?"

"Don't you see what I'm getting at?"

"If you want me to be honest, no."

"If the medium is always a young person, isn't it possible that Stevie could be the medium for a poltergeist here? Wouldn't that explain the things that were thrown, and his denial of it?"

"Oh, really. You said yourself he was in a foul temper."

"I know, but isn't it *possible* he could be telling the truth?"

"Stevie a medium? Don't be ridiculous."

"I'm not! I've just been telling you that all over the world—"

Kathryn began to laugh. "That's the most fantastic idea I've ever heard. You mean he could wrap himself in a sheet, and hold séances, and commune with the dead—Stephen, you've been drinking."

"I have not! Well—yes, but that has nothing to do with it. It's not that kind of medium. I think the words he used were that the child had 'strange, if unconscious, mediumistic powers.' In other words—" He stopped, as he saw Stevie in the door. "Hi," he said. "What can I do for you?"

"Is there any root beer in the house?" Stevie asked.

"I'll put it on the list," said Kathryn. She started to write it down, and from Stevie's room came the crash and clatter of phonograph records. Powell and Kathryn jumped up and followed Stevie into his room, around which records were strewn as though hit by an explosion.

"Hey, what's going on here?" Stevie shouted. "Look at my records!"

"Where did you leave them?" Kathryn asked.

"Right here. I had them in a pile right on the table, and I was sorting through them."

"The pile toppled, that's all. You probably had it too high."

"I didn't! I was very careful."

Kathryn looked around the room. "There's no other explanation," she said. "I think it would be better if you put them in two piles, or better yet a rack. Tomorrow we'll see if we can buy a rack in town."

Powell said nothing, and went slowly back to the living room. In a few moments Kathryn joined him, and there was a short silence before he said, "Now do you see what I mean?"

"I see Stevie piles his records too high, if that's what you mean. What else?"

Powell sighed. "Nothing," he said.

When, at last, the three of them sat down to supper, they were in a subdued mood. Conversation was limited to the requirements of eating, and about halfway through the meal Powell made up his mind to broach the idea he'd been toying with since late afternoon. As casually as possible, he said, "How's the car fund coming, Stevie?"

Wearily, almost plaintively, Stevie said, "Hey, please, will you just *try* to call me Steve? Once a day, even? This Stevie business is driving me bughouse."

"I'm sorry," said Powell. He cleared his throat. "Tell me, Steve, how's the car fund coming?"

"Not too good. I have maybe fifty skins."

"You'll never get anything with that."

"Don't I know. What I'd like is a stripped-down Chevy frame with a Cadillac engine, and outsize rear wheels for—"

"Let's be sensible. What you'll get is an old car with a stick shift. Probably a sedan."

"I know. But I can dream, can't I?"

"You're going to need at least three hundred dollars to get anything you can pass your test in. It occurs to me that the best way to do that is to get a job."

Both Stevie and Kathryn stared at him, and Stevie was the first to speak. "A *job?*" he said. "Doing what?"

"I don't know, but I'll make a bargain with you. If you get a job, I'll match whatever you make a week, and put it in the car fund. That way, you should have enough money by August."

Stevie considered this for a moment. "You're on," he said. "Suppose I get a job for five hundred a week—will you match that?"

"Uh—yes," said Powell, knowing he was safe.

"Hot spitooley," said Stevie. "What do I do, advertise?"

"The best thing is to go to the village and ask around. I'll see if Mr. Lasker has any ideas."

For the first time in a long while, Stevie showed enthusiasm. "If I get five hundred and you give me five hundred, that's a thousand a week; from now to August is like eight weeks—that's eight thousand skins, maybe nine—"

"I wouldn't count on five hundred," said Powell. "You'll be lucky if you get fifty."

"I know, but five hundred is an easier number to figure with."

Powell didn't say anything, because he realized that even at fifty dollars a week he had committed himself to more money than he had on hand. I'm going to have to start thinking about a job for myself, he thought. And the real problem is there's nothing around here I can do. I'm a specialist, with no place to specialize.

They went to bed early and Powell lay awake, staring into the unfamiliar darkness and wondering what he was going to do. He was so immersed in his own problems that he forgot the stories about the house, and when the cellar door swung open with a bang, he assumed it was Stevie moving about in the kitchen.

Five.

He found the door open next morning, and figured what it needed was a new latch. There was nothing visibly wrong with the present one, but it was annoying to have to keep closing the door, and the draft from the cellar was faintly chilling. I wonder what's down there, he thought. If there's nothing important I might even nail the door closed, or get a lock for it. He started down the stairs, looking for a light, and after three steps he stopped. There was a smell that was something like lilacs but with indescribably unpleasant overtones, and the back of his neck became so cold he started to shiver. The hell with this, he thought. There's nothing here I want. He went back up, closed the door, and examined the latch to see how to secure it. He decided that a simple bolt would be the answer, and made a mental note to buy one when he saw Ed Lasker about Stevie's job. Steve's job. He'd have to remember to stop calling him Stevie. Pleased with the idea of having a project, he made orange juice for himself and his still-sleeping family, cooked and ate a large breakfast, and stacked the dishes in the sink. All at once he felt better than he'd felt in years. I guess this is what I need, he thought. Get away from the rat race, and putter about the house. It's too bad I can't make a little money while I'm at it.

He went outside, and inhaled deeply. The air smelled of brine and seaweed, and was warmer than yesterday. The sea was calm, and reflected the morning sun in his eyes, but the horizon was obscured by low-lying fog that blurred the details farther out. Quiet, gentle swells came slowly out of the fog and broke on the rocks of the cove. From somewhere far down the coast, a foghorn hooted hollowly. On an impulse, Powell set out to explore the cove, and see if there was some easy way to get to the water. His back had been better recently, and he reasoned that if there was any kind of path he'd have no trouble.

He found a path, which led steeply down across the rocks, and when he got to the bottom there was a flat space like a platform, from which projected the remnants of a dock. The shape of the cove protected the dock from the direct force of the sea, but the water rose and fell with each wave, and Powell knew that in a heavy sea the place would be all hell for a small boat. Which was probably why the dock had been allowed to disintegrate. Looking around, he saw behind him a cleft in the rock unlike any of the blowholes made by the sea, and he went to it and peered inside. It was large enough to admit a man, and as far as he could see the footing was even, so he squeezed inside and moved cautiously forward. Very shortly he was in darkness, and from the quality of the air he could tell it was a tunnel that went on for a considerable distance. Suddenly there was a blast of air against him, and the same ugly lilac smell that had come from the cellar, and Powell ran out of the tunnel and into the daylight, gasping and shivering and possessed by a nameless terror. He stood for several minutes, looking at the entrance and trying to find an explanation for his fear, but none came to him. It was now clear what the tunnel was; it led from the cove up to the cellar of the house, and the sea-driven wind was what kept opening the cellar door. But why the smell, and why the fear? He finally concluded that the smell must be rotting vegetation of some sort—probably not lilacs, but something that gave the same impression—and the fear simply came from the suddenness with which the blast hit him. There could be no other reason; it was the fear of the unknown. If he were to go in there again he'd know what to expect, and it would be all right. He thought for a moment of testing the theory, then decided there was no need to. As long as he knew what it was, there was nothing to be afraid of. He turned and climbed slowly up the path to the house.

In the village he bought a brass bolt and screws, and then went to see Ed Lasker. He told him his idea for Steve, and Lasker gave him three or four people to call. Then, in an offhand way, Powell said, "I went down to the cove this morning."

Lasker eyed him quietly. "Oh?" he said. "Why?"

"Just looking around. I gather someone used to keep a boat there."

"That place is no good for boats. You'd best stay clear of it."

"Why?"

"Them rocks get slippery. You fall off there and crack your head, and next thing you know you're crab bait."

"There's a tunnel that goes up to the house, isn't there?"

"Used to be. It's been bricked up."

"But there's a breeze that comes through. It keeps opening the cellar door."

Lasker shook his head. "Been bricked up for years," he said.

"Then what opens the door?"

"Probably warped. Them old houses don't fit so good in the joints."

"Well, I'm going to put a bolt on it. I hope the owners won't mind."

"Not at all. Put on anything you want."

When he got back to the house, Kathryn was finishing her breakfast. She was still in her dressing gown, but she had put on rudimentary makeup and wore a scarf around her hair, and the scars of sleep on her face showed how deeply she had slept. She looked fresh, and pretty, and ten years younger than she had the day before. "Good morning!" she said. "When did you get up?"

"Around seven," Powell replied. "The sun woke me, so I figured I might as well get up." He took the bolt and screws out of the envelope, and went to the cellar door to measure for screw holes. "This bloody door keeps flying open," he said. "I got Lasker's permission to put a bolt on it."

"You know something?" Kathryn said. "I really don't mind this house. It's ugly, and it's in awful shape, but I think it's got a funny kind of charm. Do you know what I mean?"

Powell started the first screw into the wood. "Not exactly," he said.

"It's hard to explain. But its very ugliness gives it personality."

Powell tightened the screw, and started another. "Uh huh," he said. "Personality I'll grant you."

"But you don't like it?"

"I didn't say that. But I don't see us buying it."

"I don't know. If we were suddenly to fall into a lot of money, I could see buying this and doing it over, and I'll bet in a few years we'd have something pretty great. And that's not even considering the view."

"Well, we'll think about that when we fall into a lot of money. Right now, all I have to worry about is making enough to match whatever Steve makes."

She left the sink and came to him. "Look at me," she said, and he straightened up. "One thing I don't want you to do is worry. We've got enough to keep us going, and anything you make is so much gravy. But I don't want you to worry about it because worrying is just going to make you sick again, **and** you'll be worse off than before."

"I'll try," said Powell. "But I don't think worry ever slipped a disc."

She put her arms around his neck. "Just don't worry," she said. "Don't worry about anything, and try to pretend this is a sixty-foot yawl." She kissed him.

The door to the maid's room opened, and Steve came out. His hair was tousled, and his eyes were bleary, and he had apparently slept in a pair of old track pants. "Holy cow," he said. "Don't you people ever sleep?"

"I was saying good morning to your father," Kathryn replied. "And it's perfectly legal, so don't complain."

"That's O.K. by me, but you do have to run around the house all night to prove it?"

"What do you mean?"

"I mean whoever was hacking around the kitchen last night made so much noise I couldn't sleep."

Kathryn glanced at Powell. "Let that be a lesson to you," she said. "When you raid the icebox, do it quietly."

"I didn't raid the icebox," Powell replied. "I never got out of bed."

"Maybe you walk in your sleep," said Steve. "Somebody was down here, that's for sure."

"I thought it was you," said Powell. "I heard a door, and thought you'd got up."

"This was more than a door," said Steve, reaching for a box of cereal. "This was somebody walking—back and forth, up and down, in and out—I thought I'd go nuts." He poured the cereal into a dish, and slumped down at the kitchen table.

"You must have been having a nightmare," Kathryn said. "First night in a new house, you often dream strange things."

Steve shook his head. "Not this time," he said.

"The cellar door was open when I came down," said Powell. "But I don't think that—proves anything."

"Have you looked down there?" Kathryn asked.

"There's nothing there," he replied quickly. "I went down once, but there's no light, and—that's all. That's why I'm putting on the bolt."

Kathryn looked at him. "I don't understand," she said. "What has that to do with it?"

"I told you. The door keeps coming open."

She thought about this. "Could anyone get into the house through there?" she asked. "Is there a door to the outside?"

"No. They tell me there used to be a tunnel, but it's been bricked up."

"I think I'll go look," said Kathryn. "Where's the flashlight?"

"I tell you there's nothing there! There's nothing to see!"

"I'm just curious. You don't mind, do you?" She looked around the kitchen, and spotted the flashlight on a shelf. "There it is," she said. She tested it, and headed for the cellar stairs.

"I'll come with you," said Powell.

With Kathryn in the lead, they went down into the dank and clammy cellar. The lilac smell was gone, and although Powell's nerve-ends were tingling with anticipation, he got none of the feeling he'd had before. The floor was dirt and the walls were stone, and the whole area was considerably smaller than the house. It was as though it had been built as a storage bin and a place for the furnace, the skeleton of which gaped, black and hollow, in one corner. Empty boxes and barrels were piled about as though they had been thrown from the stairs, and a pickaxe and some rust-rotted garden tools were stacked against one wall. On the far side, away from the stairs, the stone stopped abruptly, and there was a semicircle of brick about five feet high. Kathryn's light darted around it, and at the ground beneath it.

"That must be it," said Powell. "Ed Lasker told me it used to lead to the cove." He saw something on the floor, and reached down and picked it up. "What do you know?" he said, sniffing it. "It's seaweed. And it's still wet."

"I guess anything would stay wet down here," said Kathryn, flicking her light about. "Well, there's no place anybody could have got in, so Stevie must have been dreaming." She headed back toward the stairs, with Powell close behind.

"See what you can do about calling him Steve," he said. "It's good for his morale." He still held the damp piece of kelp, and on a sudden instinct he flung it away, and wiped his hand on his trousers.

Back in the kitchen, Powell closed the door and started putting the last screw in the bolt. Kathryn replaced the flashlight and said, "Sorry, old boy, but I guess you were dreaming. There's no way anyone could have got in."

"Then it was some dream," said Steve. "I even went to the can."

"Dreams can be very realistic," Kathryn replied, and shook detergent into the sink.

Six.

The poltergeist phenomena stopped as soon as Steve got a job. Nothing more was thrown or broken, and although Powell couldn't say it wasn't coincidence, he was content to let the matter ride. So long as the commotion stopped, he didn't care what the reason was.

And Steve, with a definite goal to aim at, was happy in his work. After considering all the prospects—and reconciling himself to something less than five hundred a week—he signed as a general apprentice with Doc Mellish's construction crew, at $1.50 an hour. Because of the bargain with his father this turned out to be $3.00 an hour, which wasn't bad for an eight-hour day, but the work was spotty and dependent on the weather, so he couldn't say for sure how much he would make on the summer. Still it was better than nothing, and it gave him something to do.

One day, he was helping a carpenter named Zeke Frobisher repair a porch, and had just fetched a cross-cut saw from the truck when Frobisher took the nails out of his mouth and said, "How d'you like your house?"

"It's a dump," replied Steve.

Frobisher was a lean, wind-scarred man, with milky blue

49

eyes and hands the size of catcher's mitts. He ticked off a measurement on a plank, put it on a sawhorse, and began to cut. "See anything at night?" he asked.

"What do you mean?"

"I guess you don't know about the house, then."

"I know it's a dump. What else?"

"That house is so haunted there ain't more'n two-three people around here'll go near it. I wouldn't go up there for a hundred dollars."

Steve swallowed. "Why not?" he said.

Frobisher completed his cut, and rubbed his thumb along the edge. "I know what's good for me," he said. "People've died up there, just like *that*." He snapped his fingers. "Most of 'em of fright, they say."

"Ah," said Steve uneasily. "There's nothing there."

"You wait, sonny. You just wait. And don't say I didn't tell you."

Steve paused. "What kind of ghost is it?" he asked.

"Lots of kinds. There's moaning and shrieking and hollering like all get out. Must've something pretty bad happened there to get a place haunted like that."

"Does anyone know?"

"They say old Twitchell murdered his wife and bricked her up in the basement, but there's nothing to prove it."

"That's not so bad. I mean—just one murder shouldn't cause all that fuss."

"Weren't just one. People live there a while, they go kind of crazy, and anything's like to happen. Oh, that's some bugged-up house, that is. Blood on the floors, blood on the walls—"

"Stop trying to kid me," said Steve. "I've been all through it, and there's no blood anywhere."

"It ain't there all the time—it sort of comes and goes, like.

They say if someone's about to die, his name gets writ in blood on the wall."

"Ah, come on. Don't try to give me that."

"I ain't trying to give you nothing, sonny. I'm just telling you what they say. And that cove, there; you know what's good for you, you'll keep clear of it."

"Why?"

"Just keep clear, less'n you want 'em to find you floating face down like Art Crannish."

"Who's he?"

"He was. He went down there, and the next day they found him on the west tide. You might of said he was face down, except the fish had et his face."

"Maybe he slipped."

"Maybe. Maybe not."

"Well, all I know is I haven't seen anything."

"Heard anything?"

"No—well—no." Steve didn't think the footsteps in the kitchen quite matched up to what Frobisher was describing. "Nothing really."

"You'll know when you do. Sometimes there's screeching and hollering, and sometimes it just sounds like people walking around, but whatever it is, it's there. You'll know."

"I've heard people walking around," said Steve. "But I think it was my parents."

"You think? Don't you know?"

"Well—they said they thought it was me."

Frobisher cackled. "That's the ghost," he said. "Probably the one they call Walking Jenny."

"Who's she?" Steve's neck began to tingle.

"Walking Jenny was an old hoor used to walk between here and Cranton, back in my granddaddy's time. They say the only time she got off her feet was when she was working; the rest of the time she'd be on the hoof—here to Cranton, Cranton back here again, then twice around the village green and off to Cranton. Used to pick up a lot of trade along the road, they say. Had legs like a kangaroo."

"How'd she die?"

"No one rightly knows. One night she was plying her trade, chipper as a spring colt, and the next night a feller name of Sam Sweetser sees her on the road about halfway to Cranton. He says, 'Evenin', Jenny, got time for a lark?' and she smiles at him like always, so he goes up to take her arm and by God if he don't put his hand right through her! Nothing there but the night air. Naturally he considers this calls off all bets, so he just tips his hat and takes off for town, and don't stop running till he's in his own bed. Even then, his feet kept twitching; kept his wife awake most of the night."

"Did he tell his wife about it?"

Frobisher looked thoughtfully at Steve for a moment. "No, it ain't likely he did," he said. "But he told the boys down to the firehouse, and that got the word out."

"Well, why should her ghost be in our house?"

"Like I said, she was a girl who got around. And after old Twitchell bricked up his wife, it's more'n likely Jenny did a little walking up the hill. Could be she's got a sentimental attachment to the place—best bed she ever slept in, most likely."

Steve considered this. "I don't know," he said at last. "You hear a lot of ghost stories, but I don't know anyone who's actually seen one. Have you?"

"Like I say, sonny, I know what's good for me. I keep away from them places, and I stay healthy. No, I ain't seen no ghosts, and I don't intend to. But you—it seems to me like you're asking for it."

"This wasn't *my* idea. My parents had the brilliant thought, and there wasn't anything I could do about it."

"Well, you better tell 'em if they find you dead of fright in bed it's their fault. That is, if they ain't dead themselves."

"Thanks. That's nice to hear."

"Don't mention it. Now stop standing there with your mouth open, and fetch me a drawknife."

Fog came in later that afternoon, and blotted out the landscape in a white, clammy blanket. Wisps of fog eddied around the porch, and the wind that drove it was chilling. Frobisher looked around and shivered. "The hell with this," he said. "No point getting the tools wet. Let's go." He and Steve packed the tools and put them in the pickup truck, and drove off. Frobisher was quiet for a while. "How you fixing to get home?" he asked finally.

"Walk," Steve replied. "I can't get a car till August."

Frobisher was silent again, and then he said, "Tell you what. This ain't no day for nobody to be walking, especially where you're going. I said I wouldn't go near that house, but I'll take you as far as the driveway. O.K.?"

"That's fine," said Steve. "That'll be perfect."

Frobisher clutched the wheel and a grim look came over his face, as though he were already regretting the offer. As they drove through the town they passed the Heart's Ease Café, and he suddenly slammed on the brakes and pulled the truck to the curb. "Let's go into Mother's a minute," he said. "I need something to warm me."

"Is this *your* mother's?" Steve asked, as he got out of the truck.

Frobisher laughed. "I wish it was," he said.

There were several people in the bar, and they looked around as Frobisher and Steve came in. The bartender started to draw a beer, but Frobisher held up his hand. "Give me a shot, Mother," he said. "I need something to take the chill off."

"I'll give you a shot, but I can't serve the kid at the bar," Mother replied. "He'll have to take a table."

"This," Frobisher announced, "is young Mr. Powell. I am taking him up to his house, and I need something for the cold. Don't give me no arguments, please."

Mother looked at Steve. "No kidding," he said, with interest. "What'll you have, sonny?"

Steve put his foot on the brass rail, and his elbow on the bar. "I'll have a 7-Up," he said. "Straight."

Mother reached below the bar, uncapped a bottle, and set it in front of Steve. "Well, well," he said, as he poured Frobisher's drink. "How do you like it up there?"

"I already ast him," Frobisher replied. "He's heard Walking Jenny, but that's all." He slapped some money on the bar and took his drink.

"Seen any blood on the walls?" asked a man down the bar.

"Shut up, Flicker," said Mother. "You'll get the kid all jumpy."

"I ast him about that, too," said Frobisher. "No blood yet." He slid his empty shot glass forward, and Mother refilled it.

Steve, who was reveling in the attention, took a casual swallow of his drink and set the bottle down. "As a matter of fact, there has been a little blood," he said. "But not enough to mention."

Frobisher stared at him. "You told me you hadn't seen none," he said.

"I'd forgotten. It was just a little patch."

"Did it look like it made letters?"

Steve pretended to think for a moment. "Now that you mention it, yes," he said. "There was a kind of zigzag streak, like a Z, and then one that could have been an E or an F. It was kind of blurred."

Frobisher gripped the bar, and his face turned the color of

clay. A few stools away, a man laughed. "That wouldn't be your name, would it, Zeke?" he said.

"Holy Jesus," Frobisher said prayerfully. "Oh, Holy Jesus."

"I could be wrong," said Steve. "It was just a little bit, and it was pretty blurry."

"I ain't going near that house," Frobisher whispered. "I ain't going within three miles of it."

"You said you were taking the kid home," said the man. "What are you going to do—leave him walk?"

"He was set to walk anyway," Frobisher replied. "I just made the offer because—" He stopped, and pushed his glass across to Mother.

"I was taught if a man makes a bargain he sticks to it," said the man, grinning. "You wouldn't want to be known as a welsher, now, would you?"

Frobisher glared at him. "You want to take him?" he asked. "My truck's out front, and you're welcome to it."

"I wasn't the one made the bargain," the man replied. "If I'd said I would, then sure, I'd take him and glad to, but it just so happens I didn't open my mouth. Looks like you've got the job."

Frobisher turned beseechingly to Steve. "If I was to call your daddy, would he come get you?" he asked.

"He's out," said Steve glibly. "He had to see the doctor about his back."

Frobisher drained his glass and gripped the bar, shivering. Then he slammed a fist down, and turned away. "All right, God damn it," he said. "Let's go."

Steve followed him out and into the truck, and Frobisher started off with a lurch that was caused part by whisky and part by panic. He drove wildly out the fog-shrouded road that led to the bluff, and Steve began to get nervous. The truck's tires skittered off the edge of the road on the curves, spraying stone and gravel like the wave from a ship, and twice oncoming cars loomed out of the fog ahead, missing collision by inches. Steve decided the joke had gone far enough.

"Look," he said. "I think I ought to tell you, I was only kidding about that blood."

Frobisher was quiet for a few moments, and then said, "What do you mean?"

"Well, I figured you'd been kidding me with all your stories, so I thought I'd kid you a little in return. There never was any blood on the walls."

Frobisher said nothing, and gradually the truck slowed down. "I oughta throw you right outa the car," he said at last.

"Why? Wasn't that fair?"

"That ain't no subject to kid about, sonny. And don't you never do that again. Never."

"But weren't you kidding me?"

"I told you! No! Now, shut up and stop talking about it!"

They drove the rest of the way in silence, and at the entrance to the driveway Frobisher stopped the truck. Steve opened his door, and hesitated. "Thank you for the ride," he said. "And for the drink—and—I'm sorry."

Frobisher stared stonily ahead and said nothing, and Steve got out and closed the door. The truck drove off in a flurry of gravel, and disappeared in the fog.

When Steve entered the house, his mother was in the kitchen and his father was trying to start a fireplace fire with wet wood. They were both preoccupied with what they were doing, and he was interested in what their reactions would be to his announcement. Standing in the door between the two rooms, he said, "I suppose you know this house is haunted." Nobody said anything, and he went on, "You should have heard the stories I heard today. Old Man Twitchell killed his wife and bricked her up in the cellar, and an old whore named Walking Jenny used to—"

"Stephen, that's enough," said his mother. "Where did you hear this?"

"Zeke Frobisher told me. Everybody knows it." Steve glanced to where his father was wadding newspaper under the smoking logs. "What do you think about it, Pop?" he asked.

"I wouldn't know," Powell replied.

"There are no such things as ghosts," Kathryn said. "That's the one thing you can be sure of."

"A guy named Art Crannish went down to the cove once," Steve said. "Next day they found him, and the fish had eaten his face."

"Stephen!" Kathryn exclaimed. "If you don't mind!"

"Have you been down to the cove, Pop?" Steve asked.

"Uh—yes," said Powell. "Once."

"What's it like?"

"Like—any other cove, I guess. I wouldn't go down there again, though. The path's not too good."

"I'd like to see it sometime."

"By the way," said Kathryn, "while you're standing there doing nothing you might straighten up your room. It'll get your mind on pleasanter subjects."

"What needs straightening?" said Steve. "I made my bed."

"There are clothes all over it, and you've done something to the wall. I don't know what you put on it, but it's going to take soap and water to get it off."

"I didn't put anything on the wall," said Steve. "I just hung my banner and my pictures, but I didn't do anything else."

"Go look and see."

Steve went into his room, looked at the smear on the wall, and began to tremble. Oh, no, he thought. It can't be. He looked more closely, and started to touch it, then put his hand behind him and backed away. "Hey, Pop!" he called.

Both Powell and Kathryn appeared in the door, and saw

Steve, looking pale and shaken, staring at the wall. "What's the matter?" Powell asked.

"It's blood!" said Steve. "It means somebody's going to be killed!"

"Oh, really," said Kathryn. "I could kill that Zeke Frobisher."

Powell examined the smear on the wall. "Darned if it doesn't look like blood," he said.

"How could it be blood?" Kathryn asked. "Be reasonable."

"I didn't say it was; I said it looked like it. Got a rag?" She handed him a dishrag, and he scrubbed the stain until it was almost gone. Then he looked at Steve. "What else did Frobisher tell you?" he said.

"Not much," Steve replied hesitantly. "That was about all."

The telephone rang, and Kathryn went to answer it. They heard her say "Yes?" and then her voice took on the shade-louder tone that goes with talking long-distance. "This is she. . . . Uncle George? How wonderful to hear from you! Where are you? . . . I see. . . . Oh, we'd *love* to see you! . . . . Yes, plenty of room. . . . On your boat? Wait a minute." She covered the mouthpiece and called to Powell, "It's Uncle George. He wants to know if there's a place here he can land his boat."

"It depends on how big it is," Powell replied. "But, knowing him, if there isn't a place he'll make one."

"He says yes, there's plenty of room," Kathryn said into the phone. "There's a cove right below us, where you can anchor. When can we expect you? . . . Oh, wonderful. We can't wait. . . . Goodbye." She hung up, and came back into Steve's room. "He's coming," she said. "There wasn't much I could do."

"When does he get here?" Powell asked.

"Some time late Friday. He's sailing up the coast, so he

can't be sure exactly." Then she looked at Steve and said, "And if you listen to one more word Zeke Frobisher tells you, I'll shoot you both. There's no excuse for this."

"I'm sorry," Steve replied. "I guess I got kind of jumpy."

"It's no wonder, the stories he's been feeding you."

"I think I'll go down to the Atheneum tomorrow," said Powell. "I want to do some research."

"About what?" Kathryn asked.

"This house. Old Man Twitchell. Whatever I can find. I have a feeling I might come up with something interesting."

She turned away. "Well, good luck," she said. "But if you come up with any more ghost stories, please don't bring them back."

Seven.

Next day. Powell went to the Atheneum. It was deserted except for the librarian, but in spite of—or possibly because of—its emptiness Powell still felt he should lower his voice. There was something about the building that compelled him to whisper.

"That book about Ebenezer Twitchell," he said. "May I see it?"

She smiled. "Of course," she said, in a normal voice. "But you must understand it's incomplete."

"In what way?"

"It just gives the historical details. The—well, the more personal aspects of his life are omitted. And rightly, too."

"Where could I find out about them?"

She smiled again, and indicated a chair next to her. "Sit down," she said. "Do you have a few minutes?"

Ebenezer Twitchell ran away to sea during the War of 1812, and for the rest of his life was never very far from the water. This was partially because his father Obadiah, a harnessmaker, used to beat him with a snaffle bit every chance he got, and by the time Ebenezer was strong enough to make it an equal contest his father had died. By then it was too late

60

for Ebenezer to do anything except be a sailor, and he almost reluctantly set about the business of making a living at sea. Near the end of each voyage he would vow never to go out again, and then a chance would come for a promotion, or a lucrative voyage, and he would sign on for one more trip. He had his second mate's papers when he was twenty-two, and with them came the chance of becoming a master, and Ebenezer gave up even pretending not to go back to sea. If he could be a master, then he might in some way get revenge for all he had suffered at the hands of his father.

At about this time he married Felicity Mayhew, an unattractive girl of twenty-eight whose father had each year offered a larger and larger dowry in the hope of getting rid of her, but whom none of the local youths would touch with a frigate's bowsprit. Ebenezer, however, aware that his voyages were going to become longer and longer, and the intervals ashore shorter and shorter, reasoned that he could put up with Felicity for a week or so every year, in return for what was by now not only a great deal of money but also a fine piece of seaside property, which her father had thrown in as a final raising of the ante. Furthermore, once he became master he might be able to get a whaling ship, and their voyages sometimes lasted three years. He went to Felicity's father and announced he would like to marry her, and the old man grasped his hand in a bone-crushing grip and tearfully called him Son.

Felicity, unattractive though she was, was no fool, and she saw through Ebenezer's offer and also saw what kind of person lay beneath the surface, and what he was likely to become. She reasoned that if she'd kept her virginity this long (although with no difficulty whatsoever) there was no point throwing it away on someone who would be gone most of the time, and would become increasingly savage in the short intervals he was home. The day of the wedding she ran away, but her father put the dogs on her, and they caught her in the swamp the other side of Cranton. That night, she locked herself in the bedroom before Ebenezer could get a foot in the door, and he, after thinking a moment, shrugged his shoulders and went into town.

Felicity was right; Ebenezer did become more savage, not only at home but also at sea, where he felt that everything and everybody were conspiring against him. When, finally, he became a full-fledged master, his reputation for harshness had spread so that it was difficult for the owner to sign on a crew. But there was no denying he made money; any ship he commanded was taut almost to the breaking point, and his cargoes were bigger and were delivered more efficiently than any others along the coast. At last he got a whaling ship, and sailed for the South Seas without saying goodbye to either Felicity or her father, who counted this among their greater blessings for that week.

His whaling career was, by some standards, short, although it was five years before he returned home. Several hundred miles east of the Solomons his ship was rammed and sunk by an enraged bull whale, and he and a few survivors drifted about in an open boat for nearly a month before they landed on an uninhabited island. When, after more than a year, they were picked up by an outgoing whaler, there were only two survivors: the cook, who had gone crazy, and Ebenezer.

When he got back Felicity's father had died, allegedly from too prolonged exposure to his daughter, and although this didn't affect Ebenezer much he was dismayed to find he was no longer in demand as a ship's captain. The feeling was his luck had run out; that his five years in the Pacific had taken the edge off his efficiency, and it wouldn't be worth the trouble necessary to scour up a crew who would sail with him. He tried three owners and got the same reply from them all, so he said the hell with it, and retired. He built a house on the property that had come with Felicity's dowry, and told her she could stay where she was or move in with him; it was all the same to him. For some reason never clearly understood, Felicity sold her father's house and moved in with Ebenezer, possibly out of nothing more than rank curiosity. But moving in meant into the house only; she kept herself locked in her own bedroom at night, and this was perfectly splendid as far as Ebenezer was concerned.

Many years before, on one of his periodic jaunts into town, he had seen a plump blonde circling the village green. Plump blondes were rare locally, and Ebenezer, invigorated by a couple of hours at the tavern, decided to investigate. He found out what he wanted to know almost immediately, and from then on he looked her up whenever he was in port. Looking her up was easy; the only difficulty was that she had no permanent lodgings, and taking her back to the house where Felicity and her father were asleep was obviously out of the question. This made their rendezvous something of a fair-weather proposition; on rainy nights, or when there was too much snow on the ground, Ebenezer would stay in the tavern and wish he were back at sea.

One night after his retirement, he lay in his solo bed and reflected that, although his life had been full in some respects, it had been miserably wanting in his relations with women. This naturally reminded him of the plump blonde, whose name was Jane, or Jenny, and he decided to look around and see if she was still in the neighborhood. He was afraid that by this time she might be a bit long in the tooth, but in view of his other opportunities it certainly wouldn't do any harm to look. On this note he went to sleep, and dreamed that he found Jenny, and she had turned into a South Sea Islander.

He did indeed find her, late in the afternoon, and he was surprised to see that the years had treated her kindly. Since hers was basically an outdoor existence, she had developed more stamina than her housebound sisters; her complexion was good, she seemed fit and strong, and she recognized him instantly.

"Well!" she said. "I thought you'd never get back. Where've you been?"

"Never mind that," said Ebenezer. "Where can we go?"

She looked at him curiously. "You mean you still don't have a house of your own?"

"I have a house of my own, but—" He stopped and thought. There was a maid's room downstairs that was empty at the moment because of the sudden departure of the maid, and Felicity was usually asleep in her own locked room by nine-thirty. "Could you be there at four bells?" he asked.

Jenny's eyes narrowed. "Is this a *church*?"

"Four bells! The time! Ten o'clock!"

"You don't need to shout. I can understand when you speak English. Yes, I suppose I could make it by then, if I'm in the vicinity."

"See that you are."

Jenny pouted. "I'm not used to being ordered around," she said. "I'll be there if I'm not otherwise occupied."

At ten-thirty, the commotion in the maid's room was such that neither Jenny nor Ebenezer heard Felicity descend the stairs, cross the kitchen, and fling open the door. Then she screamed, and they hurled themselves into opposite corners of the room. She started after Jenny, but one kick from Jenny's powerful leg sent her spinning against the wall, and she retreated into the kitchen and returned with a cleaver. This time she went for Ebenezer, and all the hatred that had built up over twenty-five years went into the blow she aimed at his head. But Ebenezer had had some experience with mutinous crews, and he parried Felicity's blow, wrenched the cleaver from her hand, and fetched her a slice on the side of her head that opened her from jawbone to temple and spattered the wall with blood. She sank into an untidy heap on the floor.

"You've killed her!" Jenny shrieked. "Good Godamighty, you've gone and killed her!"

"It was her or me," Ebenezer replied, breathing deeply. "You saw her." His mind was racing ahead, trying to decide what to do, and then he remembered that when the house had been built the men digging the cellar had run into an underground stream, flowing from the hills above down to the cove, and they had had to dam the upstream side before continuing with the cellar. The downstream side remained open. "You stay here," he said. "Start cleaning up." He took the lantern that Felicity had brought, and with that in one hand and his wife's limp foot in another, he dragged her across the kitchen and down the cellar stairs.

It was almost daylight by the time he and Jenny finished cleaning the walls and floors, and the only spot they couldn't completely eradicate was the one on the wall, where Felicity's head had hit.

With Felicity out of the way, there was nothing to keep him from seeing Jenny as much as he wanted; the only problem was that Jenny wanted to see him more than he did her. More exactly, Jenny grew to like the house, and saw no reason why she shouldn't spend all her off-duty time there. Years of living in the fresh air had done wonders for her constitution, but one hip was developing rheumatoid symptoms, which were not helped by contact with the bare ground. One afternoon, at a time when business was slack, she went up to the house and found Ebenezer on the porch, staring morosely through his spyglass. She settled herself in a rocking chair and sighed.

"What a day this has been," she said.

"Already?" Ebenezer replied, his eye still to the glass.

"I mean my hip," said Jenny. "Since first thing this morning it's been on fire. Coming back from Cranton, I thought I'd never make it."

"Don't move around so much. Get yourself a place, and settle down."

"That's just what I was thinking of! How did you know?"

"There's nothing to know. It just makes sense."

"I've got a few clothes and things, down at Barney's. I'll get them, and bring them right up." She rose and started to leave, and for the first time Ebenezer took his eye from the spyglass and looked at her.

"You mean *here?*" he said.

"Of course. Isn't that what you meant?"

"I did not. I meant get yourself a place of your own."

"Well, I like that! After all I've done for you, it seems to me I've as much right in this house as you have."

Ebenezer's face turned a mottled red. "Listen, woman—" he began, but Jenny cut him off.

"What's more," she said, her voice rising, "if I was to tell a few people what I know about this house, you wouldn't be living here much longer yourself! You'd be hanging from the gibbet with your tongue sticking out!"

Ebenezer had started to reach for her, and he stopped. "And you'd be there with me," he said. "You're in this as much as me."

"I am not! I was an honest woman earning my living, and I saw you clip your wife with a cleaver and kill her! I had nothing to do with it—I was all the way across the room!"

Ebenezer realized she had a point, and regardless of whether or not she was implicated she could make it very messy for him. His story of self-defense wouldn't hold up without corroboration, and the long and the short of it was that she had him, as securely as though there were a ring through his nose. His only chance was to play along, and wait for a chance to put her out of the way. "All right," he said. "But do me one favor—don't tell anyone you're staying here."

Jenny looked at him with contempt. "Afraid of your reputation?"

"No. I don't want your friends hanging around here."

"What's the matter with my friends? I have some of the finest friends a woman could—"

"I said don't tell anyone!" Ebenezer bellowed, in his quarterdeck voice. "If I find any of your friends hanging around here I'll shoot them for trespass!"

"All right," said Jenny. "I wasn't going to, anyway."

So she moved in, and Ebenezer spent most of his time on the porch with his spyglass, trying to think of a foolproof way to kill her. It wasn't that he minded having her around; it was just that she had the power of life or death over him, and the ability to make him do what she wanted, and this was intolerable. There was also the danger that she might inadvertently, either in her cups or in the pursuit of her trade, blurt out enough to prove his undoing. But the trouble was that her hours were so irregular it was impossible to work out a plan in advance. Then he remembered about bees.

A long time ago, Jenny had told him that the one occupational hazard that worried her most was the chance of being stung by a bee. She had been stung once, with near-fatal results, and the doctor told her she was one of those luckless people who are sensitive to bee-sting, and that another sting would probably prove fatal. Since then she had stayed as far away as she could from clover, flowers, and other places bees might be, and she never lay on the ground without checking first to make sure there were no bees in the grass. She had tried various forms of repellants, but they repelled people as well as bees, and she finally had to accept the risk. With a plan slowly taking shape in his mind, Ebenezer went into the village and bought a fine-mesh net, then returned and got a preserve jar, and went bee-hunting.

When he had collected a dozen bees, and been stung twice (he waited anxiously after the first sting to see if he, too, might be sensitive), he went into the house. After thinking a few moments he went upstairs, took a jar of Jenny's facial cream from the shelf where she kept it, and put it in the medicine cabinet. Then he put the jar full of bees in the cabinet, removed the top, and very quickly closed the cabinet door. After that he took his spyglass and went onto the porch.

Jenny usually came home for a light snack at suppertime, but on this day darkness fell and there was still no sign of her. Ebenezer waited for a while, staring into the glass in which he could see nothing, and then folded it up and went inside, hoping the bees wouldn't go to sleep. If they did, and she found them and wasn't stung, she'd know what he was trying to do and he'd have to kill her quickly, with his own hands. The idea didn't appeal to him. He was moodily cooking a piece of codfish when Jenny came in, limping and exhausted. She tossed her bonnet on the table and sank into a chair.

"Do you know the expression 'It never rains but it pours'?" she said.

"I've heard of it," replied Ebenezer.

"Well, that's what today was like. Nothing at all at first, and then around a quarter to six—my!" She sucked thoughtfully on a tooth, then said, "Come to think of it, I should have known. It's payday at the mill."

"You going out again?"

"Lord love a duck, I should hope so," she replied, getting stiffly to her feet. "It's not often a girl has a chance like this to sweeten her hope chest." She laughed throatily and went upstairs.

Ebenezer heard her walking around, opening closets and slamming dresser drawers, and he burned his codfish waiting for the scream that never came. Finally he heard her coming down the stairs, and he sagged in disappointment. She looked into the kitchen.

"You haven't seen my face cream anywhere, have you?" she asked.

"Why should I?" he replied, stabbing at the burned fish. "I don't use it."

"I just thought you might have seen it."

"Have you looked in the medicine cabinet?"

She thought briefly, then shook her head. "No," she said. "I don't keep it there. It was on the shelf." She shrugged and turned away. "Well, no matter. My public will have to take me as I am."

She left, and Ebenezer had a sullen supper of bread and cheese. Then he went upstairs and very cautiously opened the medicine cabinet, and saw what a narrow escape he'd had. The bees were asleep, some in and some out of the jar, and he very carefully replaced those that were out and recapped the jar. After thinking a moment, he went into Jenny's room, drew back the covers on her bed, and after uncapping the jar put it down near the foot. Then he remade the bed, and went to his room.

The screams seemed to have been going on for a long time when he finally woke up. They came first from a great distance, and then closer and closer, and then Jenny was on his bed, flailing at him with her fists and screaming, "You bastard! You bastard! You bastard!" He pushed her away, and her screams turned to gasps as the swelling in her throat cut off her breath, and she tottered to the head of the stairs and fell, making a sound like large rocks as she rolled down. Ebenezer waited for a long time, until everything was absolutely quiet, and then he went back to sleep.

He lived for another five years, and those who saw him remarked that he seemed to be getting progressively more depressed. He snapped at children, and had a morbid aversion to flowers, and once when a storekeeper asked if he'd like to try a new batch of honey, he flew into a rage that could be heard on both sides of town. He bought a dory, and built a dock for it in the cove and took to rowing out to sea, returning at dusk each day. Then one morning the dory was discovered bumping gently against the dock, with Ebenezer lying stiff and purple-faced in the bow. The dory's painter had been secured to a cleat on the dock, and the loose end had been knotted around Ebenezer's throat, and drawn tight. So tight, in fact, that it almost took off his head.

Subsequent owners discovered the tunnel and tried to make use of it as an access to the cove, but the whole arrangement was unsatisfactory and they finally had the entrance bricked up, and eventually sold the house. Everybody who owned it tried to find out more about it, but the books in the Atheneum gave only the historical facts, with emphasis on Ebenezer's shipwreck and subsequent ordeal. The more intimate details of his life were never printed.

"I see," said Powell, when the librarian had finished. "And how do you know all this?"

Her eyes crinkled, and she said, "I have my ways."

"What happened to the bodies?"

"Nobody knows. Not even I"—she hitched her chair closer to him, and her eyes grew wide with excitement—"but I'd give anything if I could find out! It might explain—oh, it might explain any number of things!"

"Like what?"

"Well, for one thing, I'm sure they weren't given a Christian burial."

"So?"

"Don't you see? No, I guess you don't."

"Does it make a difference?"

"Everything makes a difference! If I could only find out!"
Powell began to wonder if she was crazy. "Well, if I run
across one I'll let you know," he said. The moment he said it
he was afraid he'd been too sarcastic, but she was in deadly
earnest.

"Please do," she said. "I'd count it a favor."

On his way home he reflected that the woman *was* slightly
crazy, and he wondered how much of her story he ought to
believe. Probably not much. A lonely old woman, with nothing but time on her hands, she had doubtless let her mind
wander for years, reading books on psychic phenomena and
inventing stories to go along with them. He'd do better to
stick to the published facts, and leave the guesswork for
others.

Then, a few days later, he had to make a sharp re-evalua-
tion of his judgment, when he became the first in his family
to see the ghost—or, to be more precise, one of the three
ghosts.

Eight.

It wasn't much of a ghost, really, but it unsettled Powell and paved the way for his complete acceptance of anything else he saw, or thought he saw. If he had any doubt at the beginning he had none now, and was resigned to the fact that he was surrounded by elements he could neither explain nor understand, except in the most perfunctory and traditional terms.

It was the morning of the day Uncle George was due to arrive, and Powell had slept later than usual. Kathryn was downstairs making breakfast, and he went into the bathroom and stared foggily at himself, trying to decide whether to shave now or wait until later in the day. He decided to do it now, because Uncle George might arrive at any hour and then there wouldn't be time, and he had just finished soaping his face when the back of his neck felt cold, and in the mirror he saw someone standing behind him. It was a thin woman, wearing a long gray dress, and she was staring into Powell's eyes in the mirror. He whirled around, and there was nobody there. Then he looked back in the mirror, but the figure had disappeared, and he put his hands on the washbasin and breathed deeply, trying to slow the racing of his heart. After a while he straightened up and took his razor and started to shave, but his hand was trembling so hard he cut himself on the first stroke. He put the razor down, dried his face, and hurried downstairs.

Kathryn was cooking bacon when he came into the kitchen. He sat heavily at the table, and she looked at him and said, "Good morning." Then she looked again, and said, "Are you all right?"

"Sure," said Powell, rubbing his hands together. "I'm fine."

"You don't look it. You look just awful."

"I'm great! I'm fine!"

Kathryn turned back to the stove and was quiet. Then she said, "How's the back been lately?"

"All right."

She lifted the bacon onto a paper towel. "How would you like your eggs?"

"No eggs today. Just a piece of bacon."

Quietly, Kathryn turned from the stove. "Listen to me," she said. "I've been married to you long enough to know when you're feeling well and when you're not. Either you're sick, or something has upset you, and I wish you'd tell me what it is because I can't help you if I don't know the trouble."

Powell took a deep breath. "All right," he said. "If you must know, I've just seen a ghost."

"I see. Where?"

"In the bathroom. She was looking at me in the mirror."

"She?"

"An ugly-looking woman in a gray dress. She was looking right at me."

"And then?"

"Then she was gone."

Kathryn was silent for several moments. "Dear," she said gently, "don't you think you ought to see a doctor?"

"No! There's nothing a doctor could do!"

"Yes, there is. I'm sure Dr. Gerlock could give you the name of someone."

"What do you mean, someone?"

"A—well, a specialist."

"If you mean psychiatrist, no! I'm not having a nervous breakdown and I'm not crazy and I don't need to be analyzed! I just happen to have seen a ghost!"

"I know, dear, I know."

"If you have any other explanation, I'd be glad to hear it."

"I think you've been tired, and probably nervous—"

"Tired from what? I haven't done anything in months!"

"I know. Maybe that's what's worrying you."

Powell stood up. "There is nothing worrying me," he said. "This happens to be the first time I've seen a ghost and it was something of a shock, but I'm sure that in time I'll get used to it, and maybe even come to like it. Now please stop treating me like a child." He picked up a piece of bacon, put it in his mouth, and headed for the door.

"Where are you going?" Kathryn asked.

"To the Atheneum."

"What about Uncle George?"

"If he gets here before I'm back, say I'm doing some research. Say anything you like, but don't say I need a psychiatrist."

The Cranton librarian smiled at Powell when he came in, and nodded as though she'd been expecting him. Her sneakered feet touched together under the desk in a gesture of anticipation, as she watched which of the books he selected. She smiled to herself as he took James Reynolds' *Ghosts in American Houses*. He sat down and leafed through the contents, looking first to see if the Twitchell house was mentioned. It wasn't, and he went on to read of other American ghosts, most of which came from the South. There were a few instances in New England, one of which the author himself had witnessed, but none of the ghosts was particularly virulent, or dangerous. But when he got to *Ghosts in Irish Houses,* he found ghosts that could strangle people, knock them down, hurl stones at them, and drive them insane. Irish ghosts, with many centuries behind them, were considerably more menacing than their American cousins, and Powell was glad he hadn't decided to rent a house in Ireland for the summer.

At noon the librarian was relieved by a younger woman, and she scampered silently across to where Powell was reading. Her eyes were bright with excitement as she whispered, "Which one have you seen?"

"I beg your pardon," Powell replied. "What do you mean?"

"Which ghost?"

Powell swallowed. "I don't know. How did you—?"

"We can't talk here. Are you having lunch?"

He looked at his watch. "I guess so. But—"

"Come on. I'll tell you outside."

He rose and followed her, and when they hit the hot sunshine he felt that the ghosts were very far away. But the librarian was a-twitter with anticipation, and she almost danced as she led him across the street to a restaurant.

"Now," she said, when they were seated. "Was it Felicity?"

"I suppose so," he replied. "Are there others?"

"Oh, my, yes. There's Ebenezer himself, and there's Jenny. She was a—well—a you-know-what."

"So I gathered."

"I must say she tells the funniest stories, though." The librarian threw up her hands and laughed a silent laugh. "My sakes! Some of the things that girl knows!"

A waitress came to their table, and the librarian ordered a lobster roll and blueberry pie. Powell settled on a hamburger, and when the waitress had left he said, "Is it all right if I ask how you know all this?"

"Of course. I talk with them. Felicity and Jenny, that is. I've never been able to get a civil word out of Ebenezer."

Powell had the feeling he was going crazy. "How?" he asked. "How do you talk to them?"

"Well, first you have to believe. It's no good if you don't believe. Then you put yourself in a trance, and pretty soon there they are—or one of them, at any rate. They never come on together."

Powell stared out the window with an almost trancelike sensation creeping over him. Outside in the sunshine, people were walking past about their business: a mother dragging a small child with a balloon, two girls in shorts eating ice-cream cones, the local policeman hurrying to the barber shop in his lunch hour, and three men in dungarees headed for a saloon, and they were all part of a totally different world. Powell knew that what he was hearing was preposterous, and that the woman was a psychic nut, and yet she seemed to know things other people didn't, and to have an extra level of perception somewhere. "This trance," he said. "How do you go about that?"

She closed her eyes, and smiled. "It's easy. You simply imagine a long, long Turkish carpet, with all the designs and scrollwork on it, and you imagine that you're being wrapped in this carpet, fold after fold after fold after fold—" She opened her eyes. "Oops," she said. "I almost got carried away there. Now tell me—what did you see?"

"Just this woman in the mirror. She was standing behind me."

The librarian nodded. "That's right," she said. "She told me she was going to do that. Just a little peek at first, to see how you took it. Some people scream, and that spoils it."

"Did she tell you anything else?"

"Well—" The librarian hesitated. "Not much. She seems to be kind of upset about something, and sort of grouchy, so it was hard to make out. I'm going to get hold of Jenny tonight, though, and she'll probably tell me more. Would you like to come?"

"Not tonight, thank you," Powell said quickly. "My wife's uncle is arriving."

"That's right. I'd forgotten."

Powell stared at her a moment, then said, "Tell me—are any of these ghosts malignant?"

"Why?" She appeared to dislike the question.

"A couple of times I've had a presentment of real evil. Down at the cove once, and also in the cellar.

"Stay away from that cove," she said. "No good will come there."

"Then they are malignant?" Powell's sense of unreality was now complete, and he found himself talking about ghosts as though he were discussing baby-sitters.

"No," said the librarian. "Not all of them. Felicity's mean, and tends to be surly, but I wouldn't say there's any evil about her. Jenny, in spite of her past, is my favorite, although for obvious reasons she and Felicity don't get on too well. There's no evil in Jenny—just a rowdy kind of fun. As for Ebenezer, I've told you I can't get a civil word out of him, and I think maybe that's just as well. I have a hunch Ebenezer is *very* evil."

"Thanks," said Powell. "I just like to be prepared."

"You have nothing to worry about with the ladies." Then, as an afterthought, she added, "So long as you play along with them."

Their food arrived, and Powell ate his hamburger in silence. The librarian took a large bite of lobster roll, then said, "You've no idea the fun it's been, over the years, to watch people come and go in that house. Most of them last only a few weeks, but some have stuck it out the whole summer. Not many, though. One couple even went crazy. But I suppose I shouldn't be telling you that."

"On the contrary," said Powell. "As I said, I like to be prepared."

"All you need is to believe. It's the people who don't believe who go crazy, because they have no way to explain what they've seen."

"That's what I'm thinking about," said Powell. "And I don't quite know what to do about it."

"You'll be all right," said the librarian. "It's your wife I'm not so sure about."

George W. Merkimer, otherwise known as Uncle George, had made his money in porcelain bathroom fixtures, at a time when the income tax was negligible and money multiplied by itself if left alone. He survived the stock market crash by refusing to recognize it, and his whole life was based on the premise that he did what he wanted, and left the world to its own affairs. Now in his late seventies, he was a lean, rangy man with a mop of white hair, and only slightly less vigorous then he had been in his fifties. He had survived two wives, and his present wife, Estelle, was roughly twenty years younger than he. He had met her at a circus fire in Waukegan, and had been attracted by her red hair and her ample pectoral development. It wasn't until after they were married that he learned she'd been part of the trained-dog act. He had no children by any of his marriages, a situation he attributed to having had the bad luck to marry three barren women. That it could have been his fault was never considered. His philosophy was summed up in the rear-view mirror of his car, which he kept tilted upward on the theory that other motorists were no worry of his, and should look out for themselves.

His boat was a fifty-five-foot diesel cabin cruiser, and there was just enough room in the cove for it to swing at anchor. He and Estelle were rowed ashore by the boat captain, and he was faintly irritated that there was nobody on the dock to greet them. "I told her we were coming today," he said. "You'd think the least they could do would be to get down here."

"Maybe they didn't see the boat," said Estelle, as she started up the path.

He glanced back at where the boat lay, sleek and white and clean, its reflection shimmering on the smooth water of the cove. "Anybody who can't see that must be blind," he said. "And I damn well told her I was coming Friday."

They reached the top of the path, and Kathryn came hurrying across the lawn. "Welcome to Wuthering Heights!" she said. "It's good to see you!"

"This isn't much of a reception committee," said Uncle George. "Where's the rest of the family?"

Kathryn kissed him and Estelle, then took them both by the arm. "Big Steve is at the Atheneum in Cranton doing some research, and little Steve has a job. He's saving up to buy a car."

Uncle George looked at the house. "Is this the best you could do?" he asked.

"I know it looks hideous on the outside, but it's really rather comfortable. And of course the view"—she turned, and indicated the sweep of the landscape—"the view alone is worth the price of admission."

"How's Stephen's health?"

"Oh, fine—" She hesitated. "His back kicked up a little last week, but aside from that he's—he's all right."

"It doesn't sound that way. What's the matter?"

"Nothing. He's—well, I think he'd like to get another job. He hasn't been happy at the magazine for a long time."

Uncle George snorted. "If you're not making any money

you're not going to be happy," he said. "I told you, you should have married that young man at the bank."

"George, that's **no** way to talk," said Estelle. "Kathryn wouldn't be happy with anyone but Stephen, and you know it."

"He's not making any money," said Uncle George. "I can get him a decent job, if he wants it."

"Actually, he's had several offers," Kathryn lied. "It's just the enforced idleness that's getting him down."

They went inside, and Kathryn started to make some tea. Uncle George sat in the living room and glared at the furniture, and Estelle came into the kitchen to join Kathryn. "Is that your caretaker?" she asked.

"Who?" said Kathryn, measuring tea into a pot.

"The man with the spyglass."

"Not that I know of. Where is he?"

"He was on the porch as we came in."

Kathryn stopped, and looked at her. "On *our* porch?" she said.

"You must have seen him. He was right there, looking out to sea with his spyglass."

Kathryn went to the window, and Estelle followed her. "There's nobody there now," she said.

"I guess he's gone," said Estelle.

Thoughtfully, Kathryn continued to make the tea, and she had just loaded the tray when from the living room came a shout, and then a crash of glass. Both women hurried into the room, and saw Uncle George standing, livid with rage, with the pieces of a flower vase scattered on and around him.

"What the hell's going on here?" he shouted. "Estelle, did you throw that vase at me?"

"Don't be silly," she said. "Nobody threw anything at you."

"They sure as hell did! I was sitting here minding my own business, and suddenly this vase hit the wall behind my head.

Somebody threw it, and I don't think Kathryn's aim is that good."

At that moment the front door opened, and Powell came in. "Well!" he said brightly. "Welcome!"

Uncle George glared at him. "I'll bet you're the one that did it," he said.

For the first time, Powell saw the debris. "Oh-oh," he said. "He's back again."

"Who is?"

"Our poltergeist. I thought we'd got rid of him."

"What the hell are you talking about?"

"Really, Stephen," said Kathryn. "This isn't a joking matter."

"Who's joking?" Powell replied. "Remember what happened before?"

"That was Stevie," she said, trying to sound as though she meant it.

"Well, neither Steve nor I were here just now, so it was either the poltergeist or one of you who threw it. Take your choice."

"I'll still bet you did it," said Uncle George. "That was a man's aim."

"Sure—through a closed window," Powell replied. "If you can't think of anything better than that, let's drop it." He turned and went into the kitchen, leaving three silent people behind. He noticed that the bolt on the cellar door was drawn back, and the door was ajar. "Did you open the cellar door?" he called to Kathryn.

"No," she replied. "Why?"

"I just wondered." He closed and bolted the door. I guess I'll have to wire that bolt, he thought. And then we'll see what happens. He shivered, and made a drink.

They were halfway through dinner when the boat captain appeared, and knocked at the back door. "May I speak to Mr.

Merkimer, please?" he said to Kathryn, who had answered the knock.

"Of course," she said. "Come in."

He had a flat, weatherbeaten, Scandinavian face, and when he took off his cap his blond hair stood straight up, giving him a look of frightened surprise. He went tentatively into the dining room and said, "I'm sorry to disturb you, sir, but I thought you ought to know. There's a malfunction on one of the seacocks, and we're taking on water."

"Are the pumps working?" Uncle George asked.

"Yes, sir. I started up the pumps and we're holding our own all right, but I thought you ought to know about the seacock. I can't see what happened."

"We'll give the yard hell when we get back," said Uncle George.

"Yes, sir," said the captain.

"All right, Pedersen," said Uncle George. "Just keep her afloat till I get there. I'll be down after dinner."

The captain looked as though he wanted to say something else, but he just said, "Yes, sir," and turned and, almost reluctantly, left the room.

They all went down to the boat after dinner, and while Uncle George and the captain crawled through the bilges Estelle showed the Powells the rest of the boat. It was an elegant affair, with separate master cabins, bulkhead-to-bulkhead carpeting, and all the latest navigational equipment. That something as relatively simple as a seacock should malfunction seemed preposterous, and Powell wondered idly if poltergeists knew anything about nautical mechanisms. Finally Uncle George came in, his hands stained with grease and bilge water. "I'm staying on board tonight," he said. "I don't know what's the matter with the damn thing, but I won't sleep easy if I'm not here."

"I'll keep you company," said Estelle. She had wondered how she could avoid sleeping in the house, which had made her uneasy the moment she entered it, and this was her excuse.

"Why?" said Uncle George. "What could you do?"

"Nothing. Just so you won't be lonely."

Uncle George snorted. "You're always saying how you can't wait to sleep in a real bed again, and now you turn down the chance. Women are crazy."

"Do you *mind* if I stay here?"

"Hell, no. Suit yourself."

Estelle looked at Kathryn and smiled. "Romantic, isn't he?"

Kathryn, relieved at not having to house Uncle George, also smiled. "I imagine he could be," she said.

"Flattery'll get you nowhere," said Uncle George. "One of you threw that vase at me, and don't think I'm going to forget it."

"I'll tell you one thing," said Powell evenly. "If I *had* been the one to throw it, I wouldn't have missed."

"Stephen, we've got to be going," Kathryn said, standing up.

"I kind of like that," said Uncle George. "You're not as much of a punk as I thought."

"Come on, Stephen," said Kathryn. "Good night, Uncle George. Good night, Estelle."

The boat captain silently rowed them ashore, and when they reached the dock Powell shone his flashlight in all directions, ending on the cleft in the rock that marked the tunnel entrance. The rocks glittered in the reflected light, and the hole seemed small and harmless. He turned up his collar.

"How do you feel?" Kathryn asked, as they started up the path.

"Fine."

"I've been thinking; this really isn't a very stimulating life for you, holed away from everybody, and everything."

"I don't mind."

"But summer is supposed to be for fun, and parties, and things like that. I think we should get people down for weekends, and have picnics, and all the rest of it."

"O.K., but don't do it on my account."

"I think we'd all be happier."

"Isn't it going to get kind of expensive?"

"We won't worry about that."

He stopped and looked at her in the darkness. "You haven't taken any money from Uncle George, have you?"

"No, I haven't! And I turned him down when he offered you a job! I lied and said you had lots of offers, and were just waiting for your back to get better!" She was more violent than she intended, and realized she'd secretly been hoping Uncle George would help in a way that would be acceptable to Powell. She knew he'd feel much better once he was back at work.

"All right," he said. "You don't have to shout. You just seemed awfully glib about it."

"I was only thinking of you."

He took a deep breath, and continued up the path. "You know the place is haunted, don't you?" he said.

"I know it's supposed to be."

"It is."

She thought for a moment, and then, choosing her words very carefully, said, "That's another reason for having people here. Maybe it's haunted because nobody's been here for a long time; maybe it just needs a little life and gayety to get rid of—the haunts."

"But you'll admit it's haunted?"

"Dearest, let's not argue about it now. I'll admit that things could be a lot more cheerful, and if that's what's meant by being haunted, then yes, I'll admit it is."

It's a starter, Powell thought, as they crossed the lawn to the looming hulk of the house. It isn't much, but it's a starter.

Estelle had been asleep in her cabin for perhaps an hour, when she was awakened by the sound of footsteps scuffling about in the passageway. She rose and went to the door, and opened it just in time to see the figure of a plump, naked woman emerge from Uncle George's cabin and vanish up the companionway. It was a moment or two before Estelle could get her breath, and then she strode across and opened the door. The cabin was in darkness, but she could see the form of her husband sprawled across the bunk. "George Merkimer, you swine!" she shouted.

"Whuh?" said Uncle George, struggling up from the depths of sleep. "Whozzat?"

"Is that why you wanted to stay on board? Is that why you tried to get me to sleep at the house? It was a pretty stupid trick, if you thought you could get away with it."

"Whur you talking about?"

"You know damn well what I'm talking about, and when I think of all I've had to put up with from you and then have *this* added to it—*this*, this degradation, this sneaking, whore-mongering—"

"Now, wait a minute!" said Uncle George, by now fully awake. "Start from the beginning, and fill me in."

"I'll fill you in, all right. I'll fill you into a six-foot hole if I can find a shovel. Who do you think you are—Frank Harris? What makes you think you can get away with it?"

"Get away with *what*? Damn it, woman, come to your senses and speak English!"

"Has she been following us all along the coast? Has she been coming aboard every night? Because if she has I'm getting off this boat right now, and you'll never see me again!"

"Who in the *hell* are you talking about?"

"I'm talking about that fat blonde I saw coming out of your room with no clothes on. And don't tell me you didn't know she was here."

Uncle George lay back, and pulled the covers up to his chin. "Go to bed," he said. "You've been dreaming."

"I have not! I was wide awake as I am now! There was a great to-do in the corridor, and when I looked out she was coming out of your room!"

"Sure, sure. Good night."

"Don't try to kiss me off!"

"WILL YOU SHUT UP AND GO TO BED?"

She backed out of the cabin, her ears ringing with the sound of his bellow, and neither of them had heard the splash at the stern, or the captain's cries for help.

Nine.

Estelle lay awake the rest of the night, wondering if it was possible she'd been dreaming. She was sure she'd seen it, and yet George had been so obviously confused that if there *had* been a woman in his room, he didn't know it. Then she thought of seeing the man with the spyglass, a man nobody else had seen, and she began to wonder if she were having hallucinations. This so unsettled her that she didn't notice the boat listing slightly, and a faint sloshing noise that was growing louder. Finally, as the first daylight seeped through the porthole and filled the cabin with grayish light, she could see a small trickle of water coming under the door and snaking across the carpet. She leaped out of bed, and opened the door. The whole passageway was awash.

"George!" she screamed. "Wake up!" We're sinking!" She ran across and flung open his door, bracing herself against the increasing list.

"*Now* what?" said Uncle George, from beneath the covers. "Don't you ever sleep?"

"We're sinking, George, sinking!" she shrieked, and ran back to her cabin to get her clothes.

Uncle George sprang from bed, his arms and legs flailing like propellers, and took one look at the passageway. He grabbed a pair of trousers and started to run. "Come on!" he shouted, as he passed Estelle's door. "You don't have time for that!"

"I'll be right there," she called back. "I just want to find my jewel box."

"Damn it, woman, get moving! We're going under! Where the hell is that Pedersen? *Pedersen, where are you?*" He reached the afterdeck just as the boat lurched and began to roll, and he climbed onto the high rail and started making his way forward. Estelle came out of the companionway clutching her jewel box and with her red hair streaming out behind her, and he paused long enough to put a foot down for her to grasp. She pulled herself up, and together they crawled toward the highest part of the boat. There was another lurch, and a low rumbling of air, and bubbles began to thunder inside the boat as it sank lower in the water. It rolled back to an even keel, then its bow rose, and with a sigh and a gurgle it slid backward under the surface. There was a bump as the stern hit bottom, and then the bow settled until only the mast was above water. Uncle George and Estelle clung to the crosstrees and looked at each other. The water was cold and oily, and for a few moments neither of them spoke.

"I will be everlastingly damned," said Uncle George at last.

Estelle began to cry. "My new coat," she blubbered. "And all my summer wordrobe—all ruined!"

"Oh, shut up," snapped Uncle George. "I'd like to know what happened to Pedersen. If he'd been on the job, this wouldn't have happened."

"What are we going to do now?" said Estelle through her tears. "I can't swim and hold my jewel box at the same time."

"The hell with your jewel box. I wonder where the dinghy is." He put his head under water, and faintly, through the murk, perceived the dinghy, sticking straight up like a balloon on a string, held by its painter to the stern of the yacht. "It's down there," he said. "Which means Pedersen must be on board." He thought for a moment, then said, "Damn. He was a good boatman, too. Now I'll have to train another."

Estelle sneezed. "I think I'm catching cold," she said.

"You'd be a lot healthier if you quit running around the boat all night," Uncle George observed sourly. "What was all that about, anyway?"

"I don't know," she replied, and began to cry again. "I just don't know."

"If you don't know, it was damn bad judgment to wake me up. I've never heard such a wild-eyed routine in my life."

"I'm sorry! But I'll swear I saw someone come out of your room!" She sneezed again. "Do you have a handkerchief?"

Grumbling, Uncle George reached in the pocket of the trousers he was clutching, and produced a sodden handkerchief. "Here," he said. "Wring it out first."

"I can't! I can't let go of my jewel box!"

"Will you do me a favor and drop that damn jewel box? We can recover it when the boat is raised."

"Never! I wouldn't give it up for anything in the world!"

"Give it to me, then. I'll drop it."

"Don't you touch it!" She clasped it in both arms, almost losing her hold on the crosstrees.

"Who gave it to you in the first place?" said Uncle George, reaching out. "I'll get you a new set."

"You will not! Let go!"

"Listen, woman, we'll spend the day in the water if you keep this up. Give me the jewels, and let's get out of here."

They were tugging back and forth at the jewel box when Powell, who had risen early, appeared at the rim of the cove. He hurried down the path, and watched in silence from the dock. Finally they saw him.

"I suppose it would be silly to ask what happened," he said.

"You're damned right it would," said Uncle George. "Get us a boat, and get us off this damn mast."

"I don't have a boat," Powell replied. "I don't know where I could find one."

Uncle George turned to Estelle. "Listen," he said. "I'm going to swim to shore. You can either drop that box and follow me, or you can stay here until someone finds a boat. It's up to you."

"George, I'll never forgive you for this," Estelle said, beginning to cry again.

"Forgive *me*? What have I got to do with it?"

"You always said if I stuck to you everything would be all right, that nobody would ever beat you at anything. Well, I stuck to you, and now look at me! I was better off with the trained dogs!"

"Shut up! Are you coming, or aren't you?"

"I'm coming." Sadly, gently, she set her jewel box on the water, then took her hands away and watched it sink and spin until it was out of sight. Then she pushed away from the mast, and followed her husband to shore.

When they reached the house, Powell took them upstairs and got towels and dry clothes for them, then woke Kathryn and told her the news. She put on a dressing gown, and came down to make breakfast. "What's going to happen?" she asked. "What are they going to do now?"

"Whatever it is, it's not going to be by boat. Or, at any rate, by that boat. That's out of commission for quite awhile."

"I guess we should look up trains. Or maybe he'll want to hire a car."

Powell looked at his watch. "I don't know if there's a car rental place here. Ed Lasker'd know, but it's too early to call."

"I imagine what he'll do is call a limousine from Boston. I somehow don't see them riding a train."

Uncle George came down, wearing the slacks and sweat-shirt that Powell had given him. There were no shoes or socks in the house that fit him, and his bare feet looked like long white flippers. "You got a phone?" he snarled.

"It's right there," Powell replied. "But I don't think the rental places are open yet."

"What rental places? I'm calling the salvage people."

There was a pause while Uncle George opened the phone book, and then Powell said "Oh." After another pause, he said, "What are you going to do for transportation?"

"I won't need any transportation until the boat's raised. That'll be quite a while, so I won't worry about that now."

Powell and Kathryn looked at each other while Uncle George put through the call, and they continued to look at each other as they heard him say, "What do you mean, no answer? This is an emergency.... All right, let me speak to the supervisor...." Finally, when the chief operator had assured him there was no way to get an answer in a vacant building, he slammed down the receiver and turned away. "If I was there you can bet it'd be a different story. They wouldn't give me any of this no-answer rigmarole then."

"We can arrange to get you there, if you want," Powell said gently. "The taxi service will be open pretty soon."

"No point in that. By that time they'll be answering the phone."

"What about your captain?" Kathryn asked. "Where will he be staying?"

Uncle George cleared his throat. "It looks as though he's staying on board," he said. "He must have got caught down below somewhere."

Kathryn closed her eyes, and bowed her head over the stove.

"I suppose somebody should make sure," Powell said. "The salvage people may not get here right away."

"I'm sure," Uncle George replied. "The dinghy was made fast, which means he was aboard, and I didn't see him top-side, which means he was down below."

"Still, that isn't proof."

"It's all the proof I need."

"Does he have a family?"

"Don't ask me. I hired him to run the boat."

"I think we should get a diver to go down and look."

"Any diver who goes on that boat had better be bonded. There's a lot of valuable stuff there."

Powell turned abruptly away, and went to Kathryn. "Anything I can do to help?"

"Just hold on," she said, in a quiet voice. "Be strong, and we'll all survive."

After breakfast, Powell went down to Ed Lasker's office. Lasker looked apprehensive, as he always did when Powell came in, and Powell reflected that, everything considered, he had good reason to. "Good morning," Powell said. "Do you know anyone around here who's a diver?"

Lasker's eyes narrowed. "What for?"

"A boat sank in the cove last night, and we think there's someone still on board."

"Who?"

"The boat captain. Man named Pedersen."

Lasker considered this. "Fess Dorple, on Doc Mellish's crew, might do it," he said. "He was one of those opened your house, so he ain't—ah—squeamish, and I hear he's done a bit of that skin-diving. I'll find out, and let you know."

When word got around that Fess Dorple was going to dive for a body in Twitchell's cove, the town turned out as though for a carnival. People forgot their aversion to the cove, and came and stood on the cliffs that ringed it, and stared down at the mast that rose, like a long, thin finger, from the water.

The sunlight glinted on the varnish, and beneath it could be seen the blurred white outline of the boat. The adults talked quietly among themselves, exchanging reminiscences and folklore, and the children, after a cursory look at the mast, ran about and wrestled and played, while their dogs barked wildly and snapped at their heels. Girls with curlers in their hair chewed gum and wondered what the body would look like, and boys with transistor radios pressed against their ears invented gory tales of other accidents they had seen. The absolute stillness of the mast, and the gentle motion of the bright water, made it difficult to realize an accident had taken place, and the boys felt called upon to inject the note of drama they somehow felt was lacking.

Then a truck arrived and Dorple got out, self-conscious in his bathing suit and sneakers, and began to unload his diving gear. People called to him and one or two made jokes, but Dorple paid them no attention as, with Rabbit Warren helping him, he carried his mask, oxygen tank, weighted belt, and flippers down the path to the water. The children stopped playing and crowded close to the edge of the cliff, and they were immediately pulled back and shushed by angry parents. Absolute silence descended on the cove as Dorple, looking now like some gangling marine animal, lowered himself off the dock and slowly swam toward the mast. The gasping, bubbling sound of his breathing could be heard by the farthest watchers. When he reached the mast he paused, then jackknifed and headed down, his flippers flailing in the wake of bubbles that streamed up behind him. People held their breath, watching the trail of bubbles that rose at regular intervals, and when they could no longer hold their breath some found they were breathing in rhythm with the bubbles, unconsciously synchronizing with Dorple down below. The silence lasted several minutes, and then a child said, "What's he doing, Ma?"

"Be quiet!" replied the mother. "He's looking for a body."

More minutes passed, and the trail of bubbles went from one end of the sunken boat to the limit of the other end, and people began to mutter and wonder how long Dorple's oxygen would last. One wit suggested that he might have got into the liquor supply, and maybe they should set a match to the bubbles and see if they burned, but nobody even pretended to laugh, and the wit went back to looking at the water. Finally, after what seemed like an hour, Dorple's masked head rose slowly to the surface, and people craned forward to see what he brought with him. He brought nothing. They watched him swim toward the dock, and their disappointment began to be tinged with irritation. Who had said there was a body down there, anyway? Was this some kind of a joke, or something? Did this what's-his-name Powell think they had nothing better to do than stand around the cove all day? Some people drifted disgustedly away, but others stayed to hear from Dorple what he'd found. It might be that the body was jammed under something, and he couldn't get it out. But no. He shook his head and spread his hands, and Rabbit Warren helped him take off his tank. The crowd dispersed, and only one or two remained to be convinced.

When Dorple reported to Powell at the house, Powell turned to Uncle George and said, "Well, there you are. Now what do you suggest?"

Uncle George glared at Dorple. "He wasn't in his bunk?"

"No, sir. And he wasn't in the engine compartment. I went through the whole boat. There's nobody there."

Uncle George's lips tightened. "Sonofabitch must've swum to shore," he said. "Left us out there to die like rats."

Young Steve, whom Kathryn had forbidden to go near the cove during the diving, was bursting with frustration. "Why should he swim?" he asked. "Why didn't he take the dinghy?"

"You keep out of this," snapped Uncle George.

"Is it all right if I go out now?" Steve said to his mother.

"Yes," said Kathryn. "Just be careful."

Steve went rocketing through the door, and Powell turned to Dorple. "Well, thank you anyway," he said, and handed him some folded bills. "This'll pay you for your time."

"I don't know why you paid him," said Uncle George, when Dorple had left. "He was hired to find a body, and he didn't do it."

"Did he see my jewel box?" asked Estelle, who had just come into the room.

"No," Powell replied. "He wasn't looking for it."

Estelle sighed. "I wish you'd told him before he went down," she said.

Even under the best of conditions, salvaging a sunken vessel is a tricky operation. The method most commonly used, if the water is shallow, is to work chains or cables under the ship, attach these to pontoons that are brought along either side, then sink the pontoons and tighten up on the cables. When all is secure, the pontoons are pumped dry again and they rise to the surface, bringing the ship with them. There are, however, a staggering number of things that can go wrong, and in the case of Uncle George's yacht they were compounded by the fact that there was limited maneuvering room in the cove, and the pontoons, the barge, and the other equipment were always in danger of collision. Also, the sea in the cove was extremely rough with certain winds, which made work impossible. The salvage master, after surveying the scene, advised Uncle George to tack a flag to the mast and leave it there, but Uncle George was not amused.

"The boat went down," he said, "and she's damn well going to come up."

"It's going to be expensive," the salvage master warned.

"Don't think you can frighten me with that. If you don't want to do it, I'll get another firm that will."

"We'll do it. But don't hold your breath."

The first diver who went down, to tunnel a hole for the cable to be passed under the boat, came up again within five minutes. He was furious. "All right," he said. "Who's the wise guy?"

"What do you mean?" asked the foreman. "What's biting you?"

"Somebody goosed me."

"Cut it out, Charlie, and get back to work," the foreman said. "There wasn't nobody else down there."

"Don't give me that. I know a goose when I feel one."

"Well, it wasn't none of us. If you got a friend down there, that's your worry."

The diver glared at the others on the barge, then turned back to the water. "I'm taking a knife with me," he said. "Anyone who tries it again is going to get his hand cut off."

He was back again in ten minutes. "Now what's the matter?" said the foreman.

"I quit," he replied, taking off his tank.

"What are you talking about?"

"Just that. I quit."

"Why?"

"If you want to know, you go down there. I've had it."

Another diver was sent down, and he stayed about fifteen minutes. When he got back on the barge he removed his mask and breathed deeply. "The first tunnel's dug," he said. "You can put the forward cable through." Then he went over and sat next to the other diver, who was moodily smoking a cigarette. "I know what you mean," he said.

The first man glanced at him. "Have a cigarette."

The two smoked in silence for a while, and then the foreman came over to them. "All right, off your butts," he said. "The cable's rigged and ready to go under."

"You do it," said the second man. "We're tired."

"What kind of talk is that? Get down there before I throw you both overboard!"

"Try it," said the first. "Let's see you try."

The foreman glared at them, then snatched up a mask and oxygen tank, and began to strap himself into it. "A bunch of wise guys," he said. "If you think you're going to get paid for sitting around smoking, you got another think. You're gonna be docked a day's pay, and if I had anything to do with it you'd turn in your flippers and go back to walking. Bunch of lazy bums think they can get away with anything just because they're qualified divers. Well, I'm a qualified diver, too, back from the days when you wore a fifty-pound helmet, and no couple of young punks are going to tell me they're tired after one lousy dive. I'll put that whole damn cable through myself, and tell the company we don't *need* no other divers, and I'll collect the pay for both of you. How do you like that?"

"Great," said the first diver. "Let's see you do it."

The foreman went over the side, and the divers watched with mild interest as the cable was slowly reeled out. After about a half hour a buoy bobbed to the surface on the other side of the wreck, and in a few minutes the foreman appeared. He hoisted himself wearily onto the barge. Without looking at the two divers he said, "That's all for today."

"What's the matter, boss?" the first man said. "Tired?"

"I said that's all for today!" the foreman snapped. "I got the goddam cable under, and it's too late to start digging for the other! You want to sit around here all night?"

"No, boss, we don't. We just thought you might."

The foreman dropped his belt, and unstrapped his tank and set it by the air compressor. "Wise guy," he said.

The divers grinned at him. "You still gonna dock us a day's pay?" the second one asked.

"If you don't shut up I'll hit you both in the mouth," the foreman replied. "I was down there longer than the both of you put together."

Next day it was found the cable had slipped loose and slid back under the wreck, so it had to be passed through again and resecured. For some reason it was much harder this time, and three divers worked most of the morning before it was done. Then in the afternoon a brisk wind sprang up, and all work had to be stopped. On the following morning the cable had once again come adrift. The foreman made a decision.

"All right," he said. "This time, we're gonna put it under and bring the sonofabitch all the way back to the barge, so we have both ends here. Then there'll be no way for her to slip out."

They did as he directed, and the next day it was found that the cable had broken, at exactly the spot where it went under the boat. "O.K.," said the foreman, breathing heavily. "If that's the way it's gonna be, we'll use chain."

With some difficulty they got several lengths of chain beneath the boat, then warped the pontoons alongside and attached them. Very carefully they were sunk, and the chains shortened, and then began the job of pumping the pontoons out. First the pilot house of the boat appeared above the surface, with water pouring out its windows, and in the torrent were charts, pencils, and sodden books. Then the cabin began to appear, and the debris that cascaded out included pillows, clothes, magazines, and hats. The surface of the cove became covered with flotsam, and a crowd began to gather on the hills around. Finally the foreman gave the order to stop.

"O.K.," he said. "Now let's get some pumps on, and clean her out."

Two men dragged a heavy pump aboard, and were setting up

the connections when there was a crack, and a thud, and the boat lurched and began to go down by the stern. The men scrambled for the rail, leaving the pump behind.

"Stop her!" the foreman screamed. "Stop her! For God's sake don't let her go!" He became wild-eyed and incoherent, as the boat slid backward out of its cradle, and settled beneath the water. A few bubbles belched up, and rocked the debris on the surface.

"What happened?" gasped one of the men who had scrambled back to the barge.

"Search me," said a diver. "I guess one of the chains must of bust."

"If you ask me," said the diver named Charlie, "I'd say it was her that did it."

"Who's her?" said the pump man.

"Nobody you know," replied Charlie.

The pump man looked at him for a moment, then spat. "You been diving too long," he said. "You got water on the brain."

Ten.

By the end of the first week, Estelle and Uncle George were barely speaking. Accustomed to separate rooms, they got on each other's nerves in the one that Kathryn allotted them, yet the bed in the only other room was so uncomfortable that neither of them could sleep in it. Uncle George spent several hours each day down at the cove, harassing the salvage people to the point where the foreman twice threatened to quit, and when he came back to the house he took out his frustration on whoever happened to be around. For this reason people stayed away as much as they could: Powell spent most of every day in the Cranton Atheneum, Steve took to hanging out in the Heart's Ease Café after work, and Kathryn invented long shopping trips that occupied the time when she wasn't cooking. She was hampered by the fact that Powell had the car, but she came to like the walk into town, which gave her time to meditate on the shambles of what she had hoped would be a pleasant summer. She was sure Powell's preoccupation with ghosts came from nothing more than his worry about the future; she had read how insecure people imagined fantastic things to explain their troubles, and she had hoped that by encouraging and pampering him she could give him the self-confidence he needed. In the circumstances this was impossible, and it worried her to watch him drift to tales of the supernatural for his escape.

It was Estelle, who couldn't possibly walk to town and was therefore trapped in the house, who bore the brunt of Uncle George's temper. She had thought, in the ten years she'd been married to him, that she'd learned how to handle his various moods, but she had never before seen him frustrated, and this unlocked a whole new side to his nature. He became as unbearable as possible without breaking some fundamental law; he committed no felony, but the effect on those around him was almost enough to indict him for attempted manslaughter. Finally, when she could stand it no longer, Estelle gathered up her cosmetics and moved into the vacant room.

Her first night there, she fell asleep quickly in spite of the bed, out of the sheer, glorious relief of being away from her husband. She woke up at one point and, unaccustomed to the strange surroundings, came fully awake to find out where she was. Then, satisfied, she had started to drift off again when she heard a shuffling noise in the corridor. It sounded familiar, and it was a few moments before she identified it as the same noise she had heard on the boat. She got up and, very slowly, went to the door and peeked out. There was the same figure as before, disappearing down the hall, and Estelle decided to follow it and find out, once and for all, what was happening. The figure was apparently unaware of her, and it went to the stairs and descended, with Estelle following on tiptoe. She was, strangely, not frightened; her curiosity was so overpowering that it left room for no other sensation. Down the stairs, and through the hall, and into the kitchen, and then the figure went through the open cellar door and out of sight. Estelle hesitated only briefly before she, too, went through the door, and she had no sooner reached the foot of the cellar stairs than she began to scream. Piercing, shattering, full-lunged screams; she didn't know why, but everything in her body contorted itself and became knotted with terror, and the screams tore from her throat in an attempt to release whatever was strangling her. Still screaming, she staggered up the stairs into the kitchen, just as the rest of the household, in various stages of undress, arrived and began turning on lights. Uncle George took her shoulders and shook her, but she kept on screaming until he hit her twice across the face. Then she stopped, but her eyes remained wide, and wild-looking.

"What in the hell is the matter with *you?*" Uncle George shouted. "What have you been doing?"

She stared at him for several moments, and he shook her again and repeated the question, and finally she said, "I don't know. I just wanted to find out."

"Find out what?"

"I saw her again."

"Who?" said Powell quickly. "Whom did you see?"

Uncle George looked at him. "She's had some idiot dream about a woman in my room. She had it the last night on the boat, and woke me out of a sound sleep."

"Is she a blonde?" Powell said to Estelle.

"Yes," she replied, looking at him with wonder.

"And plump?"

"Yes. How did you know?"

"I guessed."

Young Steve, who had been so terrified by Estelle's screams that he was at first unable to talk, now spoke up. "What did she look like?" he asked. "Were her clothes all bloody?"

"Steve!" Kathryn snapped. "Don't make things worse than they already are."

Estelle turned her eyes to Steve. "No," she said. "She— she didn't have anything on."

Powell smiled. "That figures," he said.

"What do you mean?" said Kathryn.

"Just that. If it's who I think it is, that figures."

"What do you mean, if it's who you think it is? You heard Uncle George say it was a dream."

"And we're not getting anywhere standing around talking about it," said Uncle George. "I'm going to bed. And you, Estelle, if you have a brain in your head you'll take a sleeping pill." He started out of the room, but Estelle stopped him.

"Please," she said. "Can I sleep in with you?"

"I don't know what for."

"I don't want to be alone."

"If you'll be quiet, you can. But I'm not going to be kept awake the rest of the night." He turned and left the room.

"Would you like some cocoa?" Kathryn asked. "That'll help you sleep."

"No, thanks," said Estelle. "I just—" There was a crash in the next room, and Uncle George began to shout.

"Who in the bloody hell did that?" he yelled, appearing with a broken beer stein in his hands. "Who threw that at me?"

"The same one as did it before," said Powell. "And we were all in this room."

"I don't give a damn where you were! Somebody threw this at me, and I'm not going to bed until I find out who!"

Powell glanced at Kathryn. "Any ideas?" he said.

She looked blank, then said, "It must have fallen off the mantel. That's all I can think of."

"Fallen, hell!" shouted Uncle George. "It came past my ear like an artillery shell!"

"I think the best thing is for everyone to go to bed," Kathryn said. "We'll all feel better in the morning." She knew her explanation wasn't very good, and it made her nervous not to find a better one.

"Nobody's going to feel better any morning," Uncle George replied. "I'm going to find out who's after me, and

I'm going to make him sorry for the day he was born. Or
she, as the case may be."

"Oh?" said Powell. "What are you going to do about it?"

"Would you like to find out?"

"Yes." Unconsciously, Powell moved closer.

"How would you like your wife to be disinherited?"

"I'd love it. I never have liked fishing for money in the
toilet."

"Stephen!" said Kathryn. "Please!"

"Toilet money's better than what you can make on your
own," Uncle George observed. "If you were left to make your
own living, you'd be lucky to *have* a toilet."

"George," said Estelle. "Let's go to bed."

"I'd prefer living in the woods to taking handouts from
you," said Powell. "If you think you can frighten me that way,
think again."

"Stevie, go to your room," Kathryn said. "It's way past your
bedtime."

"I want to watch," Steve replied. "I hope Pop pokes him
one in the snoot."

"I said go to bed!"

"Slug him one, Pop," said Steve, as he went toward his
room. "Don't let him get away with that kind of talk."

"I'll tell you one thing," Uncle George said to Powell. "If I
were twenty years younger, I'd show you a thing or two you
wouldn't forget."

"You're safe in that threat," Powell replied. "You're never
going to get a day younger—you've about run the course as it
is."

"Stephen!" Kathryn shouted.

"I think I'm going to be sick," said Estelle. "George, take
me upstairs."

"That's your worry," Uncle George told her. Then, to Powell, "'If you've been counting on any of my money, you can

stop right now. Not one nickel will ever enter this house."

"I've told you how I feel about that," said Powell. "That's the best news I've heard all week."

"Both of you, stop it!" cried Kathryn, on the verge of tears. "Please! Let's go to bed!"

There was a silence while the two men glared at each other, and then Uncle George whirled around and left the room.

"I'm sorry," said Estelle to the Powells. "I'm really dreadfully sorry. We'll be out of here in the morning."

"I'm sorry, too," said Powell. "I shouldn't have sounded off."

"Frankly, I liked it," Estelle replied. "It's time somebody stood up to him." She hesitated, then said, "Tell me—did I really see someone, or was I just imagining things?"

Powell looked at Kathryn, then said, "I don't know. You might possibly have seen a ghost."

"Really, Stephen," said Kathryn. "That's no way to make her sleep."

"You knew what she looked like," Estelle said to Powell. "Have you seen her?"

"Not this one. I've seen another."

"You mean there are *two?*"

"I'm told there are three."

"Don't believe him," Kathryn put in quickly. "He's been reading a lot of nonsense."

"It doesn't look like nonsense tonight," said Powell.

"Please, dear, let's drop it. You'll get Estelle so worked up she'll never sleep."

"I'm not sure I will, anyway," said Estelle. "I don't want to be alone, but if I go in with George I'll just lie there and listen to him snore." She turned and started upstairs, then stopped. "You know," she said, "this marrying for money isn't all it's cracked up to be. I'd rather be you two than have all the money in the world."

She left, and Powell watched her go. "She earns every nickel she gets," he said. He paused, then added, "I am sorry I blew up. I can take just so much of that man, and then I explode."

"I know," said Kathryn. "It's been a strain on all of us."

"That's why you've got to believe me about these ghosts. Maybe you can't see them, but that doesn't mean they're not there, and you can drive yourself crazy if you try to rationalize things like that. I mean that, literally."

"I'm sure you do, dear."

"Then will you believe me?"

"Yes, of course. Now, let's go to bed."

They went upstairs, and as she turned out the bedroom light Kathryn said, "I imagine if I had to live with Uncle George, I'd have bad dreams, too."

Estelle's announcement that they would be out of there in the morning turned out to be slightly premature. By the time they got up, the entire Powell family had vanished in various directions, and Estelle and Uncle George had their breakfast together in the kitchen. They ate in silence, and it wasn't until after Uncle George had finished his coffee that he spoke.

"I've been thinking," he said.

Estelle waited, but he said nothing more, so she said, "Yes?"

"I've been thinking maybe I misjudged Stephen Powell. He's not good for much but at least he isn't a grifter, and I like that."

"He certainly isn't a grifter."

"And it takes guts to give me backtalk the way he did. Not many men would tell me things like that to my face."

"No, they wouldn't." Estelle didn't know where the conversation was headed, but she was optimistic.

"I think I'll tell him so," Uncle George went on. "If we're going to be staying here we might at least try to be friendly, no matter what we think."

"Well—" Estelle hesitated, then said, "I told them we were leaving today."

He looked at her in amazement. "What made you say that?"

"I didn't think we *could* stay, after what you and he said to each other."

"Nonsense. Just an honest difference of opinion. No need to bear any grudges over that."

"Still, wouldn't it be better if we went somewhere else?"

"How can I supervise the salvage if I'm not here?"

"Look at it this way, then. I hate this house. I've hated it since the first minute I set foot in it. That's why I wanted to sleep on the boat that night."

"What's the matter with it? It's run-down, but that's nothing a little money couldn't cure."

"That's not it. It's—I don't know how to say it, but I feel there are other people here. Evil people. People I can't see— mostly."

"Estelle, that's a lot of hogwash and you know it. If you don't like the beds that's one thing, but don't give me any of that 'evil people' drivel. Stephen Powell may be a failure, but he's not evil."

"I didn't mean him! I mean—"

"I don't care what you mean. I'm not going to pay money to stay in a hotel when there's a perfectly good house right here."

"It *isn't* a good house! It frightens me!"

"Then go home."

She looked at him for several moments, and then she said, "I'll tell you one thing, George Merkimer. If I go home it'll

be for good, and it won't be the home you're thinking of. If I
go home it'll be to Fond du Lac, Wisconsin, and anyone who
wants me will have to take a dog team to find me."

He returned her stare, and for a while there was silence.
"Go ahead," he said at last. "I dare you."

She rose from the table. "Will you call a cab?"

"Call your own cab. This is your idea."

"Very well." She looked up the telephone number and
made a call, and he watched in silence. Then she hung up,
and glared at him defiantly. "Make my excuses to Kathryn,
will you?" she said. "Tell her I'll write a bread-and-butter
letter shortly."

His face tightened into an icy smile. "And what do you
think you're going to use for money?"

"And now I'll tell you another thing," she said. "Your
whole world revolves around money; you can't even look at a
tree or a pond or a cloud without wondering how much it
would cost to buy it. Well, there's a big section of the world
that get's along very nicely without money, and I'm going
back to it."

"Very pretty. Will a speech like that buy you a ticket to
Upper Moose Jaw, or wherever?"

"I've also put away enough, over the last ten years, to buy
my own transportation."

His smile broadened into a grin. "So money comes in
handy, after all," he said. "You wouldn't be so brave without
it."

"You wouldn't be anything without it. Nobody would look
at you twice, and God knows nobody would put *up* with you."

He looked out the window for a minute or two, then said,
"How did you manage to put away any money? You can't
have done it on what I gave you."

"You're right I couldn't. I did it by padding the household
accounts—a little here, a little there, and over the years it

added up. I had a feeling it might come in handy, and I was right."

"You bitch."

"What did you expect? I earned it—I earned it five times over, and just because you're too cheap to give it to me doesn't mean I didn't have it coming. And I thank whatever ghosts are in this house for getting me out of the whole messy arrangement before I lost my mind. At least where I'm going I'll have some self-respect, and not be what I was with you. It's a big relief, and I'm here to tell you I feel better already."

For the first time it occurred to him she was actually leaving. He had been indulgent at first, believing that in the long run he had the upper hand, but now it appeared that not only was she in grim earnest, but also that he had no way of stopping her. He rose from the table and stretched. "All right," he said, with a yawn. "Joke's over. Go back to your room."

"I will not."

"Do as you're told, woman, or I'll lock you up. And if you want to argue, I'll have you arrested as a common thief. Now shut up and go to your room." It was a transparent bluff, and he saw it hadn't worked, so he moved closer to take hold of her. Then he saw her eyes widen, and she screamed.

"George!" she shrieked. "Look behind you!"

Instinctively he turned and looked, but saw only the cellar door swinging slowly open. A cold draft came up the stairs, and he slammed the door and bolted it, just as he heard Estelle run out the front door. He followed as far as the living room, and saw her run down the driveway and hail the taxi that was coming up the hill. She got in, and the taxi turned around and sped off. He watched it until it was out of sight.

Eleven.

Fess Dorple became something of a celebrity as a result of his skin-diving in the cove. Previously, people had thought of him as a well-meaning but slightly slow youth, who would never be more than one of Doc Mellish's workmen; now he had an aura of adventure about him, and people liked to be seen talking to him. This brought out hitherto unknown qualities: where he had once been quiet and retiring, he now blossomed forth as a raconteur, revealing incidents in his past that nobody would have guessed possible.

One afternoon he was in the Heart's Ease Café, regaling the customers with an account of an abortive moose hunt, when Rabbit Warren came in and slid onto the stool next to him. Mother automatically uncapped a bottle of ale, and Warren sipped it slowly while Dorple finished his story. Then Warren said, "I know where you can do some more diving, if you've a mind to."

"Where?" said Dorple.

"A couple of divers quit the salvage job, and they're looking for replacements. The company don't have no divers they can spare."

Dorple thought this over. "What's the money in it?" he asked.

"I ain't doing the hiring. I just heard they could use a diver."

Down the bar, Gloria Tritt spoke up. "Fess Dorple, if you take that job you'll never come to the surface again. You go down, and you won't come up."

"Well," said Dorple, defensively. "I did it once. There's nothing to it." He hadn't particularly liked the dive, expecting as he did to find a body, and the thought of returning to the boat didn't appeal to him.

"You were lucky once," said Gloria. "In that cove, nobody's luck holds more'n once."

This, clearly, was a challenge, but Dorple would have preferred not to take it up. He was therefore grateful when Mother said, "What kind of talk is that? If a man did it once, it stands to reason he can do it again."

"Mother, you don't know what you're talking about," Gloria snapped. "That cove's so full of haunts it's a wonder there's room for the fish."

"You'll believe anything," replied Mother. "If someone was to tell you frogs had wings, you'd pass it on as gospel."

"All I know is what happens," Gloria said. "Too many people's died in that cove."

"You thought the house was haunted, too," Warren put in. "I took you all through it, and you didn't see one damn spook."

"That was daytime."

"Well, Fess ain't going to be diving at night," said Mother. "He's going to do it in daytime, just like the rest of them."

"So why'd they quit?"

"I hear the old man's a bastard."

The door opened and Zeke Frobisher came in, followed by Steve. "Looks like we're late," he said. "Nobody work today?"

To Mother, Gloria said, "Ask Zeke. He'll tell you I'm right."

"What's that?" said Frobisher.

"Fess is going to do some diving in the cove, and Gloria's trying to tell him it's haunted. She thinks ghosts can go under water."

Dorple realized that, as far as the rest of them were concerned, he had accepted the job. He started to say something, but Frobisher spoke first.

"Any man'd go in that cove is outa his mind," Frobisher said. "That cove ain't nothing but a death trap."

"Then how come Fess got away with it?" Mother asked. Turning to Dorple, he said, "What about it, Fess? Did you see any ghosts when you was down there?"

"Not exactly," Dorple replied. "But I ain't said I'd do it—"

"You see?" Mother said to Frobisher. "The one man who's been down there says there's no ghosts."

"As a matter of fact," Dorple began, "I don't know if the money'll be enough to—"

"Then what happened to the boat captain?" Gloria persisted. "How come he disappeared?"

"Probably went over the hill," said Mother. "All I know is no ghosts can go under water. And I'll bet you even money Fess don't see one single ghost all the time he's diving there."

"You got a bet," Gloria replied. "And I'll give you three to one he don't come back."

"Is that all right with you?" Mother asked Dorple. "Will you tell us if you see a ghost?" Dorple nodded numbly, and Mother turned back to Gloria. "O.K. A buck even, he don't see no ghost."

"A buck even," said Gloria. "And three to one he don't come back."

Mother thought a moment. "If he don't come back, how'll we know he seen a ghost?"

Gloria laughed. "That'll be obvious," she said.

"All right," said Mother. "You got a bet."

Dorple went down to the cove next day, hoping they'd have found some other replacement, but the foreman signed him on immediately. They were going to try once more, the foreman explained, to put chains under the boat, and then lessen the strain by blowing compressed air into the flooded spaces. Uncle George stood on the dock and shouted instructions, which were ignored. "You got it clear now?" the foreman said. "You know what you gotta do?"

Dorple nodded, adjusting the straps on his weighted belt. Then a thought that had been nagging at him since yesterday returned, and he said, "What happened to the other divers?"

The foreman waved a hand in disgust. "Temperamental bastards," he said. "They wanted everything their own way."

It was an unsatisfactory answer but it was all he was going to get, so Dorple pulled down his face mask, took the soft rubber breathing tube in his mouth, and adjusted the valves to his air tanks. The air was cold and tasted tinny, and he breathed experimentally a few times before he clambered down the ladder and dropped backward into the water. He flipped his fins and jacknifed under.

The moment he got below the surface he was afraid. He didn't know of what, because the water looked no different from the time before, but a numbing fear gripped his chest and made his breath come faster. Below him, in the murky gloom, he could see the white outline of the boat like the underbelly of a shark, and on all sides the water disappeared into darkness that seemed to hide a thousand terrors. Everything looked unnaturally large, and menacing. He assured himself it was just the stories the people had told him at the bar, and that it was impossible for ghosts to be under water, but the fact remained that all his instincts urged him to get to the surface. He waited, about ten feet down, for his heart to return to normal, and he concentrated on the necessity of breathing regularly, while his eyes searched the gloom for any signs of danger. There were kelp-covered rocks, and a small cave in front of which he could see a lobster waiting, and there was the quick flash of a school of minnows darting past. Strands of reddish seaweed undulated slowly in the current, and he could hear the rattling sound of the waves breaking against the rocks. The sounds of his own breathing were loudest of all, hissing and rumbling in his ears. Cautiously, keeping his head moving from side to side, he flippered downward and circled the sunken boat, then touched bottom at the spot where a length of chain lay beneath the keel. He worked for a while on the chain, remembering what the foreman had told him to do, and he was so absorbed in his work that he failed to notice a school of small squid, which appeared in formation and hovered behind his shoulder. They were perhaps six inches long, and white, and they moved in such perfect unison that they might have been a single organism. They darted back and forth, their stabilizing fins fluttering madly, and then suddenly Dorple saw them and let out a bubbly, strangled scream, and they vanished. He backed against the hull and sank slowly to the sand, unable to gather the strength even to kick himself free and rise to the surface. His breath came in great, labored gasps, and he knew he was using too much oxygen, but he was powerless to do anything until he recovered from the shock of seeing what looked like thirty thousand tiny eyes staring at him out of an acre of tentacles. Finally his heart returned to normal, and he started to get up. Beneath him, something twitched at his behind, and he swirled around and saw he'd been sitting on a horseshoe crab, which now glided off across the sand, its spikelike tail forking defiantly upward. He hung onto the side of the wreck for a moment, smiling because he now knew there were no ghosts; what had frightened the others were natural phenomena of the sea. They had frightened him, too, but he'd been able to conquer the fear, and was now master of himself. Looking down, he saw the edge of a small box, and he stopped and tugged at it. It came away with a sucking motion and a cloud of sand, and he brushed it clean and opened it, and for a moment his breathing stopped and the bubbles ceased to rise from his mask. With a great effort he resumed normal breathing, so as not to disrupt his flow of air, and he stared at the box in his hands. He was looking into a cask of jewels such as he had never seen; there were gold clips, and diamond bracelets, and ruby pendants, and sapphire chokers, and an assortment of odds and ends of precious stones and gold and silver knicknacks that looked like the contents of a pirate's chest. But this was a new box, and Dorple felt it probably belonged to the owner of the yacht.

But suppose it didn't? Suppose it had come from another wreck, or had been dropped by someone else, what would be his chances of keeping it if he reported it? Pretty small, pretty damned small indeed. Most likely the foreman would claim it, and to hell with who had owned it to begin with. Better than to throw it away by reporting it, he should hide it for now, and come back at night and recover it. He looked for a hiding place, and saw the small cave with the lobster in front of it. The lobster retreated to one side, raising its claws over its head, as Dorple swam over and placed the box in the mouth of the cave. Then he returned to the wreck and glanced up at the surface, which looked like a muddied window pane, and slowly began his ascent.

"You took your time about it," the foreman said, as Dorple hauled himself up the ladder. "What kept you?"

Dorple raised his mask, spat, and began to unfasten his weights. "It ain't easy," he replied. "You should try it yourself sometime."

"I did," said the foreman. "I been down there myself, so you can't tell me nothing."

Dorple glanced at him, and smiled. "That's what you think," he said.

All the regulars were at the Heart's Ease Café when he walked in. Mother looked up, and his face broke into a leathery smile. "Ha!" he said. "He's here! Gloria you owe me four bucks!"

Gloria swiveled on her bar stool, and surveyed Dorple sourly. "Sonofabitch," she said. "I'd never of thought it."

"Four bucks even," said Mother. "Pay up."

"Not so fast," Gloria replied, as Dorple leaned casually against the bar. "He ain't said if he seen no ghosts."

"What about it, Fess?" said Mother, grinning. "Did you see one?"

Dorple examined his fingernails, determined to milk every possible bit of suspense out of the situation. "That's hard to say," he replied. "For a moment there, I wasn't so sure."

"Well, did you or didn't you?" said Mother impatiently. "There's money riding on this."

"I'll tell you how it was," Dorple replied. "Gimme a beer first."

"This one's on the house," said Mother, uncapping a bottle and setting it on the bar.

Dorple took a long swallow and wiped his mouth. "Well, it was like this," he said. "The minute I get down there, I know something's wrong. I can't describe it—it's just a feeling, like when you come in a dark room and know there's someone there."

"So!" said Gloria, triumphantly. "A ghost!"

"So I get down to the wreck," Dorple went on, ignoring her, "and all around I see things moving—the shadows are moving, the seaweed is moving, and things are creeping and crawling along the bottom. Things I never see before, and all of them are kind of moving and floating around, like— "

"Any corpses?" asked Gloria. "Was there any bodies, or skeletons?"

"None that I seen," Dorple replied. "There coulda been, though. I didn't go too far from the wreck."

"You coulda been standing on a skeleton and not know it," Gloria said, darkly. "They sink into the sand."

"Gloria, shut up and let him tell the story," said Rabbit Warren. "He knows what he seen and what he didn't."

"At any rate, I'm working on the chain," said Dorple, "and suddenly I get this feeling there's something behind me. At first I don't wanta turn around, but I figure I might as well know if there's something gonna jump me, so I look back"— he stopped, and took another long swallow of beer—"I look back, and there's this big blob of white, with thousands of eyes staring at me, and then—VOOM! It's gone! Like that." He snapped his fingers. "Vanished. I thought I'd like to die."

"It was a ghost!" Gloria shouted. "I win the bet!"

"Wait a minute," said Mother. "What do you think it was, Fess? Do you think it was a ghost?"

Dorple paused, and looked at the ceiling. "I got to be honest with you," he said, at last. "I think it was a school of squid."

"Squid my ass!" shrieked Gloria. "If it was squid, where'd they go to?"

"They move pretty fast," said Dorple. "First you see 'em, then you don't."

"You just said it was a big blob!" Gloria protested. "A big blob of white!"

"That's what it looked like. They was packed kinda close together, and when I first looked at 'em all I could see was white."

"There ain't no squids get that close together," said Gloria. "This was a ghost."

"Well, maybe." Dorple drained his beer, and slid the glass forward. "Gimme another," he said.

"Now, don't go backing off like that," Mother said, uncapping another bottle. "Either it was a ghost or it wasn't; we can't leave it open when there's money on it."

"It was a ghost," said Gloria. "And nobody's gonna tell me different."

"Well, he's here, so you owe me three bucks on that bet," said Mother. "You can't get around the fact he's here."

"I owe you two bucks, and not a nickel more. I win the bet he seen a ghost, so that knocks a buck off the three."

Mother took a deep breath. "All right, then, two bucks," he said. "Pay me."

"Put it on the bill," said Gloria, and tilted her head back and finished her drink.

Dorple was trembling with excitement when, that night, he parked his car at the edge of the cove. He had driven the last part of the way without headlights, and his eyes were accustomed enough to the darkness so he could see the beginning of the path that led down to the dock. There had been a moon earlier, but now heavy black clouds blotted it out, and the wind from the sea smelled of rain. The night was restless, and changing, like some giant animal stirring in its sleep, and Dorple had the feeling there'd be no diving tomorrow. In fact he wished he'd come a little earlier, when there still was a moon and the sea was calm. He put on his weighted belt and his tanks and then, with his mask on top of his head and carrying his flippers and a waterproof flashlight, he carefully picked his way down the path. The water in the cove was black, and oily, and he located it more by sound and smell than by sight.

Once on the dock he felt free to use his flashlight, and he put on his flippers and made the final adjustment with more than usual care. He knew that diving alone was risky, and that to do it at night was foolhardy, but there was no one he could trust with his secret, and the prize was well worth the risk. He estimated there was a hundred thousand dollars in that box, and he didn't intend to share it with anyone. He pulled down the mask, took the rubber tube in his mouth, and breathed in and out until he had the flow of air regulated. Then, taking the flashlight, he let himself into the water and went under.

If it had been dark above the water, it was trebly dark below; he was suspended in an infinity of blackness, through which the beam of his light made only a small and feeble glow. He picked out a few meaningless details on the bottom and flippered toward them, forgetting as he did to blow out his ears and equalize the pressure. Suddenly his ears and sinuses felt tight and began to ache, and he stopped, blocked his nose, and blew hard. The pressure eased, and he cursed himself for being careless. This was the one time he couldn't afford to be careless, and he resolved to go slowly, and think twice before he did anything. He got to the bottom and rested, playing his flashlight about in search of identifying marks. He knew the general direction of the cave, but the details looked different at night. Something touched him from behind, and his skin went cold and he whirled around and stared into the glowing eyes of a sea bass, which had been attracted by his light. The bass flicked its tail and disappeared, and Dorple breathed deeply to try to stop the hammering of his heart. Breathe deeply and regularly, he told himself. Deeply and regularly, or your air may stop and you'll suffocate.

After a while his heart calmed down, and he moved in a slow circle to the left, looking for the cave. It seemed like an hour before he found it, and he had begun to have the unreal feeling he was living through a nightmare. The circular glow of his light against the rocks had hypnotized him, and if it hadn't been for the distinctive shape of the cave he might very well have passed on by, turning in an endless arc out to sea. He reached inside and felt the box, and as he lifted it there was a quick flurry, and something closed like a trap on his wrist. He screamed into his mask and jerked his hand back, bringing with it the lobster that had clamped its needle-toothed claw onto him. Gasping and choking, Dorple hammered at the lobster's head with his flashlight, then dropped the light and tried to tear the animal loose. It was like sawing his wrist with a knife, but it finally came off, and in slow motion he hurled it from him. He retrieved the light, seeing blood spreading like reddish smoke from his wrist, and he snatched up the box and kicked his way toward the surface. But after a while he couldn't see the surface; the water was equally black in all directions, and the only way to tell which way was up was to watch his bubbles, and follow them. His ears were ringing and his heart was pounding, and he had the feeling he was about to lose consciousness, when finally he broke water and saw the night sky. He ripped off his mask, dropping the flashlight in his hurry, and drew in deep, roaring lungfulls of fresh air. He didn't care what happened now; he had the box clutched to his chest and he was safe on the surface, and he didn't even watch the light as it spiraled and twinkled down until it came to rest on the bottom. When at last he had his breath back, he flippered slowly toward the dock, noticing that the wind had risen and the waves were larger than before. He reached up and put the box on the dock, then hauled himself up and lay, exhausted, on his face on the planks. He had no idea how long he lay there; it might have been five minutes or it might have been an hour, but all at once he was surrounded by a foul-smelling wind that engulfed him and buffeted him and turned his stomach cold with terror. It seemed almost to be pushing him into the water, and he stood up, stumbled, and knocked the box off the dock. His only thought was to get away, to run, to fight off the force that was clawing at him. His skin crawled and he began to cry, and he ran, his frog-feet flapping and tripping him. He ran and scrambled and clawed his way up the path, sobbing and whimpering, and he flung himself into his car and, stamping the pedals with his flippered feet, he somehow got it started, and roared off into the night. At the bottom of the cove, the flashlight winked once, and then went out.

Twelve.

The storm that night turned into a whole gale. Powell, who had gone outside at the sound of Dorple's automobile, saw the lights careening away and then looked up at the sky, which was black and loud with wind. He shivered and went back inside, where Kathryn was working on a needlepoint design. From the other room came the sound of Steve's record player.

"Did you see who it was?" Kathryn asked, without looking up.

"No," Powell replied. "I don't know how long he'd been there, but he was certainly leaving in a hurry."

"Probably some kids on a date."

"Could be. Whoever it was, they'd better get home soon. We're in for a storm."

"Good. I like storms."

"It'll be interesting to see how the house holds up. Maybe we should get out some pans, in case."

"There are plenty of pots and pans. Wait till a leak starts before we drag them out."

"How about candles? Do we have enough?"

She looked at him and smiled. "What's the matter?" she

said. "You sound as though the place were going to fall apart."

"I just like to be prepared," he said defensively. "It's easier to look for candles now than after the power goes off."

"Who says it's going to go off?"

"It just might, that's all! Is there anything wrong in being prepared?"

Without a word Kathryn put down her needlepoint and went into the kitchen, returning a few moments later with a handful of stubby candles. "There," she said, putting them on the mantel. "Does that make you feel safer?"

Powell went over to her as she sat down. "Look," he said, "I didn't mean to snap. I'd just rather find the candles now than later. Is that wrong?"

She sighed, and thought a moment before answering. "No," she said. "I guess everybody's nerves are raw."

"They'd be a lot better if we could get rid of Uncle George."

"I'm aware of that. But beyond that, there's—I don't know how to put it—we seem to be operating on different levels, somehow. I wish I could get it straightened out."

"You mean you wish you could get me straightened out."

"I didn't say that! I said 'it,' and by 'it' I meant our disagreement about lots of things. I hate it, and I wish it would stop."

"I know."

"Then let's *do* something! It's no good to sit here and snarl at each other when we both know it's wrong!"

"O.K. What should we do?"

She thought for several seconds, her face knotted with frustration. "If you'd only be *reasonable!*" she burst out at last. "If you'd only see that—no, that isn't going to do it. I'm sorry. You can't help what you think, any more than I can."

"Then what do we do?"

"I don't know. I honestly don't know."

Powell hesitated, then said, "I'm going to talk to the librarian tomorrow."

"Isn't she a spiritualist?"

"Uh-huh."

"But that's the whole trouble! The more you get filled up with that stuff the worse it is!"

"This is different. It's just an idea, but it might help."

"Well, if it helps, I'm for it. Believe me, I'm tired of living like this."

There was a rattle of rain against the windows, and from outside came the sound of a wind-blown chair careening across the porch. "Oh-oh," said Powell. "Here she comes. We'd better start buttoning up."

They secured the living-room windows, and had moved into the kitchen when there came the flap of feet on the stairs and Uncle George appeared, dressed in a nightshirt. "My goddamn ceiling leaks," he said.

Powell took a dishpan and followed Uncle George up to his room, where a brown spot was spreading on the ceiling. He waited for a couple of drops to fall, then set the dishpan in place, and the next drop hit it with a musical clang.

"That's great," said Uncle George. "How am I supposed to sleep with that noise?"

"There's going to be a lot more noise than this," Powell replied. "If I were you I'd plug my ears."

"Why don't you call your caretaker? Isn't he supposed to fix this kind of stuff?"

"On a night like this, I doubt if I could get a doctor. The caretaker would laugh in my face."

"Not in mine, he wouldn't. He'd damn well get over here."

Powell started to say something, then cut it short and went downstairs, leaving Uncle George to climb, cursing, back into bed. Kathryn had locked the kitchen windows, and was putting towels along the sills where water had already started to bubble through the cracks. "This is going to be a beaut," Powell said. Instinctively he looked at the cellar door, and pushed the bolt to make sure it was tight. "If we've got one leak already, I hate to think what we'll have by the time the storm is over."

The lights flickered, and dimmed, then came bright again. "I apologize for anything I said," Kathryn remarked, as she opened a drawer for more towels. "You may have as many candles as you please."

"I guess I'll light one," said Powell. He started for the living room as the lights flickered again, and went out. Somewhere, a door banged. "Damn," he said, and groped his way in the darkness. His neck felt cold, and for the first time he felt the icy fingers of panic beginning to clutch at him. Take it easy, he told himself. You're supposed to be the man in the house, so get a grip on yourself.

He found the candles, and when he lighted one he noticed that his hands were shaking. He lighted another from the first, then went back and gave one to Kathryn. She saw his trembling, and looked at him. "What's the matter?" she asked. "Are you all right?"

He turned away, searching for a candlestick. "Of course. I'm fine."

"Do you feel all right?"

"I feel great! Where the hell are the candlesticks?"

"On the top shelf of the closet," she said quietly. "And there are more in the living room."

He felt better once he had lighted and set up the candles, but an uneasy fear continued to gnaw at him, and he wished the night were over. Normally he liked storms as much as Kathryn did, but this one was different; he had the feeling that more than the usual elements were involved, and he was alone and lost. It was like a dream he had whenever he was sick, a dream in which something infinitesimally small, like an electric spark, was contrasted with something overwhelmingly large, like a tidal wave, or the side of a mountain. It was a terrifying dream, and he invariably woke up burning with fever. His sensation now was that he was the small element, at the mercy of a dark, towering tidal wave, which could be seen coming from a great distance, its foaming top almost lost in the sky. "What about a drink?" he said to Kathryn. "Would you like one?"

"A fine idea," she said.

Steve came out of his room and looked around. "What happened to the lights?" he asked.

"The storm knocked them out," Kathryn replied. "Take a candle."

"Some crummy setup, when a little rain knocks out the lights," said Steve. "Am I supposed to play my record player with a candle, too?" Powell turned on him and started to say something, and Steve hurriedly added, "Only kidding, Pop. Only kidding." He took a candle and returned to his room.

There was a crash upstairs, and the sound of bare feet pounding on the floor, and Uncle George shouting curses. Powell took a candle and ran for the stairs, and the minute he hit the staircase a gust of wind blew out the candle. The banging and cursing increased, as he went back for another. "It's all right!" he shouted. "I'll be right there!" This time he shielded the candle with one hand and climbed the stairs into an icy wind, with Kathryn following. They reached Uncle George's room in time to see him stamp into the water-filled dishpan, lose his balance, and fall heavily against the foot of the bed.

"Son of an everlasting, spun-glass BITCH!" he shouted. "Get me out of here before they kill me!" His window was wide open and rain was pouring in horizontally, making the curtains billow out like sails on a windjammer. Kathryn ran to the window and closed it.

"Who are you talking about?" Powell asked. "There's nobody here."

"I don't know who did it, but somebody threw water on me when I was in bed," Uncle George snarled. "Hit me right on the forehead."

Powell looked at the bed, and at the ceiling over it, and saw a dark stain above the pillow. A drop of water formed, then fell with a small plop onto the bed. "That's what hit you," he said. "There's a leak right over your head."

"Then who turned out the lights?" Uncle George demanded. "Who turned out the lights and opened my window?"

"The storm knocked out the lights," Powell replied. "And I assume you opened the window."

"You think I'm crazy, opening a window on a night like this? You think I want to catch my death?"

Powell said nothing, and looked at Kathryn. "We'd better move him to the other room," he said. "He'll never get any sleep in here."

"I'll never sleep anywhere, in this house," Uncle George retorted. "This is the most bitched-up house I've ever seen. Why don't you spend a little money and fix it?"

"I'm told there's a good hotel in town," said Powell. "Completely watertight, and twenty-four-hour maid service. Why not give it a whirl?"

"Come on, Uncle George," Kathryn said quickly. "I'll make up the bed in the spare room and you can sleep there."

"That's the one Estelle used," said Uncle George. "She said it was like concrete."

"Then sleep in with us," said Powell. "I snore and Kathryn kicks, but you shouldn't mind a little thing like that."

Uncle George looked at him sourly. "Don't talk so fast, or I might," he said.

Powell pushed the bed out from under the leak, while

Kathryn made up a fresh bed in the spare room. Then, with Uncle George once more settled down, they went into their own room and closed the door. The house shook and rattled, and the wind made a low, periodic whistle in the eaves. A door banged again.

"I'd better find that door," Powell said. "That, if nothing else, will keep us awake." Shielding his candle, he went into the hall and listened. For a while he heard nothing but the noises of the storm, the buffeting of the wind, and the rattling slash of the rain, and then he began to hear other noises. A stair creaked, a floorboard groaned, and the whole house seemed to be writhing under the attack. There was a crash as more porch furniture blew over, and then, once again, a door slammed. Damn, thought Powell. That's downstairs. His skin began to itch as he descended the stairs, checked carefully to see that the cellar door was locked, then tested the door to Steve's room. Everything was tight, which left only the door to the study, off the living room. He went around to it, and arrived in time to see it slowly swing open, and his candle went out. Then the door slammed, hard, and Powell turned and fled upstairs, bumping into furniture and slipping on rugs as he ran. Kathryn was in bed when he returned, and he closed the door and leaned against it for a moment.

"Did you find it?" she asked.

He nodded, and took a deep breath. "I think there's something wrong with the catch," he said. "I'll fix it in the morning."

"Put a chair against it," she suggested. "That'll keep it for tonight."

Powell shook his head, and began to undress. "It's closed now," he said. "We'll just hope it stays that way." The door banged again. "The hell with it," he said. "Let it bang."

Kathryn got out of bed, and took her candle. "There's no point in that," she said. "I'll go down and fix it."

Powell started to say something but the words wouldn't form themselves, and he waited, listening, as Kathryn went down the stairs and around to the study. He heard her drag a chair to the door, and then heard the soft padding of her returning footsteps. He continued to undress, feeling slightly ashamed and glad he hadn't said anything.

When they were both in bed, and the candles were out, they lay and listened to the storm. The house shook with each blast, and the whistling in the eaves had reached a high shriek, but aside from the few leaks there seemed to be no trouble. The house had stood for more than a hundred years, and had weathered worse storms than this, so there was no reason to expect more than routine trouble tonight. But Powell still couldn't rid himself of the nagging fear, the inability to relax, and he listened to every sound and analyzed it carefully. The muscles in his shoulders and neck ached with tension, and the more he tried to relax the more tense he became. His insteps were perspiring, and he could feel little puddles of perspiration beneath his shoulders and buttocks. Kathryn moved closer, and reached out and held his hand.

"This is a good storm," she said.

"Uh-huh."

There was a silence, then she said, "How's your back?"

"O.K."

Another silence. "I'm sorry we argued."

"So am I."

"Let's promise never to do it again, all right?"

"All right."

"Are you mad about anything?"

"Of course not."

"What's the matter?"

"Nothing."

"I'm fond of you, you know."

"I'm fond of you."

"Sometimes it's hard to tell."

"Listen! What was that?"

"What?"

"It sounded like footsteps."

"It's probably the floorboards."

"Could be."

"Remember the first storm we spent together?"

"Uh—I guess so."

"What do you mean, you guess so? It was on our honey-moon."

"That's right. Oh, sure."

"I've liked storms ever since."

"Uh-huh."

She let go his hand, and turned over. "Good night," she said.

"Good night."

He wasn't aware of going to sleep but he must have, because all at once Steve was screaming, and Uncle George was cursing, and there were bangs and crashes that sounded as though people were throwing furniture down the stairs. Powell leaped from bed, instinctively tried to turn on the light, then groped in the darkness for his candle and matches. There was a sudden light as Kathryn struck a match to her candle, but when she opened the door a blast of wind blew the candle out, and there was darkness again. Steve's screams continued at a regular pitch, and were mingled with the unmistakable sounds of Uncle George falling downstairs. Powell finally got his candle lighted, and when he and Kathryn ran into the hall they were greeted by an icy wind that swirled through the house and ripped at their nightclothes. It carried with it the familiar fetid smell, and Powell knew before he got there that the cellar door was open. He slammed it closed, bolted it, and then went into Steve's room, where Kathryn was holding the sobbing boy close to her and trying to calm him. Uncle George came limping and cursing into the kitchen, but nobody paid any attention to him.

"What happened?" Powell asked Steve. "What frightened you?"

"I don't know," Steve replied, shivering.

"It was a nightmare," Kathryn said, as she stroked the boy's head. "The storm gave him a nightmare. It's all right now. Everything's going to be all right."

For the first time, Powell listened for the sounds of the storm, and could tell it was still blowing. The wind in the house had stopped when he closed the cellar door, but the wind outside continued with increasing fury, and the house shuddered and creaked under its blows. He looked at Uncle George. "Are you all right?" he asked.

"Hell, no," replied Uncle George. "Like to break every bone in my body. Where'd that wind come from, anyway?"

"The cellar," said Powell, simply. Then, out of curiosity, he went into the living room and looked at the door to the study. It was wide open, and the chair Kathryn had put against it was lying on its back, halfway across the room. It occurred to him that although Kathryn might resist the idea of ghosts, it was possible and even desirable that Steve be convinced, and the sooner the better. He went back to Steve's room. "I think I'll stay up a while," he said to Kathryn. "You can go to bed."

She looked at him in surprise. "What's going on?" she asked. "Are you trying to get rid of me?"

"Of course not. I'm just not sleepy, that's all. I'll keep Steve company till he goes back to sleep."

"All right," she said, getting up slowly. Then she looked at her son and said, "Is that all right with you?"

"Sure," Steve replied. "That's fine."

She left the room hesitantly, and looked back.

"Shoo," said Powell, with a dusting motion. "You and Uncle George both. Steve and I will hold the fort."

"I still think you're trying to get rid of me," said Kathryn. "I want to know why."

"I don't give a damn why," said Uncle George. "I'm going to bed." He stamped up the stairs, and after a moment Kathryn followed him.

Powell looked at Steve. "Anything I can get you?" he asked. "Ginger ale, Coke, anything like that?"

"No, thanks," Steve replied. He, like Kathryn, was wondering what Powell had in mind, and he watched his father closely.

"I think I'll get a beer," Powell said. He took a candle and went into the kitchen, opened the dark and silent icebox, and found a can of beer. He opened it, double-checked the bolt on the cellar door, then went back to Steve's room and sat down. "Cheers," he said, and took a sip. Steve watched him. "There's something I think we ought to talk about," Powell said.

Steve's whole body relaxed. "Oh, that," he said wearily. "I know all about that."

"You do?" said Powell, in surprise. "How?"

"Everybody knows it. There's this thing called a sperm, and when that makes contact with an egg, it starts a—"

"No, no, no," said Powell hurriedly. "I wasn't talking about that. I was talking about ghosts."

Steve showed interest. "Oh?" he said. "What about them?"

"Well, first off—do you believe in them?"

Steve thought for a moment. "Do you?" he asked.

"Yes. Or put it this way: I don't think that I, or anyone else, knows enough to say it's impossible for them to exist. And I've seen some pretty good evidence that they do."

"Have you seen one?"

"Once. For a moment."

"Was that a ghost tonight?"

"I think so. I think that's why you were scared."

"What kind of ghost was it?"

"I don't know. I don't think anybody can explain them, but I sure as hell know you can't deny them. I think part of your fear comes from the unknown, and the rest"—he shrugged —"that's unknown, too. But if you accept the fact that they're possible, you're a lot better off than if you try to deny them. Animals accept them; animals won't go near a house that's haunted."

Steve was fascinated. "Well, what do you know about that?" he said. "I think I'll get a dog, and see if it'll come in this house."

"I'd check with your mother first," said Powell.

"What else do you know?" Steve asked. "Do you know any good ghost stories?"

Powell hesitated, wondering if Kathryn could hear him, and then said, "Well, I'll give you one example. It's documented, so there's got to be some truth in it. It's in Reynolds' book on ghosts in Irish houses, and it tells how a whole clan—a hundred people or so—were murdered one night in a castle; lured into what they thought was a banquet, and then ambushed by soldiers. This was back in the fifteenth century. They were buried beneath the floor of a big room, and then the room was sealed off, and every time since then that someone has unsealed the room and gone down the stairs into it they've been beaten to death with stones, or driven crazy. One man, before he died, told of seeing eyes and arms rise up from the floor, and pelt him with stones. The last time the room was opened was in 1924, and that man, one Arno Santley, was committed to the Asylum of St. John of God's, near Dublin. Reynolds saw the place, and saw the documents confirming it."

Steve's eyes were wide. "Wow!" he said. "Some swingin' deal! What else?"

Powell finished his beer. "I really don't think this is the time to go into it," he said. "The only point I wanted to make was that you shouldn't doubt their existence—or the possibility of their existence."

"Was that a ghost that threw my beer stein?"

"That was probably a poltergeist, which is another thing completely. A poltergeist is just a mischievous spirit, that likes to raise a little hell around the house. It doesn't hurt anybody."

"But a real ghost can kill you?"

Powell realized he'd used the wrong story as an illustration. "I wouldn't say that," he said uneasily. "The one I saw, for instance, just looked at me, and then disappeared. Generally speaking, I think you're safe with them."

"Those people in Ireland sure weren't safe."

"That was an exception; American ghosts just sort of wander around. I wouldn't worry about it, anyway. Accept it for what it is, and don't let it upset you."

"Sure," said Steve. "I'll accept it, all right."

Powell stood up. "And let's keep this between ourselves," he said. "I haven't convinced your mother yet, and I don't think she'd like my subverting you."

"Do you want me to help? Maybe the two of us working together could convince her."

"Thanks, anyway," Powell said, smiling. "I think I'd better do this alone."

"O.K. Whatever you say."

Powell picked up his candle. "Good night," he said.

"Good night," replied Steve, settling down. "And thanks for the bedtime story." Powell laughed and went up the stairs.

When he got in bed, he realized that Kathryn was still awake. He blew out the candle, and pulled the covers around him.

For a long while neither of them spoke. Then Powell said, "You O.K.?"

She hesitated, and said, "No."

"What's the matter?"

"I don't know. I just can't stop shaking."

He reached out and touched her, and she was trembling as though with a chill. He moved closer and put his arms around her, and suddenly she clung to him in a spasm of fear. "I'm losing my mind!" she cried. "I can feel it!"

"No, you're not," Powell said softly. "You're all right."

"I am not! I can feel my head getting tighter and tighter and tighter, until pretty soon it's going to burst! I can feel it!"

"Just relax. Relax, and don't worry." He stroked her head, and whispered in her ear, and after a while he could feel her relax. Her limbs sagged, and the shaking stopped, and then gradually she began to cling to him with a different intensity, and all the sounds of the storm vanished from his mind.

Thirteen.

The storm continued unabated next day. The rain came
smoking down, and the wind slashed the tops off the waves
and filled the air with brine. The surf thundered in the cove,
sending sheets of white water up the face of the rocks, and the
horizon was lost in a mist of driving spume. After breakfast,
Uncle George put on a sou'wester and staggered off against
the wind to the cove, where he took one look and then came
running back, his eyes wide with panic. "Get the company!"
he shouted. "Call the salvage people!"

"What's the matter?" Powell asked.

"What do you think's the matter? The storm's breaking
the boat to pieces!" He grabbed a telephone book and began
to tear through its pages, spreading water on everything
nearby.

"There's nothing they can do today," Powell said. "They
won't go near it."

"They damn well will if I tell them to," replied Uncle
George, dropping the book and picking up the telephone.
"That's what they're being paid—" He stopped, and jiggled
the hook. "No dial tone," he said.

"The phone probably went out when the lights did," said
Powell.

"Damn, damn, damn!" shouted Uncle George. He gave the hook a wild flurry of jiggles, bellowed into the instrument, then slammed it down. "Typical," he snarled, turning away. "Typical damn foul up."

"Hey, Ma, can I go look?" said Steve excitedly. "Can I look at the boat?"

"Only if your father goes with you," said Kathryn. "And don't get too near the edge."

Steve looked at his father. "O.K.?"

"O.K.," said Powell. He and Steve put on sou'westers and then, together with Uncle George, they fought their way against the wind to the edge of the cove.

The surf was like some monstrous animal. It roared into the cove, mauling the boat with each wave, then circled back and sucked against it, pulling it and nudging it and lining it up for another blow. The salvage barge had been driven onto the rocks and was slowly breaking up, and the yacht had changed position and seemed about to go on the rocks itself. The mast had been carried away, and the hull could be seen only as the backwash went out, momentarily dropping the water level in the cove. Then another wave would come smashing in, and it would disappear. The three people watched in silence for a while, and Uncle George's face, wet with rain, was like a figure chipped out of flint. His jaw muscles worked, and he muttered to himself as he watched the sea slowly beat his boat to pieces. After a while Powell turned away.

"There's nothing we can do here," he said, and started back toward the house. Uncle George stayed where he was, and Powell glanced back and said, "Are you coming?"

"Go on, if you want," Uncle George replied. "I'm staying here."

Powell beckoned to Steve, and together they made their way back. When they reached the house Steve went to his room, and Powell sought out Kathryn, who was mopping the puddles on the second floor.

"It's gone, all right," he said.

"I never thought they'd salvage it, anyway," said Kathryn. "I counted it lost when it first sank."

"Maybe this means he'll be leaving."

Kathryn looked up and smiled. "Don't think I hadn't thought of that." She took a sodden towel into the bathroom and added, "I feel kind of sorry for him, though. It isn't every day you lose a boat like that."

"It isn't every day you have one," said Powell. "He'll probably buy another this afternoon." Then he remembered the librarian, and said, "Do you want the car for anything?"

"Nothing I can think of. Why?"

"I thought I'd zip over to Cranton for a few minutes."

Kathryn was quiet. "All right," she said.

"Don't worry about this. I'm only trying to straighten things out."

"I know."

"I'll be back in a half hour—an hour at the most."

"You needn't hurry."

He knew she was against his going, but there was nothing more he could say. He turned and left, hoping the result would prove him right. If I'm wrong, he thought, then we're really in trouble.

The librarian smiled when she saw him come through the door. "I wondered when you were coming," she said. "I thought I'd be seeing you long before this."

"Things have been happening," Powell replied. He looked around to make sure the room was empty, then said, "You once offered to let me come when you talked to Jenny."

The librarian's blue eyes sparkled. "That's right," she said. "And I wish you had. We had quite a chat."

Powell cleared his throat. "I wonder if I could take you up on that now."

"Of course! When would you like?"

"As soon as possible." He had the insane feeling he was making an appointment with a dentist, and he had to keep reminding himself of the subject.

"Would this evening be all right?"

"Whatever you say." He had somehow hoped she could do it sooner, but he realized it was more complicated than picking up a telephone, and nothing she could do while at work.

"Was there anything you wanted to talk to her about?"

"Yes. I want to know what she wants. I want to know what Felicity wants, and I want to know what Ebenezer wants. I want to know why these people—these whatever they are—are haunting the house, and I want to know how I can stop it. It's going to drive either my wife or me crazy if it keeps up much longer."

The librarian nodded. "I know what you mean," she said. "It's a pretty tall order, but I'll see what I can do. Suppose you come here around five-thirty, and we'll go back to my place."

When he got home Kathryn was preparing lunch. She didn't look at him, but he knew what she was thinking, and he was aware that if she knew what he was going to do, she'd have him put in a straightjacket on the instant.

"Well!" she said, opening the oven and peering inside. "I didn't expect you so soon."

He shrugged in reply.

There was a silence, during which she produced six onions and began to peel them. "Everything satisfactory?" she asked.

"So far." He opened the refrigerator and took out a can of beer. Punching an opener into it, he added, "I've got to go back this afternoon."

There was a longer silence, and Powell took several deep swallows of beer. "Where's Uncle George?" he asked.

"I guess he's still at the cove. I haven't seen him since you went out."

He looked out the window. "He must be getting pretty wet."

Finally, Kathryn could stand it no longer. "What *happened?*" she asked. "What did you *do?*"

"I told you, I've got to go back this afternoon. All I did was make an appointment."

"For *what?*"

"Look, do you mind waiting till later? There's nothing I can tell you now."

She turned her back, slammed a skillet on the stove, and began to sauté the onions. Powell edged quietly out of the room.

He was at the Atheneum at five-thirty, and the librarian was waiting for him at the door. "I'm ready to go," she said. "I've already locked up." She was twittering with excitement, and as Powell ushered her into his car he had the uneasy thought that she might well be capable of inventing messages from the dead, whether she received them or not. She was so immersed in the subject that it took complete possession of her, and radiated out like invisible waves of electricity. "I hope Rajput is in a good mood today," she said, as they drove down the rain-swept street. "I hope this storm hasn't put him off his feed."

"Who's Rajput?" Powell asked.

"My control. He's usually a dear, but sometimes he gets a little edgy, and then he's hard to work with."

"I don't understand."

"Of course. I forgot. Your control is your contact with the outer world—the person through whom you work. I have to get to him before I can talk to anyone else."

"Oh. He's dead, too, then?"

"Heavens, yes. He's been dead two thousand years. He was a prince in India, or whatever they called it then. A fascinating man. There's my house—the next on the left."

They stopped in front of a small frame house with pansies in the window boxes, and when they got inside Powell could smell old carpets, furniture polish, and seasoned wood. There was also a faint perfumy smell, which he couldn't identify until he saw an open jar of potpourri on a table. He took off his raincoat, and looked for a place to hang it. "In the hall closet," she said from the other room, where she was pulling the shades. "Just on your right there," Powell did as she directed, wondering how she knew what was on his mind.

When the shades were drawn she beckoned him into the room, and closed the door. In the half darkness he had a sensation of being under water, and he drifted slowly to the chair she indicated for him. It was an overstuffed patent rocker, and the touch of the fabric prickled his hands. She sat in a facing chair, and between them was a small, round table, with a beaded runner. Her face, whiter than anything nearby, seemed to float in the air. "Now," she said briskly. "Was there anything else you wanted to know?"

Powell found that his palms were sweating, and his heart had begun to race. "No," he said, and swallowed. "Nothing I can think of right now."

"Very well, then. Be absolutely silent, unless I ask you something." She closed her eyes and leaned back in her chair, and he could hear her murmuring, "The carpet . . . the beautiful carpet . . . over . . . and over . . . and over . . . and over. . . ."

She was quiet for what seemed like several minutes, and then in a clear voice she said, "Rajput! Are you there, Rajput? . . . I'm sorry, you'll have to speak louder. . . . That's better. You always mumble so. Are your teeth all right? . . . Don't be silly. There hasn't been a decent dentist here in years. . . .

Well, I'll ask, but don't expect too much. Rajput, is Jenny
there? There's a gentleman with some rather important questions. And Felicity, too, although I don't suppose it's a good
idea to have them together. . . . Thank you." The smell of the
potpourri became stronger, and tinged with lilac, and Powell
felt cold. Then the woman's voice went on, "Jenny! How are
you, dear?. . . . Oh, I'm sorry to hear it. Jenny, there's a. . . .
Well, dear, I really don't know what *I* can do about *that*. If
ever anything was your business, I'd say. . . . Please! Jenny!
There's a gentleman here! . . . Yes, I know, and he has some
questions. He wants to know, first of all, what it is you want.
. . . Jenny! Be serious! He wants to know why you're haunting
his house. . . . Well, it's his for the summer, and you're just as
much a visitor as he is, if not more so. . . . Jenny, will you
please stay with the subject? I'm sure Rajput can find you
someone who'll be glad to oblige, but that's nothing to do with
Mr. Powell. He and his wife are quite distressed, and they
wish you'd stop. . . . Then who is doing it?. . . All right, give
me back to Rajput. . . . Yes, I'll tell him. . . . What? Are you
serious?. . . . Oh, come now. . . . Jenny, you're fooling me. . . .
Yes, I'll tell him. Now, please. . . . You're incorrigible. . . .
Hello, Rajput? May I speak to Felicity?" There was a long
wait, and then she said, "Oh, dear. Well, another time."
Then she seemed to be asleep, and Powell wondered what he
was supposed to do. He didn't want to leave, but he also
didn't want to stay if she was going to sleep all night. The
séance was clearly over, and nothing much had been accomplished. He stirred in his chair, and the librarian began to
wake up. She opened her eyes, and looked at him for several
moments before speaking.

"It was a mistake to ask her what she wanted," she said at
last. "That girl is insatiable."

"I gather there's nothing I can do," said Powell.

"No-o-o, I'd say not. But aside from her—ah—main desire,

she gave me a list of things that, frankly, don't make sense. I'm completely confused."

"What kind of things?"

"Well, one thing she said she wanted was a Deering-McCormick reaper. Why should she ask for a thing like that?"

"Maybe they grow a lot of wheat out there," said Powell. "Or up there—or down—or wherever."

"Another thing was a Cozy-Doze mattress with torsion-flex inner springs," the librarian went on. "And a Hi-Gloss Lacquer Deodorant Spray with a five-day guarantee—I think she was having me on."

"It sounds as though she watches television."

"Yes, but I'm disappointed. She's usually quite straight with me."

"How about Felicity?"

"Rajput says she's nowhere to be found. He hasn't seen her or Ebenezer in days."

"Could it be because they're in my house?"

She thought about this for a while. "Maybe," she said. "That's what Jenny implied."

"Damn," said Powell. "Excuse me."

She smiled. "After what I've just heard, one little damn is nothing."

"Do you think," Powell said slowly, "that if I were to get a mattress, and a spray, and so on, and then just—well, leave them around, that it would do any good?"

"What would your wife say?"

"I hadn't thought of that."

"And where could you lay your hands on a Deering-McCormick reaper?"

"I was thinking more of token presents. But as you said, it would be hard to convince Kathryn I wasn't crazy."

"I don't think Jenny was serious, anyway. I think she was teasing, and I'm quite cross with her."

"I'll tell you frankly, I'm at the point where I'll try anything. Kathryn thinks I'm having hallucinations, but if things don't change she's the one whose reason will come unhinged. There's getting to be too much she can't explain."

"I know."

He rose. "Well, thank you, anyway," he said. "It was good of you to try."

"I'll try again tomorrow," she replied. "If anything comes up I'll let you know."

When he got outside he had the feeling he was returning from a long journey. It was still raining, although not so hard as before, but the street and the houses and his car looked faintly unfamiliar, as though they had somehow changed during his absence. He got in the car and headed for home, and at the first street intersection he saw a large, lighted drugstore. On an impulse he pulled to the curb and got out.

The druggist was a kindly, smiling man, with a high-collared white jacket and rimless glasses. "Yes, sir," he said. "May I help you?"

Powell cleared his throat and tried to sound casual, and it occurred to him that he was acting just as he had when, as a youth, he had bought his first box of contraceptives. "Do you by any chance have a spray?" he said, making a pinching motion with his thumb and fingers.

"Yes, sir," said the druggist. "A nasal spray?"

"No, a contra—a deodorant spray. You know—for deodorants."

"Of course. Is this for a room, or personal use?"

"Personal."

"If you don't mind my saying so, sir, we've found that most men prefer the stick deodorant. We have a fine line of sticks" —he produced a sample, and held it up—"this one is by far the most popular. In fact I use it myself, because in my position one can't be too careful. Rub some on your hand, and see how fresh it smells."

Powell began to perspire. "This isn't for me," he said. "It's got a special name, and I'm supposed to get it for—someone else. It's called the Hi-Gloss Lacquer Deodorant Spray, and I'm told it has a five-day guarantee."

The druggist looked at him coldly. "It certainly does," he said. "It takes five days and a pint of turpentine to scrape it off. We haven't carried it for years."

"Oh," said Powell.

"If you don't mind my asking, could you tell me who wants it? I'm curious only because it's such an old-fashioned item; it was one of the first attempts at a deodorant, and I'm told it was a ghastly failure from the beginning. It hung on only because the farmers found some use for it—probably to spray their livestock. I didn't think anybody remembered it now."

"Well, I guess you could call this an old-fashioned girl," Powell said, with a strangled attempt at a laugh.

"Ah, yes. In that case, we have a very nice lavender spray, reminiscent of lilacs in the—"

"I don't want that," Powell cut in. By now he wanted nothing so much as to get out of the store. "Give me that one," he said, pointing to an atomizer that contained a colorless fluid.

"That isn't really a—"

"Never mind. It'll have to do." He produced his wallet, and thumbed out some bills. "How much is it?"

"Five dollars. But I ought to tell you—"

"Here. Don't bother to wrap it; just give it to me." He put down a five-dollar bill and held out his hand. Slowly, the druggist gave him the atomizer, and he put it in his coat pocket and left the store. The druggist stared after him for almost a minute after he had gone.

His next stop was the Heart's Ease Café. He wanted time to

sort out his thoughts before talking to Kathryn, and he wanted particularly to think of what to tell her. He couldn't tell her the truth; it would not only be humiliating, it would also confirm her belief that he was mentally unstable. Dorple was perched on a bar stool, staring into a glass of beer, and he glanced at Powell and nodded in recognition.

"Hi," Powell said, sliding onto a stool. Then, to Mother he said, "A Scotch, please."

"I hear the boat broke up," said Mother, producing a bottle and a shot glass. "They say the storm ripped her clean in two."

"Yes, the last time I saw her she seemed about to go. I haven't checked recently."

"Don't," said Dorple. "Stay as far from that friggin' cove as you can."

Powell eyed him with interest. "Oh?" he said. "Did you see something there?"

Dorple threw back his head and drained his glass. "I didn't see nothing," he said. "But I wouldn't go back there for a million bucks." He slid the glass forward in silent command for a refill.

"What's got into you, anyway?" said Mother, reaching for a bottle. "Yesterday you come in looking like you owned the world, and giving us a big story about a school of squid, and today you creep in and start pouring down the beer like you was about to be shot. What happened last night?"

"Nothing," said Dorple. "Just gimme a beer."

Powell remembered the car he'd seen driving away from the cove, and concluded it was Dorple's. "Somebody was there last night," he said. "Just before the storm. I saw the lights as they drove off."

Mother glanced at Dorple. "Now, what silly sonofabitch would go there at night?" he said.

Dorple was quiet for a minute, and then he said, "All right, I'll tell you. Yesterday, when I was working on the wreck, I found a box of jewels on the bottom. Since they wasn't on the boat I figured they was fair game, so I stashed 'em away and came back to pick 'em up at night. I did—I picked 'em up, all right—but when I got back to the dock there was this— Jesus Christ, I don't even want to think of it." He shivered, and drained half his new beer.

"Did it come from that crack in the rock?" Powell asked.

"I don't know where it come from; all I know is I got the hell outa there before it got me. It was *after* me! Like it had hands, only it didn't!"

"What about the jewels?" Mother asked.

"I think they fell in the water. Look, let's not talk about it no more, should we?"

"I know what you mean," Powell said. He thought for a moment, then said, "Would you do me a favor?"

"I don't know," Dorple replied. "What is it?"

"Would you come and tell my wife about it? I can't convince her the place is haunted, but maybe a first-hand witness will. How about it?"

"Mister, I wouldn't go near that house for *nothing*. I don't even want to look in that direction."

"Suppose I bring her here. Will you tell her then?"

"Right now I don't want to think about it. In a month or so maybe I'll feel different. We'll see." He finished his beer, and slid the glass forward.

"I'll say one thing," said Mother. "I never seen you drink so much and stay sober. By my count, this is the twenty-third beer I poured since you come in here, and you ain't one bit drunker than when you walked through that door."

"Quit the talking and fill the glass," said Dorple.

Electrical power had been restored when Powell got home, and he could hear the tinny sounds of Steve's phonograph.

Kathryn was in the living room with her needlepoint, and she looked up at him with interest. "Well!" she said. "What luck?"

"None." He felt the bulge of the atomizer in his coat pocket, and brought it out and gave it an experimental squirt.

"What's that?" Kathryn asked.

For the first time he looked at the label. "It says 'Moth-Skram,'" he said. "I guess it's some kind of moth-repellant."

Kathryn studied him closely. "Did you just buy it?"

"Yes. It—well, it was there, and it seemed like a good idea. They didn't have what I was after."

"Who's 'they'?"

"The drugstore. In Cranton. A very nice druggist, though."

"What were you after?"

"It doesn't really matter. The whole thing was a bust."

"Sit down," said Kathryn. "Can I get you a drink?"

"I'd love one." He sank into a chair. "I had a couple at Mother's, but—"

"At *where?*" Kathryn stopped on her way to the bar, and stared at him.

"It's a bar. The man who runs it is named Mother—I mean, that's what they call him."

"Just what kind of place *is* this?" Kathryn asked in an icy voice.

"Like any other bar. Everybody goes there." He wondered if this was the time to tell her about Dorple, and decided to wait until he was on firmer ground. Nothing he'd said had made much sense, and she'd probably brush Dorple off as one more fantasy. She went slowly to the bar, and put ice in two glasses.

"Tell me about your spiritualist," she said, in a casual tone. "What did she do?"

Powell toyed with the atomizer. The hell with it, he thought. I might as well tell the truth as try to invent something. "Nothing," he replied. "She went into a trance and mumbled a lot of stuff, and that was all."

"What had you expected?" She handed him a drink.

"I don't know. I thought she might come up with some answers. You yourself said anything would be worthwhile, if it worked."

"I know. And I've been doing some thinking."

"About what?"

She sat on an arm of his chair and stirred her drink with one finger. "I've been thinking that we've been locked together too long, without seeing any outsiders. Uncle George and Estelle don't count, because they just made things worse."

"*That* is the truth," said Powell, sipping his drink.

"Well, what I thought—and please don't say anything until I'm through, because you may think I'm crazy—I thought it might be a good idea if we had a big party—a costume party, even—and got all our friends down for a Saturday night, and cut loose. We could have a few for the weekend, and the rest for just Saturday—I haven't worked out all the details, but my main point is that what this house needs is a little life, and if for once we should cut loose and have a real, go-to-hell, wing-ding of a party, it would be the answer. We haven't had one in a long time, and I think we need it."

Powell was silent, while he considered the various appalling possibilities. "Would it have to be a costume party?" he asked finally.

"I don't know. It might be nice."

"It would be expensive."

"We could manage that."

He thought some more. Should he tell her what he really thought of it, or should he try to discourage her in a tactful way? He took a deep breath and said, "I think it's a lousy idea." He felt her stiffen, and knew he'd been wrong.

"What's the matter with it?" she said.

"In the first place, the expense. In the second place, I hate big parties. In the third place—"

"You hate big parties because they're full of boring people. If we made our own list we'd have whom we liked. And I don't remember your having such a horrible time at the Gaffneys' Christmas party. If you'll remember, you were the one who wanted it to go on till Twelfth Night—and that was at five in the morning."

"That was different. That was—"

"What's different about it? It was a big party, and there were even some boring people, but you certainly had a good time. In fact, you suggested we have one like it this Christmas. Well, this isn't Christmas, but there's no reason we can't have one like it."

"But there's no *reason* for a party! There's plenty of reason at Christmas, but in the middle of the summer—"

"There's all the reason in the world!" She was standing now, and looking at him with eyes that were wide with desperation. "There's every reason you can think of! Just for openers, it could very possibly save our marriage! How do you like that for a reason?"

"What do you mean by that?"

"You heard me."

"Say it again, and explain it in detail." He was trying to be calm, but his chest felt tight.

She took three or four deep breaths, and then relaxed. "I'm sorry," she said. "I didn't mean that. What I meant was it would do something to brighten the summer, instead of our just sitting around growling at each other. What we need is a change, and this would be the best change I can think of."

Powell knew what she wasn't saying was that she thought it would be therapy for him, and this was one reason he balked. He felt like a patient who has heard the doctors talking outside his room, but can get nothing except bland smiles when he questions them. He also felt as helpless as a patient in traction. He took a long swallow of his drink and said, "Well, let's think about it. We don't have to decide right now."

"But we ought to start planning, if we're going to do it right. This isn't the kind of thing we can whip up overnight."

"O.K., then. Do whatever you want."

She came back to his chair, sat down, and kissed the top of his head. "I promise you'll like it," she said. "This will be the best party you ever had in your life."

Fourteen.

It wasn't until suppertime that it was discovered that Uncle George was missing. Kathryn had assumed he was doing something at the cove, and Powell thought he was probably sulking in his room, but when, with supper on the table, they started to look for him, he was nowhere to be found. His room was just as he had left it that morning. They called, but their only answers were echoes.

"Where did you last see him?" Powell asked, after going out on the porch to call.

"I told you this noon," Kathryn replied. "I haven't seen him since he went out with you and Stevie—Steve."

Powell glanced at his son. "And we left him at the edge of the cove," he said. "Did you see him later?"

"No," Steve replied, slightly excited. "I looked out once, but it was raining so hard I couldn't see if he was there or not."

"Maybe he went into town," Kathryn suggested. "Maybe he even went to Boston, to—to buy a new boat."

"Not in the clothes he was wearing," said Powell. "They'd have tried to sell him a fishing smack."

"Shouldn't we maybe check the cove?" said Steve. "He

could've fallen over the edge, and knocked himself cold. Maybe he's been there all afternoon, slowly bleeding to death."

"Steve, really!" said Kathryn.

"It's a possibility," said Powell, heading toward the coat closet. "We'd better check, anyway."

"Can I come, too?" Steve asked.

"Sure," said Powell. "I might need you."

Steve dove for the closet, and produced raincoats and two flashlights. "What about bandages?" he said. "And tourniquets and splints, and things like that?"

"Let's wait till we see where he is," said his father. "There's no point setting up a hospital till we know it's needed."

"A person can bleed to death in three minutes," Steve announced, stabbing one arm into the sleeve of his raincoat.

"Where did you get that choice information?" asked his mother.

"I saw it on TV. They had a guy bleed to death, right in front of the camera."

"Probably an extra," said Powell. "They got him for scale."

"He wasn't *really* dead. But you should have seen the blood; they must have used five gallons of ketchup, all over the place."

"There's one blessing to this summer," Kathryn said quietly. "We have no TV."

"You know a funny thing?" said Steve, as he and Powell went out the door. "When I don't have the TV, I don't miss it."

"It's not funny," his father replied. "It's just that you're growing up."

Steve thought a moment, then said, "Now that you mention it, maybe you're right. I never looked at it that way." He squared his shoulders, cleared his throat, and strode off into the night beside his father.

The rain had stopped, and the wind had hauled around to the southwest and died down, but the sky was still overcast and the surf in the cove was heavy. They could see the white crests of the breakers looming up in the darkness, and then the cove would dissolve into swirling foam, and for a moment everything would subside before another dim crest appeared. They shone their flashlights around the rocks and ledges, and they cupped their hands and called, but there was neither sight nor sound of Uncle George. Powell knew that if he had fallen in the water, there would be no chance of finding him until his body was washed up somewhere along the coast. If, on the other hand, he were down among the rocks some-where—

"Maybe we better go down," Steve said. "He could be hid-den down there, and we wouldn't see him from here."

"I guess you're right," Powell said reluctantly. He had hoped that the matter could be settled without having to go down, but there seemed to be no other answer. Slowly, and keeping Steve behind him, he picked his way down the path to the dock.

The rocks were wet, and covered with seaweed and flotsam flung up by the storm. Powell flashed the light on the cleft in the rock, but the tunnel was quiet and cold and dormant, and he felt nothing.

"Hey, what's that?" Steve exclaimed, shining his light on the rock. "It looks like a cave!"

"It's nothing," said Powell, quickly turning his light away. "Stay away from it."

"Why? Suppose he's in there?"

"There'd be no reason for him to be there. Just stay clear."

"I'm going to look, anyway." Steve started toward the tun-nel, but his father grabbed him.

"Don't" he snapped. "I said stay clear!"

"But why, Pop? Why can't I look?"

Powell took a deep breath, and let go of his son's arm.

"O.K.," he said. "Go ahead and look. But don't go inside." His skin prickled, as he watched Steve go to the tunnel entrance and shine the light into the blackness.

"Well, what do you know about that?" Steve said. "It looks like a regular cavern!"

"Just stay out of it," said Powell. "You can see from here he's not there."

"I'll bet there's a lot of necking goes on in there," said Steve. "Nobody'd ever find you in a million years."

Powell glanced at his son with interest. "Oh?" he said. "Do you find you're bothered by intruders?" To the best of his knowledge the only girls Steve knew were in school, and were billed as pains in the *kiester*.

Steve shrugged. "No," he said. "Nobody'll even look at me until I get a car. After that, we'll see."

Powell cleared his throat. "Anything special you have your eye on?" he asked. He tried to remember seeing any attractive girls of Steve's age around town, but they all seemed to blur together in his mind, and he could remember only blue jeans and halters and hair curlers and ice-cream cones. The thought that that gangling, giggling group contained any romantic interest for his son came as something of a shock. For that matter, it came as an equal shock to hear the clinical way his son approached the matter. He had pictured Steve's interests as being confined to phonograph records and television, and to have him staking out long-range plans for some as yet unnamed little girl was vaguely unsettling.

"Nobody in particular," Steve replied, in an offhand way. "The field here isn't what you'd call red hot."

"Well—" Powell paused as several bits of advice, all of them pompous, flashed through his mind. He remembered the rule at his prep school, whereby you were forbidden to go out with any town girls whom you would not introduce into your own home, and he wondered if there were any way of phrasing that to make it more palatable. "I'll be happy to meet her," he concluded.

"Who?" said Steve.

"Whoever—whomever you pick."

"Why do *you* want to meet her?" Steve seemed genuinely curious.

"I just meant I'd be happy if you—wanted to introduce her."

"Well, since I don't know who it is, and will probably be too late to get anything but a dog, we don't have to worry about that now."

"What do you mean, too late? Is there some kind of time limit?"

"No, but by the time I get a car all the best of them will be gone. You got to move fast if you're going to get anywhere, and you're dead without a car."

"Well, there's always another summer, isn't there?" Powell asked, already dreading the thought. The change between Steve last spring and Steve now was so enormous that he could hardly imagine what it would be like in another year. He wondered if, after all, it had been a good idea to get him a job that threw him in with the local residents.

"Who knows where I'll be next summer?" Steve replied. "We certainly won't be coming back here, will we?"

"No, I think it's safe to say we won't be here."

"Maybe next summer I'll go around the world. Ship on a freighter as a deckhand, and move around a little."

"Well, we'll let next summer take care of itself." Then Powell remembered what they'd come for, and he shone his light around in all the places where Uncle George might possibly have fallen. "I guess he's not here," he concluded. "Maybe he went to town, after all."

"My bet is he jumped," said Steve. "That boat meant more to him than he let on."

This curiously adult observation disturbed Powell, because

it was a real, though remote, possibility. Furthermore, his talk with Steve had revealed a side he never knew existed, and he wondered how much else there was he didn't know. He reflected that the lack of communication between the generations is never so pronounced as during adolescence, and it might behoove him to make an effort to avoid misunderstandings. "I hope this hasn't been too bad a summer for you," he said, as they started back up the path.

"Not as bad as I thought it'd be," Steve replied. Then he paused and said, "I don't get the picture *you've* had such a hot time, though."

"Oh—it's been all right." Powell found himself trying to defend the summer, although he knew Steve was aware of practically every problem. "Your mother's planning a big party, and that ought to liven things up a bit."

"Are you kidding? I thought you hated parties."

"This'll be different. It'll probably be a costume party, and —well, we'll see."

"Holy cow."

They reached the top and Powell paused for breath, then said, "Have you found a car that appeals to you—one you can afford?"

"I've been looking around. They're mostly pretty junky, for what I can pay."

"Maybe we can work out a deal."

"What do you mean?"

"Maybe we can work out a long-term plan, so you won't have to get a pile of junk. If you're going to get a car, you might as well get one that runs."

"That's the truth. I just didn't think—well, I didn't know about the money."

"In the long run, it's cheaper to get one that runs than to keep paying for repairs. We'll see if we can work something out."

"I tell you what," said Steve. "I got a lot of stuff I can sell, like my record player and my air pistol and all, and maybe I can raise enough extra to make up the difference."

"Let's try something else first. You don't want to strip yourself bare."

"What the hell—if it'll help, why not?"

Powell resisted an impulse to put a hand on Steve's arm. "We'll see," he said, and started across the lawn.

"Hey, look," said Steve. "In the cupola."

Powell looked, and saw a dim light in the cupola. There were lights on the ground floor, but none on the second or third, and the cupola seemed to hang over the house like a small, square moon. Then the light went out.

"I'll bet that's Uncle George," Powell said. He started to run, and he and Steve raced up the path and into the house. Kathryn was in the kitchen as they came in.

"What luck?" she asked.

"I think he's in the cupola," Powell said, and he ran upstairs, turning on lights. With Steve following, he went up through the second floor, past Uncle George's empty room, and into the unlighted attic. There was a strong smell of lilacs, and Powell's skin froze as he shone his light around the vacant, raftered space. The attic was cavernous and cold, and the shadows jumped about, exploding and receding as he flicked his light. They went on, more slowly, to the cupola, but it was dark and deserted, with the table and the rocking chair standing cold and silent, like relics in a tomb. The musty lilac smell clung all around them. Silently, Powell and Steve darted their flashlight beams about, and then Powell spotted a small bit of seaweed on the floor. "Let's get out of here," he said. Steve turned and fled, and Powell scurried after him, through the cold and reeking attic and into the welcome light below. They slowed down, and glanced at each other, then each one took a deep breath and straightened his shoulders. It would have looked as though Steve were imitating his father, had they not done it simultaneously. They switched off their lights, and returned to the kitchen.

"Was he there?" Kathryn asked.

"No," Powell replied. "It looked from outside as though there was a light up there, but I guess there wasn't." He glanced once at Steve, then went and made himself a drink.

"And no sign of him at the cove?" said Kathryn.

"Not a trace. He must have gone to town after all. We'll probably hear from him later on." He stirred his drink, then raised the bottle and silently offered it to Steve. Steve smiled, and shook his head, and Powell also smiled as he set the bottle down.

"Wouldn't you know he'd go like this?" said Kathryn. "Here we've been hoping and praying he'd leave, and now when he does go he doesn't say a word about it, so we don't know if he's gone for good or not."

"His clothes are here," said Powell. "That means we can expect him back, provided he's still alive."

"And maybe even if he isn't," said Steve.

"That's right," said Powell. "And maybe even if he isn't."

The two of them began to laugh, and they laughed so hard that Kathryn joined in, too, although she had no idea what it was about.

Fifteen.

Uncle George had indeed gone off to buy a new boat. He stayed at the cove, cursing silently, while the sea beat his old boat to pieces, and when, finally, the stern section slid off the rocks and vanished into deeper water he turned and walked toward town. He hired a taxi, and told the driver to take him to the Ritz-Carlton, in Boston.

An imperceptible quiver ran through the lobby of the Ritz as Uncle George, clad in his sweatshirt, boots, and glistening yellow sou'wester, entered through a revolving door marked "Not an Accredited Egress," and headed for the reservation desk. An elevator had just arrived at the ground floor, and from its discreetly perfumed interior emerged three Boston ladies, complete with hats; they stopped in their tracks, and one of them gave a little squeak like a chipmunk. An elderly gentleman, coming up from the bar, said, "I'm damned," and went back down to the bar again, and two girls who had just come out of the pharmacy burst into uncontrollable giggles. The sounds of a string quartet, drifting faintly down the curved staircase from the floor above, lent a further incongruity to the scene. Two sleek young men in morning coats waited behind the desk as Uncle George approached them, and from their expressions they might well have been watching the arrival of a hooded cobra.

"I want a room," Uncle George announced. "A suite, if you've got one."

"Yes, sir," said the younger and paler of the clerks. "Do you have a reservation?"

"No, damn it, I don't; if I did I'd have told you. Just give me a room, and stop the fiddle-faddle."

"I'm sorry, sir, we're all booked up."

"Don't give me that," snapped Uncle George. "No hotel in the world is booked solid. I'll bet you've got a dozen rooms and two suites right this minute."

"I'm sorry, sir," said the clerk, his lips tightening.

"All right," said Uncle George. "Get me the manager. And be quick about it; I'm wet through to my drawers, and I've got to get some clothes."

"I'm sorry, sir, the manager's out," the clerk replied. "You can speak to the assistant manager, if you'd like." He indicated the young man on his left. Uncle George glared at him.

"O.K.," said Uncle George. "If that's the way you want to play. I'll buy your goddam hotel and fire you both. How much is it?"

"I'm afraid it's not for sale," the second clerk said, with a tight smile.

"You think I'm kidding? You think I couldn't buy it?"

"No, sir, of course not." The second clerk showed signs of uneasiness, and acted as though his collar were too small.

"My name is Merkimer," said Uncle George. "George W. Merkimer. I will give you exactly three minutes to give me the key to a suite, or so help me I will buy this hotel right out from under you. Now, get moving."

The second clerk picked up a telephone, and mumbled something. Then he slid the registration pad toward Uncle

George and produced a key. "Front!" he said, and a bellhop appeared. "Take Mr. Merkimer to his room." A little of the blood returned to his face, and he smiled.

It was as though everybody in the lobby had been holding their breaths; there was an audible exhalation as Uncle George strode to the elevator, and life at the Ritz resumed its normal course.

His next stop was Brooks Brothers, a block up Newburry Street from the hotel. The clerk recognized him and smiled. "Well, Mr. Merkimer!" he said, beaming. "Been doing a little boating, have we?"

"Boating, my ass," replied Uncle George. "Give me some clothes."

The smile disappeared. "Yes, sir," said the clerk. "What would you like?"

"Everything! Shorts, shoes, socks, shirts, suits, a hat, a—"

"Yes, sir. Suppose we start at the inside and work out."

"That's what I tried to tell you," said Uncle George. "Why is that so hard to understand?"

Once he was dressed and looking like himself again, he felt better. After notifying the insurance office of the loss of his boat, he went to the yacht broker from whom he had bought it and demanded another. The broker's office was small, and paneled to look like a pilot house, and the fittings on his desk were brass miniatures of ship's hardware.

"Well, now, let's see," said the broker, picking up a letter-opener with a gold anchor on the handle. "What kind would you like this time?"

"One that floats," replied Uncle George. "That goddam thing sank right out from under me."

The broker looked blank. "What happened?" he asked.

"Don't ask me. All I know is there was trouble with the seacocks, and all of a sudden she sank. Like to drown us all."

"*Well*, then. I assume you'd like a different kind—something in a steam yacht, perhaps?" He indicated a picture on the wall, showing what looked like a small ocean liner with a bowsprit.

"I want the same kind I had before, but this time I want a guarantee it'll float. And I want a written agreement that if it sinks, I get to sink the president of the company that built it. Tie him to a rock and sink him."

The broker laughed nervously. "That may be a little hard to get in writing," he said. "An oral agreement, perhaps, but in writing—" He shook his head, and glanced thoughtfully at his cufflinks, which were gold-and-jeweled miniature port and starboard lights. They were reversed, but he couldn't change them now.

"Then I get to sink the yard foreman," said Uncle George. "I need some kind of guarantee this thing stays afloat."

The broker drew himself up and assumed a wounded air. "Mr. Merkimer," he said, "we would not handle a boat that had not been fully surveyed and found, or guaranteed by the builders."

"Then what happened to mine?"

"It was just an—uh—unfortunate accident. I can't understand it. But I assure you—"

"Never mind the assurances," Uncle George cut in. "Just get me a boat."

In the end he got a boat, more or less like the one he had lost. Finding a captain at that time of year was more difficult, but after inquiring through local yacht clubs and boat yards he signed on a burly Swede named Iverson, who claimed to know the local waters and to be familiar with the type of boat. Uncle George signed him for a week's trial period, with the understanding that he be paid nothing if it turned out he'd lied about his qualifications.

He took delivery at the Quincy Adams Yacht Yard, a large

and venerable establishment to the south of Boston harbor. It was the last week in July; Boston was like a blast furnace, and he looked forward to getting on the water and cooling off. When the final papers had been signed he went down to the dock where Iverson was loading provisions. The boat floated gently on the water, its white sides gleaming and its brasswork flashing tiny specks of fire. It looked as sleek and new as a plastic toy, and at the same time as solid as a hotel. Uncle George stepped aboard and nodded to Iverson. "All right," he said. "Shove off." Then he sat in a wicker chair on the after-deck and waited.

There came the whine of a starter, and the hollow cough as one engine took hold, then the sound was repeated with the other engine. Uncle George listened approvingly to the low, even pulsing of the engines, and he could hear the change in tone as Iverson put them in gear. The twin screws whirled beneath him, driving a churning mass of water astern, and he was aware that people were shouting. He looked at the dock, from which the boat had not moved, and saw two yard workers screaming at Iverson as they tried to cast off the stern line, which was tight as a bowstring and beginning to quiver.

"Stop!" one of them roared. "Stop the boat, you dumb bastard!"

Iverson put his head out the window. "Dumb bastard yourself! Throw off the goddam line!"

"We can't! We gotta have some slack! Stop the sonofa-bitching boat!"

Uncle George leaped up and ran forward, and pulled back the engine controls. The throbbing stopped, and he glared at Iverson. "What's the matter?" he snarled. "Haven't you ever run a boat before?"

"Sure I run a boat," said Iverson. "Those dumb bastards don't throw off the lines."

Uncle George looked back and saw that the yard workers

had got the line off the bollard, and one of them threw it scornfully at the boat. "All right," he said. "You can go ahead now." He walked aft and retrieved the line, wondering if this were an omen of any sort.

It turned out it wasn't an omen; it was a symptom.

During the remainder of the day, Iverson missed Marble-head completely and almost ran aground on Cape Ann; he missed Boston Lightship on the way back (a slight heat haze had now turned into true fog), and was saved from running aground at Scituate only by the sound of the surf ahead; and when Uncle George finally took over the navigation and got them back into Boston harbor he narrowly missed colliding with a freighter by insisting he had the right-of-way, which he didn't. When, finally, the yacht yard loomed up ahead, Uncle George was drenched with perspiration and speechless with rage. He had the controls, and as he slowed down to approach the dock he looked at Iverson and, controlling his voice with great effort, said, "I have one more order for you, and that's all. You go forward, and you take the line you'll find on that cleat—we call it the bow line—and when the front end of the boat almost touches the dock you jump off, with that line in your hand, and put the loop over whatever you see that you think might hold it. There are several posts there, called bollards, and you should be able to find at least one of them. When you have done that you turn and run up that dock as fast as you can go, and if I ever catch you near the water again I'll have you arrested as a menace to navigation. Is that clear?"

Iverson nodded. "Sure," he said. "When do we go out again?"

He finally got a competent captain, a thin, wiry man with the un-seagoing-sounding name of Gainsborough, and for a week they cruised the local waters with something approaching real pleasure. But there was one element missing; each day ended with an odd feeling of incompleteness, and by the time the week was out he forced himself to admit there ought to be a woman on board. It was all very well to have a large and comfortable yacht, to cruise at will on the summer seas and count the trillions of stars at night, but the fact remained that he had become accustomed to having a woman around, and no day was really complete without one. He tried not to think of Estelle, the only one who had ever got the better of him, but it was unavoidable and it made him grind his teeth in rage. To make matters worse she had not filed for divorce, so for the time being he was still married to her, and unable to take on a legal successor. He knew that, at his age, it would be hard to come to an understanding with any woman without first having a very specific agreement about money, but that shouldn't be too hard once he found the right person. He thought back through the list of possibilities, and was not cheered. Most of the available women he knew were getting on in years, and were likely to be too set in their ways to adapt themselves to his. He could try for something younger, but where, and how?

The next Saturday, he directed Gainsborough to take him to the anchorage of one of the larger yacht clubs along the coast, and there they dropped the hook. They hoisted the "T" flag, and presently the yacht club launch came alongside and took him off. He was wearing a yachting cap, white flannel trousers, and a blue blazer with a yacht-club emblem on the pocket. He was freshly shaved, and had doused himself liberally with cologne. If it weren't for the blue veins showing through his pale skin he would have looked almost rakish.

An orchestra was playing tea-dance music on the lawn, and after signing the visitors' book Uncle George took a seat on the terrace and ordered a Tom Collins. He looked around and surveyed the action. The tables were about half full, and seemed for the most part to be occupied by married couples. There were a few people his age, gnarled old men in Panama hats, and flabby, overpainted women in dresses that showed too much of their arms, and they watched with the silent contemplation of people who have nothing to contribute, and expect nothing in return. Then there were the middle-aged couples, most of whom wore shorts and other revealing clothing they should have stopped wearing ten years ago, and they talked too loudly and drank with a strange kind of desperation. The younger marrieds were quiet, and more serious, and they still had a kind of freshness that made their suntans seem natural, and attractive. The only single females Uncle George could find seemed to be age sixteen and under, and they were either playing tennis or lugging sailing gear across the lawn, mostly accompanied by crew-cut youths in letter sweaters. He nursed his Tom Collins for a long time, and then had another, thinking that perhaps a mature lone woman might show up during the cocktail hour, but in his heart he knew it was a losing proposition. There might be, and probably were, women there who would be delighted to take a trip with him, but without knowing who they were, and specifically how to go about springing them loose, he was wasting his time. He ate alone in a corner of the dining room, then rode the launch out to his boat and went to bed.

The next day, he and Gainsborough took the boat back to the yacht yard in Quincy, and when they had tied up he told Gainsborough he didn't know when he'd be wanting to use it again.

In desperation, he called some of the elder women he had first rejected, but they were off at their various vacation resorts, and his telephone calls rang in empty, sheeted apartments. He went to the Tavern, a men's luncheon club to which he belonged, and made guarded references to the fact

that he was on the market for a female sailing companion, but
the only response he got was the jocular suggestion that he
call the Radcliffe Employment Bureau.

He went back to his suite at the Ritz that night and lay
awake, wondering what he was going to do. It was no fun
cruising alone, but he'd invested too much money in the boat
to want to retire it for the season. Furthermore, he hated
feeling that the sea had got the best of him, and he would like
to return to the cove as though nothing had happened. Then
an idea came to him. Why hadn't he thought of it before?
Kathryn would be the perfect one to come with him! She was
a good housekeeper, she could do the cooking, and she would
probably like nothing better than to get away from that hideous house she was trapped in. There would even be room for
Powell and Steve if they wanted to come, too, but he had the
feeling that the family members had been getting on each
other's nerves, and they'd probably like a short vacation apart.
Chortling at his cleverness, he was soon asleep.

The next day, he instructed Gainsborough to load provisions and to top off the fuel and water tanks, and early the
following morning they left the yacht yard. It was a hot, cop-
pery day, and as they cruised up the coast he felt the exhilara-
tion of knowing he was no longer bound to the land. Years of
doing exactly what he wanted had dulled his appetite for normal pleasures, and only at sea could he find the kind of free-
dom that really excited him. He could go anywhere he liked
(except of course to Europe, and he might buy that steam
yacht some day and do exactly that), and with someone to
take care of the housekeeping and act as a general companion,
he could ask no more. He breathed deeply of the clean, salt
air, and felt with pleasure the way the deck surged under his
feet. He went forward and took the wheel from Gainsborough, and put the boat in a hard right turn. When it had

completed one circle he made a full turn to the left, then handed the wheel back to the astonished Gainsborough and went aft, whistling.

It was midafternoon when they reached the cove. He could see the house, brooding on the cliff above it, and through his binoculars he thought he saw someone in a window. I bet this'll give them a surprise, he thought. This'll show them it takes more than a little old storm to get me down. They entered the cove carefully, to avoid any possible wreckage, but it all seemed to have been washed into deeper water, or broken up so completely as to be harmless. They dropped the anchor, and Gainsborough rowed him ashore.

He was halfway to the house when Kathryn came out on the porch. She was singing, but when she saw him, and saw the boat, she covered her face with her hands and burst into tears. He hurried forward, and took her by the arm. "What happened?" he asked. "What's the matter?"

"Nothing," she said through her sobs. "It's just—I'm surprised to see you, that's all."

"I thought you'd be. But hell, that's nothing to cry about. Pull yourself together; I've got good news."

Gradually she stopped crying, and blew her nose. "I'm sorry," she said. "I guess it was just the shock. We thought you were dead."

He laughed. "Not this one," he said. "The storm hasn't been made that can get me. You see the new boat?"

"Yes. It's like the old one, isn't it?"

"Only one difference. There's no woman aboard."

"That's right. Has Estelle—"

"But there's going to be."

"Oh? Who?"

"You."

They had been walking toward the house, and Kathryn

stopped and looked at him. "What do you mean?" she asked.

"How would you like a vacation from everything, and join me on a cruise?"

"I couldn't leave the men; you know that."

"Well, it'd be good for them. Make them self-reliant for a change."

"No I couldn't. Besides—"

"Then bring them along, if you have to. There's plenty of room."

"Well, we've been planning a party, and—"

"Call it off. Tell everybody you've gone away."

She hesitated, wondering if it might not be a good idea to get Powell away from the house. He probably wouldn't want to come, but there might be some way she could persuade him, especially if she got Steve on her side. "I'll talk with the men," she said at last. "I'll see what they think."

Steve, after recovering from the shock of seeing Uncle George, was all for the idea. As far as he was concerned, anything different was a good thing, and if this would be nothing else it would be different from the rest of the summer. He agreed to help put pressure on his father.

Powell had been at Cranton, and had stopped off at the Heart's Ease on his way home. He hadn't been able to persuade Dorple to tell Kathryn about the cove, and he was beginning to doubt he ever would. Instead of becoming more relaxed Dorple showed signs of increasing tension, and Powell had stopped even trying to discuss the matter.

He was so preoccupied that the sight of the boat in the cove didn't register immediately, and even then he didn't connect it with Uncle George. He wondered who might have come in and anchored there, and whether people could do that without his permission, and as he entered the house he was framing a sentence to Kathryn about the possibility of putting a "No Trespassing" sign on the dock. He went into the kitchen, said, "I wonder if it mightn't be a good idea—" and then stopped, as he saw Uncle George. "My God," he said. "I thought you were dead."

"Not on your life," said Uncle George, and he laughed. "It takes more than a little old storm to get me."

"You might have told us," said Powell. "Steve and I almost got pneumonia looking for you."

"A little fresh air never hurt anybody. That's what I'm here for—to take you all on a cruise."

Powell looked at Kathryn. "Oh?" he said.

"Yes," she replied. "Steve and I have already accepted— provided you'll come, too."

"How long a cruise?"

"As long as you want," said Uncle George. "I don't have to be anywhere until after Labor Day."

"What about the party?" Powell asked Kathryn.

"We could have that another time. I haven't sent the invitations yet."

Steve came out of his room. "What about it, Pop?" he said. "Doesn't it sound swingin'?"

Then it occurred to Powell that this would be the answer to everything. It would get them away from the house, and give Kathryn a chance to rest, and let them get back to where they were before the whole ghost business came up. It wouldn't be easy living with Uncle George, but it would be no harder on the boat than in the house, and the boat would have the added advantage of not being haunted. "I think it sounds fine," he said.

Kathryn ran to him, and threw her arms around his neck. "Darling!" she cried. "I was expecting you'd put up a fight!" Her eyes were bright, and her voice quivered with happiness.

"Why should I fight?" Powell replied. "It's not every day you get invited on a cruise. When do we start?"

"Tomorrow," said Uncle George. It hadn't worked out

exactly as he'd hoped, but it was still better than nothing, and if any unpleasantness developed he could always cut it short on the pretext of a sudden business crisis. But at least he now had somebody to cook and do the housekeeping, and that made all the difference between pleasure and tedium.

He stayed for supper, and afterward they sat in the living room, going over maps and charts and planning where they would go in the more than three weeks at their disposal. Finally, around ten-thirty, Uncle George stood up. "Bedtime," he said. "I'm going to sleep aboard tonight. Are my clothes still here?"

"Yes," said Kathryn. "We packed them away, just in case."

"Bring them when you come tomorrow," he said. "There's no rush now."

He left, and when he was gone Kathryn embraced Powell again. "This is going to be the best thing in the world," she said. "It's going to be the answer to all our problems."

"I hope so," he replied, holding her tightly. "Believe me, I certainly hope so."

They went to the kitchen, and had started to put away the supper dishes when they heard the sound of someone on the front porch. They looked at each other, then went into the living room in time to see Uncle George come through the front door. He was white and drawn, and his eyes looked like the eyes of a corpse as he walked slowly past them and up the stairs. Powell had a sudden hunch, and he snatched a flashlight from the closet and ran outside. A white, full moon silvered the cliffs and made a jagged track of light on the water, and as Powell ran toward the cove he could see that his hunch had been right. The boat was no longer to be seen, and only when he reached the cove and played his flashlight on the water could he see the thin stick of the top of the mast, showing where it had sunk.

Sixteen.

Next day, a heavy fog enveloped the coast. It turned everything white and threw a clammy chill on the house, and the
only sounds were the gonging of a bell buoy and the low
groan of the distant foghorn. Uncle George stayed in his room,
and Powell and Kathryn silently dragged themselves through
the motions of breakfast. Steve had already left, and the house
felt empty, and dead. Disappointment and despair lay so
heavily on them that they didn't trust themselves to speak,
and they avoided looking at each other as though in fear of
some kind of explosion. Finally, as Kathryn was pouring her
second cup of coffee, she said, "You going to Cranton today?"

"I don't know," Powell replied tonelessly. "Why?"

"I just wondered. I've got some marketing to do, and I
don't feel much like walking."

"Take the car. I don't need it."

"Incidentally, does anyone know what happened to the
boat captain?"

"Same as the other one, I guess. He either drowned or
went over the hill."

She felt an inexplicable flash of anger. "That's an awfully
glib reply," she said. "There ought to be some way of finding
out."

"How the hell should I know?" Powell snapped. "What's so glib about it?"

"It's too pat, and it doesn't answer anything. If he'd drowned they'd find his body, and there'd be no reason for *both* men to go over the hill. It doesn't make sense."

"Why does everything have to make sense? Do you have to have all your answers taped out for you?"

"Yes, I do!" In an uncontrollable burst of rage she slammed down her coffee cup and stood up. "There's got to be an answer for everything, and I want to know it! I don't want to be kept in the dark!"

"All right, then, he drowned!" Powell shouted. "Does that make you feel better?"

"No, because I don't believe it! I think they both went over the hill, but I want to know why! Just tell me *why*, that's all I ask!"

"How should I know? Anchor a boat in the cove, and find out for yourself!"

She felt her head tighten, the way it had the night of the storm, and a burst of panic hit her. She turned and ran out the door, jumped into the car, and drove off. Gradually, as she drove the fog-shrouded road, she became calmer, but with calmness came the realization that something utterly beyond her control was working between herself and her husband. Furthermore, she knew that unless she found some way to help him out of his mental turmoil, either he was going to have a crack-up or she was. His belief in spiritualism had reached the point where they could no longer discuss it, and their lack of communication was becoming more complete by the hour. But the harder she tried to find a solution the sooner she felt the flash of tightness in her head, and with it the fear of insanity. Why am I afraid of this? she thought. Why, suddenly, am I obsessed by this? Is it because I can't find all the answers, or is it because I really am insane, and am just showing it more often? No, that can't be. I'm a calm, rational woman, and I'm just upset by what's happening to Stephen. He's the one who needs the help, not I. Remember that always—he's the one who needs the help.

Then she remembered they had a friend, a doctor named Martin Spellick, who had switched to psychiatry a couple of years ago when his general practice hadn't proved rewarding enough. She could with complete logic invite him to the party, because they had known him for years, and he might conceivably give her a clue as to how Stephen could be helped. At least it would be worth a try, because anything would be better than living the way they were now. The lack of communication was bad enough, but the idea of having idiotic fights, like the one this morning, was more than she could bear. During all their married life they had had only one really serious fight, the result of a confused sequel to a country-club dance, and they hadn't spoken to each other for three days. She remembered those three miserable days, with neither one wanting to be the first to speak, and it occurred to her that the atmosphere had been something like that this morning. There was no anger this morning—at first, that is— but there was the same strained holding back. Then a sudden, hideous thought struck her—was it possible that Powell was carrying on with some woman in town? No, of course not. Absolutely absurd. Still, it would explain a lot of things: his constant trips to Cranton, his attitude of being withdrawn and troubled—all these would be understandable if there were some clandestine affair going on. Maybe the whole business of the librarian was a front; maybe, God willing, he didn't really believe in the spiritualism, and was just using it as a smokescreen. She felt she'd almost welcome a human rival if it got rid of the supernatural ones, and then her stomach contracted and she knew she would prefer anything to having him involved with a local woman. Maybe it was the

librarian; maybe she was beautiful and frustrated and someone he could talk to, and maybe the séances were—no, she
wouldn't let herself think of it. On the other hand, she knew
she wouldn't sleep until she had dispelled even the smallest,
nagging element of doubt. She left the laundry at the laundromat and headed for Cranton, hating herself but unable to
help herself.

The librarian looked up at her, and smiled. "I'm so glad
you've come!" she said. "I was hoping you'd see your
way!"

Kathryn was puzzled. "I'm Mrs. Stephen Powell," she said.
"I was just wondering—"

"Yes, I know!" said the librarian. "I feel as though I'd
known you all summer. Your husband talks about you all the
time."

"He does come here, then?"

"Oh my yes. And now he's persuaded you—I think it's
wonderful!"

"Well, actually—" Kathryn began, then stopped, trying to
think what to say. Looking at the librarian, she could tell that
she wasn't a menace, and if Powell really did come here it
meant her fears were unfounded, but how could she admit
the reason for her coming? She suddenly felt trapped, and
stupid, and ashamed of herself.

"He's been so worried about you," the librarian went on.
"We both have, for that matter, but of course he's much
more so, and it was only last week that—"

"Worried?" said Kathryn. "What's he worried about me
for?"

"About your disbelief. It can have very serious results, you
know."

"Oh. Well, I really don't—"

"What would you like first? We have some very good in-
troductions to the supernatural, and of course all the more ad-

vanced works, but maybe you'd rather just sit and talk a spell. When did you have your first visitation?"

"My what?"

"Your first ghost. Was it Felicity, or Jenny?"

"I haven't seen any. That's just what—"

"You mean he's convinced you without your having seen one? I think that's perfectly marvelous! Most nonbelievers have to have their noses rubbed in it before they see the light, so he must have very strong powers to convince you on his own word. But then, your husband is an unusual man, Mrs. Powell. You should be very proud of him."

"I know, yes. I am. But I'm afraid that—"

"Tell me how he did it. What did he say that tore the curtain aside? Try to remember, because it can be very important."

Kathryn took a deep breath. "He didn't say anything," she said. "I'm not convinced."

The librarian stopped, stared at her, and then sighed. "You poor dear," she said. "You poor, poor dear." She closed her eyes and leaned back in her chair.

"I'm sorry," Kathryn said. "I don't mean to be offensive, but I just can't bring myself to believe it. I know Stephen does, and it's got him very upset, and I wish there were some way he could stop. He's in over his head, and it's getting worse every day."

The librarian was quiet for a few moments, then opened her eyes and said, "And you, poor dear, came all the way out here because you thought he was mixed up with another woman. I'm the only other woman he sees, and you should be ashamed of yourself for mistrusting him. It's sad enough when you don't have belief, but when you also don't have *trust*—" She shook her head, and closed her eyes again.

"I trust him!" Kathryn said. "I trust him, but I'm afraid for him!"

Still with closed eyes, the librarian shook her head and smiled. "Then why did you come here?" she asked. Before Kathryn could answer, she went on, "Do you want me to tell you something else?"

"No," said Kathryn quickly. "I'm sorry—I mean—never mind."

The librarian opened her eyes. "You're the one you should be afraid for," she said. "You're the one who's in danger."

"How?"

"All I can say is this: your only hope lies in belief. Try as hard as you can, and perhaps things will be all right. Now, as I was saying, we have a splendid collection of books here, and you're more than welcome to—"

"I haven't time today," Kathryn said, looking at her watch. "I've got a lot of errands to do, and I have to get the car back to Stephen. Some other time, perhaps." All she wanted was to get out in the air, away from this woman who seemed to know more about her than she knew herself.

"We have an especially good volume on Extra-sensory Perception," the librarian called after her as she left. "I think you'd find it interesting."

"Thank you," said Kathryn. "I'll look it up next time."

She started the car with trembling hands, and swung it around and headed back. She tried to think how the librarian could have known what she did, or even guessed, but she couldn't find a clue. All she knew was she'd made a fool of herself, had indicated a distrust in her husband she didn't really feel, and had almost become trapped in a séance. Her desperation had been her undoing. Be reasonable, she told herself. There's a reason for everything, and if you're patient and reasonable you can always find it out.

She went first to the laundromat, and transferred the laundry from the washing machine to the dryer, then went into the supermarket next door. With her list in one hand, she pushed the glistening wire cart along the aisles, and her return to the everyday business of household matters helped settle her nerves. It occurred to her that her marketing list had been made out for three people, and she would now have to add extra food for Uncle George. She was annoyed at his assumption that he could stay as long as he liked, and the more she thought about it the angrier she became. It was not only an imposition, it was an expense, and she decided if he stayed more than a week she'd ask him to contribute toward the grocery bills. She was phrasing her speech in her mind when she realized that a man was standing next to her, waiting. She looked at him, and recognized Fess Dorple, the young man who had done the diving on the first boat. She smiled and said, "Good morning."

"May I speak to you a minute, Ma'm?" said Dorple, edging closer. He was picking his fingers with nervousness, and he lowered his voice so no one else could hear.

"Of course," said Kathryn.

Dorple looked around. A woman was coming down the aisle, selecting boxes and jars from the shelves, and he glanced toward the frozen food section, which was deserted. "Let's go over here," he said, moving away. Kathryn followed him, wondering, and he stopped at the frozen food locker and picked up a box of cod fillets. He dropped it back, wiped his fingers, and then, speaking with great effort, said, "Your husband asked I should tell you this, Ma'm, but it ain't easy." He saw a frozen lobster pie, examined it, and replaced it.

Kathryn's throat tightened with fear, and she said, "What? Where is he?"

"I don't know where he is now. This was some time ago."

"What *is* it?"

Dorple saw a box of frozen blintzes, picked it up, and began to toss it back and forth between his hands. "Well, it's like this," he said. "One day I was diving at the cove, there, and I

—well, never mind why—I decided to go back at night. I did, and—Holy Jesus, Ma'm, there's something *horrible* down there!"

"What do you mean?"

"I don't *know*. All I know is this thing kinda pushed at me and punched me and like to smother me, and almost flang me in the water. I never been so scared in all my life. I'm *still* scared." He crushed the frozen blintzes between his trembling hands, and tightened his shoulders.

"Did you see anything?"

"I didn't see nothing. I just felt it. But it was horrible."

"And you say my husband asked you to tell me?"

"That's right."

"Where did this happen?"

"On the dock there. I just come outa the water."

"Well—" Kathryn hesitated. "Thank you very much. It's very good of you to tell me."

"That's all right, Ma'm. I shoulda done it sooner, but I couldn't. I still wake up screaming nights."

She didn't know what to say. There was no doubting his sincerity, but she couldn't think of any rational advice, so she simply thanked him again. He replaced the mangled box of blintzes, wiped his hands on his trousers, tipped his hat, and walked away. She heard him breathe a deep sigh as he went.

She stood for several minutes, staring at the brightly packaged frozen foods, and then made a decision. She finished the rest of her shopping as quickly as possible, retrieved the laundry from the dryer, then got in her car and headed for the cove. The fog was still thick and cottony and she had to drive slowly, watching the side of the road. She made the turn for the cove and then, not wanting to drive too close to the edge, stopped the car and walked the rest of the way. The foghorn moaned in the distance, and the nearby bell buoy clanged in a slow and mournful cadence. Walking very carefully, Kathryn picked her way down the path to the water, which she could hear long before it loomed up as a darker spot in the fog. She stood on the dock and smelled the salty, iodine smell of seaweed, and she listened to the sucking, gurgling noise of the waves against the rocks, but she could neither feel nor hear anything out of the ordinary. Looking around, she spotted the crevasse in the rock, and she went over and peered inside. It seemed to go farther in, and she realized this must be the tunnel Powell had spoken about, the one that led up to the house. Goaded by curiosity she edged inside, and saw that it broadened out and disappeared in darkness. She went forward a few yards until the light began to grow dim, and she was turning around when a puff of wind hit her. It was cold, and reeked of decay, and she reasoned that there must be a lot of seaweed and other matter, accumulated over many years, that lay rotting far up the tunnel. She picked her way back and out into the white light of the fog, and after examining the rest of the area she returned to the car and drove it around to the house. There certainly was nothing there, she thought, as she turned off the engine. That Dorple boy must be having hallucinations, just like the rest of them. All I can do is hope and pray that Marty Spellick can come to the party—and can also come up with an answer.

Seventeen.

As soon as Kathryn left the house, Powell poured another cup of coffee and took it into the living room, where he sat and looked at the fog-whitened windows. His mind was nearly a total blank, and as he gazed away from the windows to the decor of the room—the wrought-iron lamp with the frogs and salamanders, the Morris chair, the ebony statue of the woman, the oak table with the red velvet runner—his only thoughts were how hideous everything was, and how hopeless. Not only was the furniture hideous, but the house was hideous, and his own situation was hideous, and the more he tried to do something the more hopeless it became. The foghorn, groaning in the distance, was a fitting background for his mood, and it was with no pleasure that he heard Uncle George rise from his bed and walk across the floor above. All I *don't* need right now is to talk to him, Powell thought. I'd sooner have a quiet chat with an embalmer. Then he heard Uncle George, moving slowly, climb the stairs to the floor above, and the faint hope sprang up that he might be collecting his belongings preparatory to leaving. That's really too much to hope for, Powell thought. The way things are going now, he'll probably be with us till Christmas. There must be some way to get rid of him, but I'm damned if I know what it is. I suppose we could charge him for his room and board—that should start a big enough fight to make him leave, but the sonofabitch is so unpredictable we couldn't count on it. He might just pay us the money, and sit around in a worse humor than he already is. Or we could put something in his food that would make him sick—sick, hell, why not kill him? A little rat poison, carefully administered—yes, that's a bright idea. I can see the headlines now: "Millionnaire Uncle Murdered for Money," and "Ex-Mag Man Slips the Biz to Wifey's $$Unk." No, there must be a better way.... Powell stopped, as he realized that an odd noise was coming from upstairs. It was an irregular thump, punctuated by silence, then a couple of more thumps, then silence. He got up, went to the foot of the stairs, and called. There was no answer.

Slowly, with growing uneasiness, he went up to the second floor, and looked in at Uncle George's unmade bed. The sounds still came from above, and now Powell hurried into the attic, which was empty, and up to the cupola, where the first thing he saw were Uncle George's bare feet, kicking feebly in empty air and occasionally hitting the wall. He was hanging from a rafter, the sash of his dressing gown knotted around his neck; his face was swollen and the color of wet slate, his eyes protruded, and his tongue hung out like a long piece of meat. Powell rushed up and got his shoulder under Uncle George's body, almost tripping over the capsized rocking chair, and he lifted Uncle George to take the pressure off his neck, then reached up and tried to untie the sash. He staggered about the cupola, holding the dead weight with one hand and groping for the sash with the other, and finally managed to loosen the knot. He was vaguely aware that his back hurt, but he paid no attention to it as he dropped the limp body on the floor and began to apply mouth-to-mouth respiration. He had no idea how long he knelt there, forcing air into the sagging mouth, but at last Uncle George began to breathe on his own, and the color of his face slowly dissolved into a more natural hue. His eyes, which had been glazed and unseeing, now flickered and began to move slowly from side to side. He put one hand to his throat, around which was a deep red welt. Powell stood up, feeling a stab in his back, and looked down at the figure on the floor. He was suddenly very angry.

"What the hell did you think you were doing?" he said. "What kind of lousy trick was that?"

Uncle George tried to speak but no sound came from his throat, and he shook his head.

"You don't have to say anything," Powell went on. "Just listen to me. Do you realize it could just as easily have been Kathryn who found you? And she might not have been able to get you down? And do you realize how horrible it would have been for her to see you there, all blue and with your tongue sticking out, and not be able to do anything? Is this how you repay us for putting up with you all this time? Is this what you call gratitude? You've never *known* gratitude— you've just done whatever you pleased, and the hell with everybody else. Well, I'll tell you one thing—just as soon as you can walk you're going to get out of this house, and you're not coming back. We've put up with you too long as it is, and this, by God, is the final straw. Consider yourself lucky I don't throw you out the window."

Uncle George shook his head again, and this time managed to speak. "I didn't do it," he croaked.

"What do you mean, you didn't do it?"

"I didn't."

"Well, I'm the only other one here, and although I'll admit I was thinking about—" He stopped. "Then who did do it?" he asked.

"Don't know—I was asleep—then woke up here."

"I heard you get out of bed. Do you walk in your sleep?"

Uncle George shook his head.

"This isn't something you'd do in your sleep, anyway," Powell said, more calmly. "But I can tell you nobody carried you up here. I heard your footsteps."

Uncle George shrugged.

"Don't you remember anything?" Powell insisted.

Uncle George shook his head again.

Powell took a deep breath. "Come on, I'll help you back to bed," he said. "Then I'll call a doctor."

"No doctor," said Uncle George, in a more natural voice. "I'll be all right."

"You will not. Come on." Powell lifted Uncle George from the floor and, holding one arm around his waist, guided him down the stairs. When he had put him, protesting, into bed, he drew a glass of water and left it by his side, and then went and called the local doctor. Trying to be as casual as he could, he said there'd been a slight accident, and he'd appreciate it if the doctor could drop around when he had a moment.

"I'm pretty busy right now," the doctor said. "What kind of accident was it?"

Powell hesitated. "A man hung himself," he said.

"Good God!" exclaimed the doctor. "You don't want me, you want the undertaker!"

"He isn't dead," said Powell. "I got him in time. But I think you ought to look at him."

"Sure, sure. Uh—is he conscious?"

"Yes."

"Neck broken?"

"No."

"Well, tell him to keep quiet and not do any violent exercise, and I'll be over as soon as I can. Give him a couple of aspirin, and only liquids or soft foods for lunch. A coddled egg often slips down easy. I imagine his throat's a mite sore, so—"

"Wait a minute," said Powell. "You sound as though you're giving me instructions for a week. When do you plan to get here?"

"Well, seeing as how he's out of danger, it's not an emergency. I'll get there when I can."

"Thanks."

"And remember—no violent exercise, and no stimulants. No alcohol, either, for that matter—oh, yes. How old is he?"

"I don't know. Somewhere in his seventies."

"You should have let him go. Well, keep an eye on him, anyway."

The doctor hung up, and Powell looked at the instrument for a moment and then slammed it back in its cradle. Then it occurred to him that perhaps he should watch Uncle George for the next little while, so he went back and sat in a chair next to the bed. Uncle George looked at him in silence. "I'll go," he said at last.

"You'll do nothing of the kind. You'll stay in bed till the doctor gets here."

"I don't want a doctor. I just want to get out of here."

"All in good time. Right now, you couldn't walk across the room."

Uncle George started to get out of bed, but Powell pushed him back. "Relax," he said. "You don't want me to tie you down, do you?"

Uncle George lay back and was quiet for a while, and then said, "I didn't know I was a trouble."

"Forget it," said Powell. "I was sore."

"You were right. But I thought you liked having me."

"What possibly made you think that?"

"Everybody else does."

"Everybody else is after your money."

Uncle George thought about this. "That's a hell of a thing to find out now," he said.

"You must have known it."

Uncle George thought some more. "I guess I did," he said. "Still, it's a hell of a thing to hear."

"Let's not worry about it now. Just relax, and get your strength back. You want an aspirin?"

"I do not. I want a drink."

"The doctor said no alcohol."

"The doctor's a fool. Get me a drink."

Powell shrugged, and went downstairs and made a stiff drink. After thinking a moment he also made one for himself, then took them back to the bedroom. When he got there, Uncle George was sitting on the edge of the bed, rubbing his throat. "That kind of thing raises hell with a man's neck," he said.

Powell smiled and handed him his drink. Then he raised his glass, said, "Happy recovery," and took a sip. Uncle George drank half his drink in one gulp.

"That's more like it," he said, with a shudder.

Powell sat down. "Listen," he said. "There's something we've got to get straight. You say you don't remember a thing?"

Uncle George closed his eyes and shook his head. "Noth-ing," he said. "I woke up earlier, and then I must have gone back to sleep. That's all, until I found myself hanging."

"Did you have any dreams?"

"None I remember."

"Did you by any chance dream about a man—probably an old man—in a seafaring costume? Like an old whaling captain?"

Uncle George opened his eyes. "My God," he said. "Yes."

"What did you dream?"

"I can't remember. But he was a mean bastard—" He shivered and took another swallow of his drink. "How did you know that?" he asked.

"It was a guess."

"A damn good one."

"But it could be the same person who's been throwing beer steins at you."

Uncle George stared at him, finished his drink, and held out the glass. "I'm getting out of here," he said. "Give me one more and I'll go."

"You're not going anywhere," said Powell, taking the glass. "You stay where you are."

"Don't give me any lip. Just make me a drink."

Powell went down, and made two more drinks, and when he got back Uncle George was half dressed. "I'll give you this on one condition," Powell said.

"What's that?" said Uncle George, stepping briskly into his trousers.

"That you don't leave today."

"I'll leave when I please. Now, give me the drink."

"Then at least wait till Kathryn gets back."

"All right. I ought to say goodbye to her, anyway. Apologize for being such a horse's ass."

Powell handed him the drink knowing that, in his weakened condition, it would probably stretch him flat within ten minutes. "Here you are," he said. "Why don't we go downstairs and have a little chat?"

He had underestimated Uncle George's stamina. When Kathryn got back, shortly before noon, they had finished one bottle of Scotch and were starting on another, and Uncle George seemed, if anything, to be getting stronger. Kathryn came in the kitchen door, her arms full of groceries, and stopped in mute amazement at the sight of the two men at the kitchen table, with a bottle between them, shooting Steve's air pistol at a dustpan propped in the sink. The dustpan was pocked with pellet marks, as was the wall surrounding the sink, and the floor was littered with bits of misshapen lead. "Got him!" Uncle George shouted as Kathryn came in. "Got the sonofabitch right between the eyes!" He recocked the pistol and handed it to Powell.

Powell looked around and saw Kathryn. "Oh, hello, dear," he said. "Back so soon?"

"Yes," said Kathryn. "Where's the war?"

"We're just having a little fun," Powell replied. "Something to kill the time on a foggy day." He aimed at the dustpan, the pistol made a sharp crack, and a pellet clanged into the sink. "Low," he said, recocking the pistol and handing it back.

Holding the pistol pointed at the ceiling, Uncle George looked at Kathryn. His eyes were glassy and his speech was slow, but he was coherent and under control. He spoke very precisely. "Kathryn, my dear," he said, "your husband is one of the greatest men in the world. He saved my life this morning; he literally saved my life."

"It was nothing," said Powell. "Go ahead and shoot—it's your turn."

"Not until I've had my say," pronounced Uncle George. "I am going to have my say, and nobody is going to stop me. Kathryn, I want to apologize for being such a monumental horse's—for being such an arrogant boor, and inflicting myself upon you and your family. It was thoughtless and unkind of me, and I am here now only because I promised to say goodbye to you. I shall be out of your sight before daybreak."

"Don't go," said Powell. "I haven't had so much fun in years. Besides, day's already broke."

"I mean that," Uncle George said to Kathryn. "By sundown you will have seen the last of me."

"Shut up and shoot the gun," said Powell. "I've got a shot I want to try."

"Do you think all this shooting is wise?" Kathryn asked.

"Aside from the damage you're doing to the wall, mightn't you possibly puncture each other?"

"Brought up with guns all my life," said Uncle George. "Can handle a gun as well as my own toothbrush." The pistol cracked, and a pellet drilled into the ceiling.

"So I see," said Kathryn. "But if I were you I'd keep it out of my mouth."

"It slipped," said Uncle George. "The sonofabitch is slippery."

Looking at her husband, Kathryn said, "Is there some easy explanation for this, or should we wait till later?"

"It's easy, all right," Powell replied. "I found Uncle George hanging from the rafters in the cupola."

"And he cut me down," said Uncle George. "Whipped out his Bowie knife and cut me down, with no more than a fraction of a second to spare. Another instant and I'd have been a goner."

"I see," said Kathryn. "In other words, it's complicated."

"You may think I'm kidding," said Powell. "I'm not."

"Is it all right to ask who hung him there?"

"We don't know, but we know whom to suspect."

"And?"

"Ebenezer. Ebenezer Twitchell."

Kathryn turned back to the door. "There are more groceries in the car," she said, "if either of you feels he can make it that far." Then she went out.

"She doesn't believe us," said Powell. "She thinks we're kidding."

"If I show her my neck she'll believe us," said Uncle George. "Let's help with the groceries."

They went out, jostling and laughing, and each one took a bag from the car. The bottom of Powell's bag was wet, and came apart the moment he lifted it, and there was a cascade of two dozen oranges, a bunch of celery, five boxes of frozen food, and a dozen peaches. They bumped and rolled and scattered around the driveway, and Uncle George laughed so hard he put his thumb through the box of eggs he was carrying. Kathryn began to laugh, too, and as she helped Powell retrieve his groceries she said, in a half whisper, "What *happened?* What's this all about?"

"Uncle George," said Powell, grappling with the wet boxes of frozen food, "take your thumb out of the eggs, and show Kathryn your neck."

Holding the dripping box of eggs in one hand, Uncle George loosened his collar with the other, and Kathryn gasped as she saw the red scar.

"You see?" said Powell. "You'd have a drink, too, if you'd been hanging from the rafters."

Kathryn was quiet as they collected the rest of the food, and when they finally had it all in the kitchen she said, "Well, now. What would you like for lunch?"

"Lunch is on me," said Uncle George. "Let's all go to the Ritz."

"That's a great idea," said Powell. "Should we change, or go as we are?"

"Let's have a drink first," Uncle George replied. "We can decide the formalities later. Kathryn, my dear, will you join us?"

"Isn't it a little far away?" Kathryn said cautiously. "It'll be kind of late when we get there."

"It's never late. We'll take a suite, and order from room service."

Kathryn, who knew better than to say a flat "no" in the circumstances, said, "That sounds fine. Let's have a drink first, and see how we feel."

"Splendid!" said Uncle George. "Bartender, another round of the same!"

He and Powell refilled their glasses, and Kathryn made a

short one for herself, which she sipped as she straightened up the kitchen. Powell and Uncle George went into Steve's room and began to play the phonograph, and by the time Kathryn had put away the groceries, swept up the stray pellets, and put the gun safely out of reach, she realized that the phonograph had stopped, and no sound was coming from the next room. She looked in, and saw Powell and Uncle George asleep on the bed, their arms and legs intertwined as though they had been shot in the middle of some mad dance. Quietly, she closed the door, and after making herself a cottage cheese salad, she took it into the living room and began to address the invitations to the party.

Eighteen.

By midafternoon the fog had lifted, and Kathryn decided to walk into town to mail the invitations. There was no sound from the back of the house, so she wrote a note and left it on the kitchen table, and she was just going out the door when she heard an automobile approaching, and saw a battered black sedan come up and stop in the driveway. A small man, wearing a high collar and derby hat, got out and came toward her.

"Mrs. Powell?" he said, lifting his hat.

"Yes," said Kathryn.

"My card," he said, producing a slightly crinkled business card. She took it, and read: "Dr. Hector O'Connor-Magician. Prophycist. Exorcist. All Ghostly Apparitions Expelled Forever. Fee Nominal."

Kathryn smiled and handed the card back to him. "What can I do for you?" she said.

"I think it's I who can do for you," he replied, speaking with a faint Irish accent. "I understand you're troubled with ghosts."

"Who told you that?"

"I'm not at liberty to divulge my business contacts, but I

have it on excellent authority that this house is fairly crawling with ghosts. Three of them, in fact—two benign, and one malignant." Kathryn started to speak, but he held up his hand and continued, "Before you say anything, let me show you my credentials." Reaching in an inside pocket, he produced an envelope full of yellowing newspaper clippings, and as he handed them to her he said, "These are all cases where I have successfully exorcized the resident ghosts. Castle Ballyshane, in Killarney; the bloody stones of Kerrigan's Keep, perhaps my greatest triumph; the screaming woman of Holly Loch, who for twelve hundred years had defied all efforts to lay her —to use the technical expression—and on this side of the water I've had unusual success in the old mansions of the South, known far and wide for their ghosts. All these you'll see in the press cuttings, if you'll but take the trouble to read them."

Kathryn riffled through the clippings and was about to hand them back when an idea occurred to her. "Wait here a minute," she said. "I'll talk to my husband." She gave him the envelope and went into the house, and quietly opened the door to Steve's room. Being careful not to wake Uncle George, she shook Powell's shoulder and whispered, "Steven, wake up!"

Powell opened one red eye, and looked at her. "Hmf?" he said. "What time is it?"

"Wake up!" said Kathryn. "The man is here to lay the ghosts!"

Powell opened both eyes and struggled to a sitting position, and Uncle George groaned. Powell looked at him without recognition, then got to his feet and staggered into the kitchen. "What did you say?" he asked hoarsely.

"I said the man is here to lay the ghosts," Kathryn repeated as she closed the door. "He's an exorcist. He's right outside."

Powell went to the sink and splashed cold water on his face, then combed his fingers through his hair. He ran his tongue around his mouth and tried to swallow, but the effort bogged down about halfway through, and he gave it up. "Who sent him?" he asked.

"He won't say. But he says we've got three ghosts, and that he can get rid of them—he's got clippings to prove it."

"He's right about the first part," said Powell. Then he looked at her sharply, and said, "You're not kidding me, are you?"

"Of course not! Come outside if you don't believe me."

"Let me get a beer first." He reached in the refrigerator, opened a can of beer, and followed her out to the driveway, where Dr. Hector O'Connor was waiting, Dr. O'Connor raised his hat, and Powell nodded.

"Would you tell my husband what you told me?" Kathryn asked, and Dr. O'Connor repeated his spiel, producing the card and envelope as evidence.

"Well, I don't know what we can lose," Powell said at last. "How much is this nominal fee?"

"I usually ask twenty-five dollars, but seeing as how you have three ghosts I'm afraid it should be a wee bit higher. Should we say fifty for the three?"

Powell handed the papers back. "No," he said. "Too much."

"If he gets rid of them, wouldn't it be worth it?" Kathryn asked, and Powell looked at her with interest.

"Since when have you believed in them?" he said.

"Never mind. Wouldn't it be worth it?"

"No." He couldn't understand Kathryn's position, and he suspected a trick. Was she just putting this on for his benefit, or what? Until he knew, he was reluctant to pay a lot of money. "Thirty for the three," he said. "And not a nickel more."

Dr. O'Connor sighed. "All right," he said. "But I'm losing money."

"So am I," replied Powell, "until I see if it really works."

Dr. O'Connor drew himself up and his blue eyes snapped. "I never fail," he said. "Ever."

"O.K. Then go to it."

Dr. O'Connor went to his car and opened a leather bag, out of which he took a black robe and a stole with various designs embroidered on it. He put on the robe and the stole, then from the bag produced three sections of a pole, which he fitted together like a fishing rod, and at the tip end was a gold cross. Then, with the pole in one hand and a prayerbook in the other, he said, "Ready on. Where are these ghosts most often seen?"

"All through the house," Powell replied. "From the cupola down to the cellar."

Dr. O'Connor nodded resignedly, and followed them into the house. As they passed through the living room, he said, "I can see this would be a fine place for them."

"Oddly enough," replied Powell, "it's the only room in which they haven't been seen." Then, as an afterthought, he said, "There have been some poltergeists, though."

Dr. O'Connor stopped. "Poltergeists weren't in the deal," he said. "I'm not going to be after exorcizing three ghosts *and* a poltergeist, all for thirty dollars."

"Never mind the poltergeist," said Powell. "I rather like him."

They went up to the cupola, where the sash to Uncle George's dressing gown still lay on the overturned chair. Powell retrieved it and glanced at Kathryn, and it seemed to him that she was paler than usual. There are a few things we're going to have to clear up later, he thought. There's a lot going on here I don't understand.

"Now, then," said Dr. O'Connor. "If you don't mind, I'd prefer to work alone. If you'd be so kind as to wait for me downstairs, you can show me where the cellar is after I've been through the other rooms. Will that be satisfactory?"

"Perfectly," said Powell, and he and Kathryn descended the stairs. As they went, they heard Dr. O'Connor muttering: "I adjure thee, O serpent of old, by the Judge of the living and the dead; by the Creator of the world who hath power to cast into hell, that thou depart forthwith from this house. He that commands thee, accursed demon, is He that commanded the winds, and the sea, and the storm. . . ."

"He seems to know the routine, all right," said Powell, as they went into the kitchen. "That much you've got to say for him."

"I think he's going to do it," said Kathryn. "I have a feeling he's going to succeed."

"Is it all right to ask when you started believing?" Powell said. "Last time I heard, you thought this was all nonsense."

Kathryn hesitated. "I went to the Atheneum today," she said.

"Why?"

"Well—for a number of reasons. I met your friend the librarian, and—and I must say she's quite impressive."

"You mean she convinced you?"

"Not exactly, but—well, wouldn't it be worthwhile if this man *could* get rid of the ghosts?"

"You mean my ghosts?"

"If you want to put it that way."

"Yes, it would be great. Where did you get him?"

"I told you; he just appeared. I had nothing to do with it."

Powell thought for a moment. It nettled him to be condescended to, and he had no real faith in Dr. O'Connor, but there was no denying it would be a good thing if the manifestations were stopped. "Well, O.K.," he said at last. "We'll see what happens."

"Now I'd like to ask you something," Kathryn said. "What happened to Uncle George?"

"Just what I told you. He says he went to sleep, and dreamed of an old man in a sailor's costume, and woke up hanging from the rafter. That's where I found him, and I'm inclined to believe him."

"He must be losing his mind. Could the boat have upset him that much?"

Powell shrugged. "Who knows?" he said. "All I know is I've got a spun-glass hangover as a result."

She smiled. "Two less likely drinking companions I can't imagine," she said. "But I must say you seemed to be enjoying yourselves."

"Transitory pleasure," said Powell sourly. "I'm paying for it now."

They heard Dr. O'Connor come down the stairs, still chanting, and go through the living room and library; then, as he got closer, they could hear his words: "He that commands thee is He that ordered thee to be hurled down from the heights of heaven into the lower parts of the earth. He that commands thee is He that bade thee depart from him. Hearken, then, Satan, and fear. Get thee gone, vanquished and cowed, when thou art bidden in the name of—" He came into the kitchen and started into Steve's room, just as Uncle George opened the door from the inside and appeared, gaunt and disheveled and in an ugly mood. Dr. O'Connor gave a little shriek and jumped back, and just missed spearing Uncle George with the cross on the pole.

"What the hell's going on here?" demanded Uncle George.

"We're exorcizing the ghosts," said Powell. "Stand aside, and let the gentleman pass."

"First time I ever see a man go after ghosts with a pole," said Uncle George. "What does he do—skewer 'em as he runs along?"

"Please," said Dr. O'Connor. "I can't concentrate if people are talking."

Uncle George stood by, glowering, while Dr. O'Connor repeated his chant in Steve's room, and then Powell unbolted the cellar door and opened it, and Dr. O'Connor went down and out of sight. This will be the test, Powell thought. If anything's going to happen, it's going to happen now. But all they heard was the muffled chant, and then Dr. O'Connor reappeared and gave a long sigh.

"That does it," he said. "They're all gone." He took off his gown, and began to dismember the pole.

"Just a second," Powell said. "There's one more place."

Dr. O'Connor looked up in surprise. "Where?" he said. "I covered every room in the house."

"This is a sort of adjunct to the house," said Powell. "It's a tunnel that leads to the house."

Dr. O'Connor shook his head. "That's not in the deal," he said. "Outbuildings and auxiliary entrances are another matter."

"For an extra five?"

"Ah, then. That will make it thirty-five dollars, and if you'll be so good as to pay me now, I'll do the tunnel and be on my way." He regirded himself while Powell and Kathryn got together the money, and then he put the bills in his pocket and rubbed his hands. "Now," he said. "Off to the tunnel."

"You people can clown around all you want," said Uncle George. "I'm going back to bed."

"If you'll wait till we get back I'll make you something to eat," said Kathryn. "You must be starved."

Uncle George sat down. "That's right," he said. "We didn't eat, did we?"

"We'll just be a couple of minutes," Kathryn said, as she and Powell and Dr. O'Connor went out the back door. Powell led the way to the edge of the cove, and pointed out the path.

"You go down there," he said. "And right at the bottom

you'll find a cleft in the rock. That's the passage that leads to the house, and I think you'll find it needs your attention."

Kathryn waited until Dr. O'Connor had started down, and then she said. "I went in there this morning. There's nothing there."

Powell stared at her in disbelief. "You *did?*" he said. "Why?"

"I met that young Dorple boy at the market, and he said you wanted him to tell me what happened to him. He did— although I must say he wasn't very coherent—so I decided to investigate. I went in as far as there was light, but nothing happened."

"Don't ever do that again," Powell said earnestly. "I want you to promise me—never!"

Kathryn shrugged. "I see no reason to," she said. "It wasn't particularly attractive."

"Nevertheless, will you promise me?"

"Of course, but why?"

Before Powell could answer, there came a series of shrieks and cries that echoed in the tunnel below; they became louder, and then Dr. O'Connor burst out into the daylight. He was wild-eyed and sobbing; his face was a mass of blood, and saliva frothed at his lips. He scrambled up the path, his tattered gown fluttering about him, and ran howling up the lawn to the driveway, where his car was parked. He started it, turned around in a spray of gravel, and roared off down the road and out of sight.

When Powell could speak, he looked at Kathryn, who was pale gray and clutching his arm tightly. "Now do you see what I mean?" he said.

It was several moments before she answered. "There's nothing down there," she said. "I was there this morning." She let go his arm, and started for the path.

"Where are you going?" Powell asked.

"I'm going down and look."

"You are not!" He ran after her and grabbed her around the waist. She tried to wrench free.

"Let me go!" she cried. "I've got to go down there!"

"Are you crazy?"

"There's nothing there! I know it!"

"Then stay here! For Christ's sake, stay here!"

"I have to prove it! I have to prove there's nothing there!"

She almost broke free, but Powell got one foot in front of hers and tripped her, and they both fell to the ground. His back stabbed him, but he held her in a wrestler's grip and talked into her ear. "Listen to me," he said. "Listen to me carefully. There *is* something there. I've felt it, and Fess Dorple's felt it, and God knows Dr. O'Connor felt it, and if you go down there you may very well end the way he did. I don't ask you to believe it; I just ask you to please, please remember your promise, and don't go down there. I love you, and I don't want you to end up a sobbing idiot. Remember— I'm asking this because I love you."

Slowly she relaxed, and after a few minutes he let go of his hold and helped her to her feet. By now his back was knotted with pain, and he stood up with difficulty. Kathryn was quiet, and her eyes seemed out of focus, but as Powell started to walk she noticed the way he held himself, and her eyes snapped into focus and she looked at him. "Are you all right?" she asked.

"I pulled my back this morning. It's O.K."

"It doesn't look it. Do you want my arm?"

"No, thanks."

They walked slowly, and as they neared the house she said, "I'm sorry."

"That's all right," he said. "Just remember your promise."

She said nothing, and they went into the kitchen, where Uncle George was sitting with a can of beer. "It took you long enough," he said. "What happened?"

"Dr. O'Connor ran into some trouble," Powell replied. "I don't think he'll be back."

"Your mistake was to pay him first," said Uncle George. "Never give a man a nickel until he's finished the job."

Nineteen.

Steve's birthday was a signally nonfestive affair. Powell had been put to bed for a week because of his back; Uncle George revealed an unexpected leaning toward dipsomania, and spent most of the time with a glass in his hand humming Spanish-American War tunes; and Kathryn, preoccupied with the general housework as well as the preparations for her own party, had little or no time to think of Steve. Then suddenly, the day before his birthday, she realized she had nothing for him, and went into town in a state of frenzy.

The first place she went was a sporting-goods store, and as she looked at the guns, fishing equipment, and skin-diving gear she realized she had no idea what Steve liked. She could always buy him records for his phonograph, but she wasn't sure what kind of records; those he played were the cacophonous sort that all sounded the same to her, and to get him the wrong ones would be worse than none at all. She thought back with nostalgia to the days when he was younger, and his toys were easy to buy and always appreciated. But she couldn't buy him building blocks or fire engines or airplanes now, any more than she could buy him an adult present like a tie or a sweater; he was in the in-between age where his needs and desires were his own personal secret, and no gift counselor could help her discover them. She gazed dismally at the assorted sporting goods, all of which might as well have been equipment for a nuclear physics lab as far as she was concerned, and she wished that Powell was with her. He still had enough boy in him to buy for himself and come up with something Steve liked; the air pistol had been his idea last year, and although Steve never used it now, it had been a great success when it was first opened, which was about all you could hope for in any present. A brisk clerk came up and asked if he could help her.

"I'm looking for something for a sixteen-year-old boy," she said without conviction.

"Yes, Ma'm," said the clerk. "In what line?"

"That's the trouble," she replied. "I don't know."

"Does he like scuba diving? That's very popular now."

"No," she said, thinking of the cove. "Nothing like that."

"Baseball, perhaps?" She shook her head. "Hunting?" No. "Archery is very popular with the younger group." She hesitated, then thought of arrows flying through the windows, and shook her head. "An air gun?" He has one. "Water skiing?" No. "How about croquet? The adults can use that, too." Definitely not. "A football? It's getting near fall, you know." She pictured Steve playing alone with a football, and almost wept. The clerk's earlier confidence faded, and he began to catch her depression. "What do his friends do?" he asked. "That might give us a clue."

"He doesn't have any friends," she said miserably. "I mean, not here. He does in the winter, but I don't know what they do."

The clerk looked as though he were going to burst into tears. "There's got to be *something*," he said hoarsely. "How about surfcasting? That's something he can do alone."

Katheryn had a faint spark of hope. "Maybe that's it," she said. "What does he need?"

The clerk hesitated. "That depends," he said. "He can

either get a spinning rod or a regular surf rod, and then"—he coughed slightly—"there are any number of different reels. It all depends on how much you want to—uh—invest."

"Are they expensive?"

"You can get a very good, serviceable reel for twenty dollars. Then the rod would be another—oh—thirty, and then there's the extra equipment, like the line, the leaders, the drails, the harness, and so on. The whole thing would run you maybe sixty, seventy dollars—not including the boots, of course. That's just the good, basic material. Naturally, you could spend twice that and more, if you want the best."

"Oh," said Kathryn. "I can't spend anywhere near that."

The clerk's shoulders sagged, and he cleared his throat. "Of course, we have *regular* fishing rods for much less," he said. "They're not for surfcasting, but they're perfectly good for pond fishing. You can get a nice, light rod for six-fifty."

"Let me see one of those," said Kathryn.

He took her to the back of the store, and produced what looked like a long, thin twig of red fiberglass. It was about five feet in length, and had a small reel attached. "This won't catch any swordfish," he said with forced joviality. "But it's perfectly good for perch and pickerel."

"What do you use for bait?" Kathryn asked.

"Artificial lures," he replied, opening a drawer that bristled and glittered with prefabricated minnows, frogs, and worms. Gleaming glass eyes stared out of clusters of barbed hooks, and Kathryn had the feeling they were all looking at her.

"Give me two or three of those," she said. "Whichever you think are best."

The clerk selected three brightly colored plugs, and dropped them into a paper bag. "Do you want this gift-wrapped?" he asked.

"I guess so," said Kathryn without enthusiasm, wondering how you gift-wrapped a fishing rod. The clerk disappeared, and returned a few minutes later with a long, thin box, which had been wrapped in orange-and-gold paper and tied with gold string.

"At least this will look festive," he said, attempting a smile. "That will be eight-twenty in all."

Kathryn paid him, aware that the wrapping was considerably more festive than the present, and as she was leaving the store she stopped and looked back. "By the way," she said, "you said this was for pond fishing. Are there any ponds around here?"

The clerk thought for a moment. "Yes, of course," he said. "There's a fine pond, just the other side of Cranton. Anyone there can tell you where it is."

"Thank you," Kathryn said, and left.

She went next to a record store, and bought a five-dollar gift certificate that would enable Steve to make his own selection, and then, feeling worse with each purchase, she bought him a pair of plaid socks and a necktie. These are no good, she told herself; these are no good and I know it, but he can't be without presents, and if I can't get anything good I'll simply have to settle for second-best. Then she remembered that the only thing he really wanted was an automobile, so she went to the five-and-ten, and for seventy-five cents bought a small toy car, symbolic of the real one. Happy birthday, she thought. Happy birthday, dear Stevie, and please forgive me.

The next morning, she had his presents at the table when he came down for breakfast. "I'm afraid these aren't very much—" she began, and realized he was already talking, and hadn't listened.

"Zeke said I could have the afternoon off," he was saying. "So I figured I'd take the license test this afternoon, then pick up the car after that. A guy at Mother's has a bag of bolts he'll sell me cheap."

"Can you take the test right away?" Kathryn asked. "Don't you have to practice first?"

"Hell, I can drive. And now I'm sixteen, what's to stop me?"

"I don't know, but I wouldn't get my hopes too high."

"Well, we'll see." Steve's eyes lit on the largest package, and he tore it open and took out the spindly fishing rod. "Well, hey," he said. "What do you know about that? Thanks."

"The man said it was good for pond fishing," Kathryn said hesitantly. "He says there's a pond over by Cranton that has a lot of fish in it."

"Well, we'll buzz over there and give it a whirl. What's this?" He next unwrapped the package with the socks, and examined them critically. "Cool," he said, and put them down.

"What would you like for breakfast?" Kathryn asked. "Would you like me to make some sausages?"

"No, thanks. Just a peanut-butter sandwich and a Coke."

"I've got orange juice all squeezed."

"O.K." He opened the necktie, dropped it without comment, and turned to the gift certificate. "Say," he said. "What's this?"

"I thought you might like to buy some records," she replied, putting the orange juice in front of him. "I didn't want to pick them out for you."

"Thanks. I may have to sell my machine, though."

"Why?"

"To get up the money for the car. Pop said he'd try to work something out, but"—he shrugged—"you know how it goes." He drained his orange juice and opened the toy car.

"That's just a token," Kathryn explained quickly. "That stands for the car you're going to get."

"Oh, I see. Sure." He looked at his watch. "Hey, I'm late," he said, rising.

"I'll fix your sandwich in a second."

"Never mind. I'll have something later." He started out the door, then stopped. "Thanks for the presents," he said.

"You're welcome," said Kathryn.

He went out, and as he bicycled to work he reflected that this might be the last day he would ever have to ride a bike. From now on he would drive, like other people, and have a car in which he could really go places. For some reason, the idea didn't cheer him the way it should; instead of being elated he felt progressively more depressed, and for a long time he couldn't find the reason. Then he remembered the pitiful pile of presents, and he began to realize the cause. There was something different, though; if, last year, he'd received a set of presents like that, he'd have felt let-down and cheated, but now he didn't feel anything as far as he himself was concerned. What he did feel, and it was only gradually that he realized this, was deep sorrow for his mother; he could see how hard she'd tried, and how aware she was that she'd failed. And, further and even worse, how rude he'd been. I'll have to get her something, he thought. I'll have to buy her something to show her I appreciate the fact she was trying. If only she hadn't tried so hard, I wouldn't feel so badly.

If he felt badly then, it was nothing to what he felt later that afternoon, when he went to the Motor Vehicle Inspector to apply for his license. He was told that all he could have was a learner's permit, valid only if a licensed driver were in the car with him, and that it would be a full week before he could take the test for a regular license. In the meantime, he was given a book of rules and regulations to study for the written part of the test. He bicycled slowly home, black murder in his heart and all thoughts about a present for his mother forgotten.

When he got back, Powell was sitting gingerly in a chair in the living room, and Uncle George was sprawled on the couch, humming "There'll Be a Hot Time in the Old Town

Tonight." Powell said "Happy birthday," and Steve growled a reply and stamped through to his room. Kathryn was in the kitchen, and when he came past she said, "How'd it go?"

"I've got to wait a week," he snarled, and slammed the door behind him. He dropped onto his bed and stared at the opposite wall, and then realized he was looking at the presents his mother had given him that morning. She had put them neatly on and beside his dresser, and they seemed to look back at him in mute accusation. Slowly his anger evaporated, and was replaced by the earlier sadness, and the backs of his eyes began to burn and he felt he was going to cry. The sadness fed on itself, and became worse as he pictured his mother tramping the streets of town, making tiny, ineffectual purchases in an obviously foredoomed attempt to give him a happy birthday. By now fairly wallowing in grief, he took the picture one step further, and imagined her being hit by a truck as she crossed the street with her arms full of packages, and he saw the blood in her hair and the crushed presents strewn about the street. This last was too much, and he got up and went into the kitchen, and threw his arms around her and buried his face in her neck.

"Hey," said Kathryn in surprise. "What's all this about?" He closed his eyes and shook his head, pressing her all the tighter, and with difficulty she turned around and took his face in her hands. "It can't be all that bad," she said gently. "You've waited sixteen years; another week isn't going to make all that difference."

He shook his head again, and croaked, "That isn't it."

"Then what is it?" she said. "Tell me what's wrong."

He paused, and realized he couldn't possibly tell her what had set him off. He had compromised his manhood enough as it was, and to admit he'd been having fantasies like a little schoolgirl would be unbearable. He turned and reeled back into his room, closed the door, and fell onto the bed. My

God, I wish I'd grow up, he thought. When you're an adult you never have problems like this.

Kathryn looked at his closed door for several moments, then went into the living room. "Did Steve say anything to you as he came through?" she asked Powell.

"Nothing intelligible," he replied. "He was in one of his black Irish moods."

"That's what I thought. But he's weepy, too."

"Probably been crossed in love." Powell remembered the dispassionate way Steve had discussed the local girls, and decided this wasn't the explanation, but it was all he could think of.

"If you ask me, he has a right to be sore," said Uncle George from the couch. "If ever I've seen a crummy birthday party, this is it."

"It isn't *supposed* to be a party," Kathryn snapped. "He didn't want one."

"Nevertheless. It's about as much like a birthday as a hog killing."

"If you can improve it, you're at perfect liberty to try," Kathryn replied, as her own eyes began to sting. "Anything would be better than what you're doing now."

Uncle George rose, slowly and unsteadily, from the couch. "Are there any complaints, my dear?" he asked.

"What was the story about your leaving?" said Kathryn, feeling her pent-up rage take control. "You were going to be out of here before nightfall, and that was some time last week."

Uncle George looked into the bottom of his glass. "It took me longer than I expected to recover from my—uh— shock," he said. "When you get to my age, that kind of thing can play hell with your system."

"Well, it plays hell with my household. *And* my finances.

You make a lot of noise about your money, but I haven't seen a nickel of it when it comes time to do the marketing."

"If that's all that's worrying you, I have a checkbook upstairs. I shall make out a blank check to your account."

"That's not all that's worrying me. Everything's worrying me—Stephen's back is worrying me, and Stephen's—his—

"Ghosts," put in Powell quietly.

"Yes, his ghosts, and everything that's going on, and all the upset, and fear, and suspicion—" She remembered the reason for her trip to Cranton, and went on, "It's got so I don't know my own mind any more. I'm suspicious, and confused, and I do things I shouldn't, and sometimes I think I'm going crazy. And to have you lying there, drinking rum punches and singing war songs and getting in the way, is exactly the last thing in the world I need!"

"There's nothing the matter with war songs," said Uncle George. "They stir up the blood, and raise the spirits." In a high, reedy voice, he sang, "Pack up your troubles in your old kit bag and smile, smile, smile," and moved slowly toward the bar. Kathryn whirled around and left the room. "Join me in a rum punch, Stephen?" he asked.

"No, thanks," said Powell.

Uncle George made the drink, measuring out the ingredients as though inventing it for the first time, then shuffled back and sank onto the couch. "Women are strange creatures," he said.

Twenty.

The next morning, Uncle George came down to breakfast early. He groped his way to the refrigerator and took out a can of beer, opened it, and took several long swallows. He looked at Steve, who had just finished his breakfast, and then at Kathryn, who hadn't acknowledged his presence. "I've come to a conclusion," he said. Kathryn said nothing, and he looked back at Steve. "And that is, I ought to contribute something."

"Whatever made you think of that?" said Kathryn, spreading butter on her toast.

"It just came to me," he replied. To Steve he said, "You're planning to buy a car, aren't you?"

"Yes, sir," said Steve. "I've got one all lined up."

"Is it any good?"

"As good as I can get for the money."

"Could you get a better one with more money?"

Steve looked at him. "Well, sure," he said. "Why?"

"Then get a better one. I'll put up the extra."

Steve's eyes lighted up, and Kathryn became confused. "I don't think *that's* necessary," she said. "Stephen and I have said we'd make up—"

Uncle George put up a hand. "Say no more," he said. "After breakfast we'll go down and do some shopping." He finished his beer, dropped the can in the wastebasket, and rubbed his hands together.

"I mean this," Kathryn said. "There's no need for you to—"

"I said, say no more," said Uncle George. "I have spoken."

Kathryn was quiet, realizing that after her outburst she couldn't very well refuse. She was embarrassed by what she'd said but relieved she'd said it, because it at least cleared the air. If nothing else had been accomplished, everybody now knew where they stood. She took a sip of coffee, then said, "Can I make you some breakfast?"

"Beer is all the breakfast I need," replied Uncle George. "Beer contains malt, yeast, and hops, to say nothing of the sugar in the alcohol. Any man who can't get along on that needs a crutch. Come to think of it, I may have another." He opened the refrigerator and peered inside. "Sonofabitch if we don't seem to be out of it," he said. "How could that happen?"

"There's a liquor store on your way in town," Kathryn replied. "You can get all you want while you're there."

"Very well," said Uncle George with dignity. "I shall."

As Steve drove, slowly and carefully, toward town, he looked at the gaunt figure of Uncle George beside him, and wondered what it felt like to be a millionnaire. He certainly doesn't look like one, he thought, and he doesn't talk like one, either. If you saw him in a crowd, you'd think he was just another skinny old man. If I get to be a millionnaire I think I'll be like him, so's not to have people pestering me all the time, like the Rockefellers. A millionnaire's life could be a tiring one, if you didn't play your cards right. Out loud, he said, "This is very nice of you."

Uncle George waved a limp hand in dismissal. "Nothing," he said. "The least I could do." He looked out the window and said, "What are you going to do when you grow up?"

"You mean for a living?" said Steve. "I don't know. I got the Army to think of first."

"Ah, yes, the Army." He thought briefly, then said, "There was a time when a man could have his own private army, to do what he pleased with. There was the life for you—any time you wanted something, you just called out your army and took it. A woman, a town, a country—anything was yours, provided you had a good enough army. Those were the days."

"Wasn't that a long time ago?"

"Unfortunately, yes. Once gunpowder became popular, then everybody could have an army, and it was no fun. Nothing is fun, if everybody can have it. Remember that, my boy —the only fun is in having what other people don't."

"Like cholera?" said Steve.

Uncle George glanced at him sharply, then laughed. "Yes," he said. "I suppose you could say so." Then he looked at Steve again and said, "I think you'll be all right."

"Thank you," Steve replied as he slowed the car. "This is the liquor store."

"Ah, yes. I won't be a minute." He was gone several minutes, and reappeared followed by a clerk who staggered under the weight of two cases of beer and one of rum. "Just put 'em in back," he directed, and climbed in front with Steve. "Now," he said. "Where is the automobile emporium?"

"Well, the car I was going to get is over at Joe's garage, but the regular secondhand dealer's the other side of town."

"Is there no place to buy a new car?"

Steve hesitated. "I don't know," he said. "I never thought about that."

"There must be. Let's find out."

Steve was in agony. "If you don't mind, sir, I think a new car would be—well, I'd rather not."

"In God's name, why?"

"Well, it's just that this car's kind of old, and it might look like—I don't know—showing off, or something."

Uncle George stared at him. "You mean you don't want to drive a better car than your family," he said.

"It's—I just don't want to look as though I was—was rubbing their noses in it, sort of."

"Well, I'll be a sonofabitch," said Uncle George. "Now I've heard everything."

"But thank you, anyway," said Steve. "Don't think I don't appreciate it."

"Sure, sure. O.K., let's go to the used-car place."

They found a 1958 Mercury convertible for what seemed like a satisfactory price, and Uncle George paid for it by check. Since Powell would have to sign the registration and transfer papers, the deal couldn't be closed right away, but the car was marked "Sold" and Steve was considered the owner. He ran his hands over the hood and fenders with a touch usually used on newborn babies, and his eyes were soft and adoring.

"All right," said Uncle George. "Now that's over, you can take me to the station."

"The station?" said Steve, coming out of his trance. "What for?"

"I'm going down to Boston. Some business I've got to take care of."

"When will you be back?"

"That'll depend. Tell your mother to expect me when you see me."

"O.K." They got into the family car, and as they drove to the station Steve said, "I don't know how to thank you for this."

"Don't," said Uncle George.

Suddenly Steve had a thought. "Hey," he said. "I'm not supposed to drive alone. How'll I get home?"

"Go straight home, and if anyone stops you tell 'em I told you to. Tell 'em I was taken sick, and had to leave."

"O.K.," said Steve doubtfully. "But I'd sure hate to louse myself up before I even get my license."

"You won't," said Uncle George. "If anyone gives you any trouble, refer him to me."

The railroad was seldom used, and the station was weather-beaten and dilapidated. Steve pulled up at the entrance, and stopped the car. "You're sure there's a train through here?" he said. "I don't remember ever seeing one."

"I've already checked," Uncle George replied. "There'll be one along in a few minutes."

"O.K., if you say so." Steve turned off the ignition, and settled back.

"No need to wait," said Uncle George, opening his door. "You go on back."

"I'm in no hurry."

"I said go back!" snapped Uncle George. "The sooner you get back, the less chance you'll be arrested." He got out and slammed the door.

"Yes sir," said Steve. He started the car and drove off, and looking in the mirror, he saw Uncle George walk slowly around the side of the station.

When he got home he told his parents what had happened, and they were mystified. "I'm afraid it's what I said last night," Kathryn said. "I didn't mean to lash out like that, but I suddenly thought if I saw him around one more minute I'd scream. I really shouldn't have said it."

"I wouldn't worry," Powell replied. "So long as he left anything here, he'll be back." He looked at the cases of liquor Steve had brought in, and said, "By the way, did he pay for that, or did he charge it?"

"I don't know," said Steve. "All I know is he paid for the car."

Powell examined the slip. "It looks as though he paid for this, too," he said. "Now, what do you know about that?"

"I really feel badly," Kathryn said. "I wish I'd had a chance to—" She saw the cellar door swing slowly open, and she felt a draft trickle into the room. "Now who unlocked that?" she asked.

"I didn't," replied Powell. He watched her go into the kitchen and close and bolt the door. She started to come back into the living room, but something in Steve's room caught her eye, and she stared at it.

"What's the matter?" Powell asked.

For a few seconds she didn't answer, and then she said, "That stain has come back on the wall in there."

Oh, God, Powell thought, I give up. They're after us, and sooner or later they're going to get us. If we've got a brain in our heads we'll clear out now, before something terrible happens. He started to speak, then realized there was nothing he could say, no excuse he could give for the fear that had suddenly struck him. He clasped his hands together and cracked his knuckles. All right, he thought. So be it. Just sweat it out, and see what happens. He had felt this kind of fear only once before, in a typhoon at sea, and he remembered it eventually had a numbing effect, so that you could live with it. You could even behave almost naturally, after a while.

It was more than a week before they heard from Uncle George. Then an air-mail card arrived, bearing the postmark of Guadalupe and a picture of lush, tropical vegetation, and it read:

> Got to thinking about private army after talk with young S. Possibilities in Venezuela and Peru; will let you know developments. Feel better already—Merkimer.

Powell turned the postcard over and examined it. "He must be crazy," he said.

"He's certainly been acting odd," Kathryn agreed. "Maybe the—" She stopped, and left the sentence unfinished.

"Well," said Powell, as he tossed the card on the table, "I'll be interested to hear how he makes out."

Twenty-one.

Once Steve got his driver's license, he came home to sleep and that was about all. Day and night, in fair weather and foul, he drove through the surrounding countryside, wallowing in the luxury of being his own master, able to go where he pleased. Kathryn would give him a marketing list in the morning, and he would run any number of errands provided they could be done by car, but aside from that his ties with home and family were severed as neatly as though he had joined the Foreign Legion. Even his looks underwent a change: he wore driver's sunglasses all day and sometimes at night, his left elbow became deeply tanned from resting on the door, and his hair was windblown and bleached by the sun. In addition, he attained a self-confidence he had never known before, and it showed in the way he carried himself and talked. He was now a man.

One afternoon, on his return from a jaunt to the New Hampshire beaches, he stopped at the local drugstore, more to see what was going on than for anything else. As he had predicted to his father, the local girls available at this time of year were decidedly substandard, but this didn't bother him because in his present mood his car gave him all the satisfaction a girl could have, and probably a good deal more. He could afford to take his time, and be as choosy as he liked.

He sauntered to the soda fountain, mounted a stool as though it were a motorcycle, then removed his sunglasses and looked around. At the far end of the fountain was a girl he'd seen before but never spoken to, a trim little blonde about his age who always carried a Siamese cat. She wore a boy's white shirt, and faded blue jeans that had been cut off above the knees to make shorts; her hair was in a ponytail secured by a rubber band, and her neck, as she leaned forward to sip her soda, looked as thin and white as a duck's. Her cat was curled up in her lap, asleep. Steve ordered a lemon phosphate, and tried to recall with whom he had seen her before.

The girl was aware of his scrutiny, and she kept her eyes focused into the depths of her soda by way of acknowledgment. If Steve had had more experience, he would have realized that this was nothing more than a gambit; if she had been trying to brush him off, she would have looked straight past him as though he weren't there. After looking at her for a few moments and getting no response, he swung back and inhaled loudly on his lemon phosphate.

The silence, punctuated only by sucking noises, continued for two or three minutes, then the girl put some change on the counter, picked up her cat as though it were a sweater, and started out. As she went past Steve, she said a barely audible "Hi," and continued out the door. Steve was flabbergasted. He didn't know what to say except a belated "Hi!" and by that time the girl had disappeared. He gulped the last of his phosphate, spilled some change onto the counter, and left the drugstore, reminding himself to look casual, and not to hurry. His attempt at an offhand stroll was more like a soft-shoe dance, but it got him outside at something less than a dead run. As it turned out, he could have taken his time. The girl had gone a few yards and then stopped, and with her cat draped over one arm was examining the display window of a furniture store. Steve headed for his car, which by coincidence was almost directly behind the girl, and he vaulted into the driver's seat and said, "Can I take you anywhere?" His voice sounded strange, and almost cracked.

The girl turned, and looked at him. "Oh," she said, in a small voice. "I didn't see you come out."

"Well, I did," said Steve unnecessarily. "I mean—here I am."

"Yes." She smiled. "That's a nice car. Is it new?"

"Well, it's a '58, but it's new to me. I just got it last week. You want to see how it works?"

She pretended to hesitate. "I have to be home pretty soon," she said. "It's almost suppertime."

Steve glanced professionally at the sky, as though reading the time, and saw there would probably be a good sunset. A cold, pale moon was beginning to rise in the east. "Plenty of time for that," he said. "We won't go far."

"All right, then." She approached the car tentatively, and he reached across and opened the door. "My name's Susan Tolliver," she said.

"Steve Powell here," he replied, imitating an Englishman he'd seen in a recent movie.

"Yes, I know," Susan said as she dropped into the seat. "And this is Yul," she added, as she folded the cat into her lap. "After Yul Brynner—you know, the King of Siam. This is a Siamese cat."

"Yes," said Steve. "So I see." He put the car in gear and started off, only slightly faster than normal. "Where'd you like to go?" he asked.

"I don't care. Wherever you say." She leaned back and looked at him, and Steve realized with a flash of panic that maybe This Is It. He'd never had a girl look at him that way before, but from all he'd seen in the movies and television, that was The Look That Leads to Trouble. Well, it had to come some time, he thought. You might as well face it now as later. He wondered what he was going to do, and began to wish he didn't have to find out, but it was too late to back away, and he had no choice but to go through with it. He'd be the laughingstock of the town if, now that he'd taken a step toward asserting his manhood, he were to chicken out and turn little boy again. The thought flicked across his mind that it was a lot safer and a lot more fun to be a little boy, but a chemical change was taking place in him that forced his mind into the background, and from somewhere a new and muscular man was emerging. I suppose in a few years I'll laugh at all this, he thought, but right now I wish it were over. I wish *what* were over? I don't even know what's happening. Then he realized she was talking to him, and he said, "What? I'm sorry."

"I said what's it like to live in a haunted house? Isn't it awfully scary?"

Steve shrugged, and smiled an attempt at a James Bond smile. "Sometimes," he replied.

"Did you ever see any of the ghosts?"

"Once or twice. It's not so much the seeing them as hearing them. Oh, sometimes there's blood on the walls, but that doesn't happen often."

"*Blood?* From what?"

"Nobody knows. It's supposed to mean someone's going to die."

"Have you seen it?"

"Occasionally. But so far nothing's happened."

Susan was quiet for a while. "You must be very brave," she said.

Steve smiled his Bond smile again. "It's all in how you look at it."

They drove in silence for a while, and then she said, "Where are we going?"

"There's a cove below the house, where you get a nice view. I thought we might go there." He reasoned that the cove would be as good a place as any, because there was always the sunken yacht as a conversation piece, and right now he was desperately in need of conversation. The more he became aware of her presence, and of the soft, perfumy smell of her beside him, the more his words tended to clog in his throat, and his earlier suaveness had disappeared in a turmoil of glandular activity. He'd never known a girl to smell quite this way, or to look quite so much as though she'd be good to touch, and his emotions were rioting around in an area for which he couldn't find anything like the proper words. All he could do was tremble, and try to maintain some semblance of calm.

The cove was in shadow when they arrived, and the moon had begun to glow in the smoky sky. Steve stopped the car, set the brake, and took a deep breath. She remained motionless, looking at the moon and stroking the cat in her lap. "A very lovely sight," she said.

"There's a boat sunk down there," said Steve. "If you look hard, you can see the mast."

"I heard. And a man drowned, too, didn't he?"

"Nobody knows. He just disappeared. Want to go down and look?"

"At what?"

"Well—the boat." Steve had no particular plan in mind; all he wanted was to keep things moving, and see what happened. He couldn't conceive of reaching across and trying to kiss her now, but maybe, if they were down by the water, or in the tunnel . . . well, he'd just have to let nature take its course. There must be a better way of going about this, but it was all so new that he didn't know where to begin.

"All right," said Susan hesitantly. "But I don't want to see a drowned man, or anything."

"Don't worry. Nothing's going to hurt you."

"All right then." Susan picked up the cat and opened the door.

"Does the cat have to come, too?" Steve asked. "Can't you leave him here?"

"Anywhere I go, Yul goes," she replied. "He yowls if I leave him alone, even for a second."

"Great," said Steve, without enthusiasm.

"What do you mean?"

"Nothing. I mean—it must make it pretty noisy around the house."

"No, because he sleeps with me and eats with me and even takes a bath with me. Of course he doesn't get in the water, because cats hate the water, but he sits by the side of the tub and waits for me."

Steve saw that the conversation was getting slightly side-tracked, so he pointed to the cove and said, "Here's the path, down this way. Take my arm, so you won't fall." He put out an arm and Susan took it, and when she touched him it was as though a small bolt of lightning had shot through him. He had touched girls before, at dancing class or when teasing them in school, but their touch had always been clammy and imper-sonal, and sometimes a little sweaty. Susan, on the other hand, had a touch that was charged with something wholly different, and although Steve couldn't define it, he knew that a big door had just opened somewhere. He guided her care-fully down the path, trying to sound calm. "My father and I came here one night," he said. "I want to tell you, it's pretty tricky at night."

"At *night?*" said Susan. "Good grief, why would you do that?"

"We were looking for Uncle George. We thought he might have hurt himself."

"You mean the old gink who owned the boat? Whatever became of him?"

Again feeling that the conversation was slipping away from

him, Steve said, "Anyway, I found a kind of cave down here that might interest you. Would you like to see it?"

"What's in it?"

"Nothing, but it's kind of interesting. You don't see many caves like it around here." They were at the foot of the path by now, and the shadows were dark and cold. The sky overhead was a slate-blue tinged with pink, and the moon became smaller as it grew brighter. The tunnel entrance was a black gash in the side of the rock. "Right over here," Steve said. "Take my hand, and I'll lead you in."

She let go his arm and grasped the hand he extended, and he squeezed through the entrance and brought her into the darkness. The cat, which had been lying limp across her arm, suddenly stiffened, arched its back with bristling fur, and with a sound like escaping steam dug its claws into her, struggling to escape. Its eyes were large and red, and its needle-toothed mouth was wide. Susan shrieked and clutched at it, but it tore loose, and with a long, moaning yowl streaked out of the tunnel, down the dock, and into the water. Susan followed, screaming and sobbing, and Steve felt himself propelled after her. In a matter of seconds, the cat, the girl, and the boy were struggling in the water at the end of the dock.

Powell and Kathryn had spent the afternoon working on plans for the party. It was to be a costume affair, but without any particular motif; guests had been told to dress in whatever costume was either appealing or convenient, just so long as it wasn't standard evening wear.

"I know what we're going to get," Powell said, when they were discussing it. "We're going to get fifteen pirates, eight beachcombers, and twenty-seven hula girls."

"We haven't asked that many people," Kathryn replied. "And besides, I know at least a half dozen who'll break their necks to be different."

"Like Liz McCratchney?"

"That was the hostess' fault. She insisted people come as they were when they got the invitation."

"And who opens their mail naked?"

"Evidently Liz does."

"Well, I'll be interested to see what she wears this time."

"Just remember your back, my love. You can't do anything strenuous yet."

"Of that I am more than aware." He yawned, and then, very carefully, stretched. "It's better, though," he said. "Another five years, and it ought to be cured." He stood up and sniffed. "Did you get new flowers?"

"No, but thanks for reminding me. I've got to get some for the party." She looked at her watch. "Also, it's time to put the roast in the oven."

"O.K., then. I'll get cleaned up." He went slowly upstairs, sniffing experimentally here and there, and took off his shirt and threw it on the bed. Then he went into the bathroom. The afternoon light was fading, and the shadows had begun to settle around the house, and he was just about to pull on the light over the bathroom mirror when he saw the reflection of Felicity standing behind him. This time he didn't turn around, but stood still and waited to see if she would move, while his back and neck tingled with little cold needles. She, too, stood still, staring at him in the mirror, and although her eyes were looking straight at him he could read nothing in them; they were blank and expressionless and cold. Finally, when he could stand it no longer, he turned around, and she was gone. He went out into the hall and looked both ways, but there was nothing there, and he was about to return to the bathroom when through a window he saw Steve's car, parked at the edge of the cove. He looked carefully, but couldn't see Steve anywhere, and then a sudden fear gripped him, and he ran downstairs.

"What's the matter?" Kathryn asked, from the kitchen. "Where are you going?"

"To the cove—Steve's down there!" He ran out across the lawn, and Kathryn followed. When he got to the edge he saw the figures in the water, and he ran down the path, taking off his belt as he went. Steve had hold of the hysterical girl, who had hold of the cat, and Steve was clinging to one of the pilings, unable to lift himself and his burden onto the dock. Powell threw him one end of the belt, and although it didn't accomplish much it at least gave him something else to hang on to, and when Kathryn arrived she and Powell were able to drag all three wet and shivering characters up onto the boards. It was a few minutes before Steve could explain what had happened, and when he had finished Powell looked at Kathryn.

"All right," he said. "What do you think now?"

Kathryn glanced at the tunnel entrance, which by now was barely visible in the gathering darkness. "Let's get back to the house," she said. "They'll catch pneumonia if they don't dry off."

Susan's teeth were clattering like castanets when they reached the house, and as she went onto the porch the soggy cat in her arms began to stiffen. Powell held the door open for her, but the cat arched its back and began to hiss, and Susan held off. "I guess I'd better stay out here," she said. "He looks like he's going to have a fit again."

Powell started to say something, then went inside and got a towel, which he brought out and handed to Susan. "Dry off with this," he said. "I'll get you some clothes in a minute."

"Never mind the clothes," Susan replied. "All I want is to get home." She would have looked eight years old, if it weren't for the small breasts showing through her wet shirt.

"Yes," said Powell. "I know exactly what you mean. I'll take you."

By the time he had driven her home and come back, Steve had dried himself and changed, and was sitting silently in the living room. Kathryn was busy in the kitchen. Powell made himself a drink, and then said, "I think we ought to get out of here."

"What do you mean?" said Kathryn.

"Just that. Pack up, and get the hell out. Go home."

"But why?"

"*Why?* My God, can't you see? Think of what's happened —the boat, Estelle, Fess Dorple, the ghosts—and I saw Felicity again this afternoon—Uncle George, the exorcizer, and now this, just now, when two kids could have very easily been drowned. I didn't mind it when the beer steins were flying around, but this is something different; it's getting progressively worse, and I have the feeling there's something out to get us. I'm not sure it *wasn't* Ebenezer that hanged Uncle George, and I'm damned sure it was he who almost drowned the kids."

"Oh, really," said Kathryn. "Get a grip on yourself."

"You get a grip on *yourself*. Face up and admit it—something's out to get us!"

"Nothing's going to get us, so long as we don't panic."

"Then explain the exorcizer—Dr. What's-his-name. What happened to him?"

"I haven't the faintest idea, but I assume he has a rather lurid imagination."

"All right, then, so do I, and I don't want to end up the way he did. I want to get out of here."

"In the first place, we can't get out of here because we have thirty people coming next Saturday, and in the second place the only way you'll end up in hysterics is if you talk yourself into it. Dr. O'Connor had a fit because he believed there were ghosts in there; I'd been in that same tunnel that same day, and found nothing."

Powell looked in at Steve in the other room. "What about it?" he said. "Did you feel anything?"

Steve thought for a moment. "I just don't know," he said. "It happened so fast. First I was leading her into the cave, then all of a sudden the cat hit the fan, and we were out and running down the dock. There could have been something pushing me, but I wouldn't swear it."

In spite of himself, Powell was forced to smile. "Let that be a lesson to you," he said. "Next time you take a young lady courting, get her to leave her animals behind."

"Don't think I didn't try," said Steve.

Powell took a deep breath. "All right," he said. "I'm out-voted. But if we all wind up raving maniacs, let's not say we haven't been warned." He finished his drink, and was making another when he smelled the familiar lilac smell, stronger than it had been this afternoon. He looked quickly at Kathryn, and then at Steve, but neither of them had noticed anything. All right, then, he thought, I'll pretend it's my imagination. If they can tell themselves there's nothing here, then I'm not going to be the one to make a fool of myself. This is all my imagination, and none of it is happening. There is a logical explanation for everything, including the figure I saw in the mirror, and the smell of lilacs is really the smell of the roast in the oven. Any fool knows that roast beef smells like lilacs when it's cooking. And lilacs smell like roast beef. It's all very simple, once you set your mind to it.

He finished making the drink, and when he lifted it to his lips he was annoyed to find his hand shaking so hard that the glass chattered against his teeth. Steady on, old boy, he told himself. Remember, you're the one who's going to have to stay calm.

Twenty-two.

The final preparations for the party took up so much time that Powell didn't have a chance to worry. The reputation of the house was such that it wasn't easy to recruit local help, and although Rabbit Warren agreed to serve as bartender, the problem of finding musicians appeared almost insoluble. Kathryn had thought that a trio of some sort would be nice, but local musicians were rare. Of those who could play an instrument, only one would agree to work the party, and then only if he could get off before midnight. Finally, through the librarian in Cranton, Powell managed to find three guitarists who were either innocent of, or immune to, ghosts, and although he would have preferred some other instruments he was not in a position to quibble. In recognition of her services, he invited the librarian to the party, and her eyes sparkled like fireflies as she accepted. "I think I'll come as Martha Washington," she said happily. "I've been having some very interesting chats with her recently." Then she hesitated, and said, "You haven't found any of the bodies yet, have you?"

"No," Powell replied. "Not a one."

"Good! Then this will give me a chance to look."

Powell began to regret his invitation. "If it's all the same to you, I'd rather you didn't," he said. "This is supposed to be a cheerful party. Besides, what difference does it make if you find them or not?"

"My theory is that what they need is a Christian burial," she said. "That will lay them, so to speak. If Ebenezer took them out to sea, then there's nothing for it, but if they're around the house somewhere, then who knows? We may all be in for a big surprise!"

"Do me a favor," said Powell. "Forget about the bodies, and concentrate on Martha Washington."

"Oh, I'll concentrate on *her*, all right. I'll get through to her just as soon as I go home."

Gloria Tritt reluctantly agreed to help serve the food and clean up the dishes, but only with the understanding that there never be less than five people in any room where she was working. Powell was able to promise this without reservation. The food itself would come from a local caterer, and the liquor supplied at a discount through the distributor to the Heart's Ease Café. Fess Dorple, whom Powell tried to induce to help with the decorations, refused flatly to set foot on the premises, so Powell and Steve had the job of stringing Japanese lanterns and inflating several dozen balloons. It wasn't until Saturday morning that Powell realized he hadn't thought of a costume for himself. "I guess I'll go as a pirate," he said resignedly.

Kathryn was still making last-minute arrangements when the first guests arrived. Dressed in a silver-and-blue Indian sari and wearing silver earrings, she whirled about the kitchen and gave instructions to Warren and Gloria, cautioned the guitarists against playing too loud, and inspected the utensils supplied by the caterer. To Powell she looked more beautiful than she had in years, and he reflected that, anachronistic as this party was, it was worth it for the pleasure it gave her. I guess it doesn't hurt to act young every now and then, he thought. You can put up with a lot of trouble if, just every so often, you're allowed to pretend it doesn't exist. His own costume was less becoming than hers, but it was comfortable, and it fulfilled the requirement of not being regulation evening wear. He was dressed in old white trousers and a blue-and-white striped sailor's shirt, with a red sash around his waist and a blue bandana around his head. He had rented a Civil War cavalry cutlass from the local antique store, and this flopped and jangled from his belt, occasionally swinging around and jamming itself between his legs. He intended to discard it later, after the evening got underway. He had briefly considered a false moustache, but some instinct had told him not to do it. False moustaches, his instinct said, get in the way of any number of things, and, besides, they tickle.

The first guests were George Henshaw and his wife, Muriel. Henshaw was managing editor of the magazine where Powell worked, and had been invited more out of duty than anything else. He was dressed as an American Indian, with a towering headdress, a fringed buckskin suit, and beaded moccasins, and he looked mean and miserable. Beside him, Muriel strode along in her squaw's outfit, and her step was brisk and springy. "How!" she said, as Powell came out to greet them. "This paleface lodge?"

"For God's sake, Muriel, knock it off!" Henshaw snapped. "Or at least wait till you're drunk enough to make it funny." Muriel glared at him, and Powell shook their hands. "Is there someplace we can talk?" Henshaw asked him.

"George, this is a party," Muriel put in. "This is no time to talk business."

"Might as well get it over with," Henshaw replied. "No point sitting on it all night."

All right, thought Powell, here it is. I'm going to be fired. Out loud he said, "Why don't we do it before anyone else gets here? We'll go in the library, and Muriel can talk to Kathryn."

He made two drinks, and then he and Henshaw went into the library and closed the door. Henshaw looked at the decor and shuddered, and his eagle feathers twitched. "Good Lord," he said. "How do you stand it here?"

"It's not bad once you're used to it," Powell replied, taking a sip of his drink. "Like anything else, I guess."

Henshaw cleared his throat, and from the sound of it Powell knew what he was going to say. The sentence hung, unspoken, in the air, but it might as well have been written in neon lights. Powell's mind raced ahead, knowing each word before it came out, so that he barely heard Henshaw saying, "This isn't a particularly easy thing to say, but you're smart enough to know we're trying to cut down our overhead. I'm not going to give you a long spiel because it would be an insult to your intelligence, so I'll simply get to the point and say that your job has become redundant. It looks fine on the masthead, but it doesn't shape up practical-wise. The fact that we've got along without you all summer is proof—this is no knock at you, mind you; it's just that your job was a phantom one and, frankly, not worth the money we were paying."

"I know," said Powell quietly. "I'm aware of that."

"Of course you are. You're no fool. As I told the boys in the business department, I said to them, 'Steve Powell knows the score, and he'll agree with us.' I said, 'I'll bet Steve'll be the first one to agree with us,' and by God you've proved me right. I always knew you had it in you." His feathers nodded in agreement.

"Thanks," said Powell, fingering the hilt of his cutlass.

"So that's that. As a matter of fact, the shop has already been streamlined, and the business boys are feeling happier."

"That's nice," said Powell. "It's good when they're happy."

"You can say that again. You've no idea the difference it makes, not to have the business and advertising boys bitching at me all the time. The place is getting to be one big family, which is how it ought to be."

Powell finished his drink, and looked into the glass. The ice cubes had holes in their centers, and the puddled liquid in them glistened. "I'm going to get a refill," he said. "You ready for another?"

"In a minute," said Henshaw. "There's one more thing. Now that our own shop is streamlined, the publishers are going to start another magazine—a small one, aimed at the cream of the reading public, so to speak. It'll be a prestige item, strictly a status number, and it'll probably lose a lot of money at first. But if it goes, it could be another *New Yorker*."

"And if it doesn't?"

Henshaw spread his hands, jiggling the tassels on his buckskin jacket. "If it doesn't, it doesn't. That's the chance you take."

"And?"

"If you want to be the editor, they'd be glad to have you. You won't make the money you've been making, but you'll be your own boss."

"Can I think about it?"

"Sure. They don't need an answer tonight, but they'd like to know pretty soon, so they can work out a prospectus, and dummy, and all."

"O.K. I'll let you know." As he left the room, Powell didn't know what his feelings were. He was chagrined at being fired, but relieved the decision had been made, and although it was good to be asked to edit the new magazine, he wasn't sure it wasn't a consolation prize. Still, it would be the first time in his life he'd been his own boss, and there was a lot to be said for that. He straightened his shoulders, swung his cutlass clear of his legs, and headed for the bar.

Several more guests had arrived, and among them he saw the

librarian from Cranton. She was wearing a tight black shirt-waist of mid-nineteenth-century design, and a full skirt. A quill pen was stuck through the bun at the back of her head. Powell greeted her warmly, and said, "What's the pen for? Was Martha a writer?"

"I decided against Martha because I found out she hated parties," the librarian replied. "All those official functions spoiled her for parties forever. So I changed my whole plan, and came as Harriet Beecher Stowe."

"I didn't know she was a party girl. I got the picture she was more the intense type."

The librarian threw up her hands and laughed. "La!" she exclaimed. "You should have been on those trips to England! A minister's wife has to unbend *once* in a while, you know."

"You've been talking to her?"

"Oh my, yes. The air has been crackling with visitations today. I can't wait for it to get dark, and see what happens."

"Well, I can," said Powell. "What would you like to drink?"

"Do you have any sherry?"

"I think so. I'll see." He found a bottle, and gave it to Rabbit Warren with instructions, then looked for Kathryn to tell her the news. But before he could reach her he was clutched from behind by Liz McCratchney, and he was relieved to see that she was covered at least as far as the basic portions were concerned. Clusters of paper roses adhered to her at strategic spots, and she wore a rose behind each ear.

"How do you like my costume?" she said. "It's called 'The Last Rose of Summer.'"

"You fooled me," he replied. "I thought it was 'Rosenkavalier.'"

"Silly!" She took a rose from behind her ear and threw it at him.

"My God, they're not *all* detachable, are they?" he asked.

"Find out, and see."

"Not on an empty stomach, thank you. If you don't mind, I'll wait till after dinner." Taking a firm grip on his cutlass, Powell moved off to greet the other guests. She's getting an early start, he thought. I hate to think what she'll be like by midnight.

Then he saw Dr. Martin Spellick, who had come dressed as a fig leaf. Kathryn had told him she'd invited Dr. Spellick, but he'd forgotten, and he greeted his old friend with surprise and delight. "Hey, Marty!" he said, shaking his hand. "It's good to see you!"

"Good to see *you*," replied Dr. Spellick cautiously. "How've you been?"

"Oh, all right. I could have used you a couple of times this summer; I've got a back that's trying to go out, but otherwise I'm O.K. Do you know any specifics for a bad back?"

"I'm not in general medicine any more, you know."

"You're not?"

"No. I'm in analysis."

"Oh, somebody told me that. How do you like it?"

"It's very interesting. Tell me, would you—"

"And better hours, too, I imagine."

"It's a full day. Would you say, everything considered, that you've had a good summer?"

Powell thought for a moment. "I suppose so," he said. "I mean, there's nothing either good or bad, but thinking makes it so. Five bucks for who said that."

"I beg your pardon?"

"I said, who said, 'There is nothing either good or bad, but thinking makes it so'? For five dollars."

"I haven't the faintest idea."

"Hamlet. There's a kid you should look into some day, when you've got the time—you'd have a field day. Excuse me, Marty; I see someone who looks lost. I'd better be a host."

Powell moved away, and Dr. Spellick watched him for a moment, then sought out Kathryn. "Well, I've talked to him," he said.

"What do you think?" she asked. "Can you tell anything?"

"Not without talking further. He seems to relate well, and has no surface aggressions, but as to his hallucinatory syndrome, I simply couldn't say."

"Try talking about ghosts, and see what he says."

"I'll try, but I can't promise anything under these conditions."

As it turned out, there were only two other pirate costumes besides Powell's. There was one Greek warrior, three beachcombers, one scuba diver, one Chinese mandarin, and several assorted costumes that resisted classification; and among the women there were only two hula dancers, one Marie Antoinette, three flappers, and one mermaid. In many cases, the identifying parts of the costumes were discarded by the time the food was served, so the over-all effect was of a group of people who had escaped from a midnight fire in an international hotel. The guitarists wandered about, playing melancholy folk songs, and their main effect was to make the people near them talk louder. Some people stayed in the house, near the bar; others went out on the porch, and a few seekers of solitude roamed around the lawn, where Powell and Steve had set up anti-mosquito torches on poles.

Inside, George Henshaw was talking with the man dressed as a mandarin, and discussing the effect of turbulence on jet aircraft, when suddenly the tail of his war bonnet was yanked around until it hung over his face. "Hey!" he said. "What the hell?" He spun about and looked behind him, but the only person near was Liz McCratchney, and she had her back turned and was talking to a small man wearing earmuffs and kilts. Henshaw straightened his feathers and turned back to the mandarin. "Who did that?" he said.

"Search me," said the mandarin. "I thought you did."

"How could I? I had a drink in this hand, and a cigarette in this."

The mandarin shrugged. "Beats me," he said. "It looked kind of funny, though. Maybe you should leave it that way."

Across the room the librarian was talking with the Greek warrior, who in real life was a literary agent. Holding her sherry glass in both hands like a wounded bird, she said, "Of course, the book first came out in serial form, but it wasn't until it was between hard covers that it made any kind of a splash. Then I had to write the key, which was a bore, but I suppose all in all it was worth it. I mean, when you consider the long-range effects."

"Of course," said the warrior, who had no idea what she was talking about.

"I hope the one I'm working on will be as good," the librarian went on. "But I suppose when you've had one smash it's hard to follow it with another."

"It certainly is," agreed the warrior. "Very few people make it."

"I'm not sure of the title, for one thing. And a title can be terribly important."

The warrior sipped his drink. "What's your title?" he asked. "Maybe I can help."

"I'm calling it 'Dred: A Tale of the Great Dismal Swamp.' Of course that's just the working title, until I find something better."

"Well, honey, I can tell you one thing right now—*anything* would be better than that. That would kill a book stone cold—unless it's a burlesque, or something. Is this a gag book, like?"

"It most certainly is not. It's deadly serious."

The warrior shook his head, and his plumes waved softly. "Murder," he said. "Absolute murder."

"The main trouble is it's too long," she said. "I wish I could get something simpler, like 'Life Among the Lowly.' "

"That's a little better. Why not try that?"

She smiled. "I've already used it, silly," she said. "And it sold 300,000 copies the first year, so I'm sure people would recognize it."

The warrior's mouth fell open. "A book called 'Life Among the Lowly' sold 300,000 copies in a year?" he said. "Where was I?"

"That was just the subtitle, of course. The main title was 'Uncle Tom's Cabin.' "

There was a count of about five, and then the warrior's mouth snapped shut and he stood up. "I'll be a sonofabitch," he said, and went to the bar.

Powell circulated among the guests, and from the increased noise level he could tell that the party was going well. The guitarists were almost drowned out by the general hubbub, which was a sign that people were having a good time, and as far as he could see there were no wallflowers, and nobody was stuck. There was one woman he didn't recognize, a plump blonde wearing a nineteenth-century dress that looked something like a smock, and when he saw her she was headed outside with the Chinese mandarin, a man named Selden Plaskett. Powell had a twinge of uneasiness, because Plaskett was known as a man who would take a pass at anything that walked, and he hoped the blonde was aware of what she was in for. He apparently needn't have worried, because Plaskett was back in a matter of minutes, with grass-stains on his knees and a look of stunned bewilderment on his face. As he tottered toward the bar, Powell smiled at him and said,

"What's the matter, Sel? No luck?" Plaskett, his eyes glassy, continued on without speaking.

As Powell passed the librarian, he heard her say to one of the beachcombers, "Of course, if there'd been any decent advertising, we'd have done better than 300,000," and the beachcomber, who was in the insurance business, said, "Why don't I drop around next week and explain this policy to you?" The librarian thought a moment, then said, "I'll have to talk to Calvin first. He makes all the business decisions."

Then Powell saw the blonde again, this time on her way out with a pirate, and he waited to see what would happen. The pirate came back even faster than Plaskett had, and headed for the bar. Before Powell could talk to him, Henshaw came up, his face mottled with rage and his headdress slightly askew. "May I speak with you a minute?" he said.

"Sure," Powell replied. "What's on your mind?"

"There's a practical joker at work here," said Henshaw. "And I don't think it's very funny."

"What's happened?" Powell asked, a hollow feeling in his stomach.

"For one thing, I just was goosed," said Henshaw. "It made me spill my drink all over that woman with the flowers."

"You didn't see who did it?" said Powell, knowing the answer in advance.

"There was nobody near me. He must have done it with a pole or something, but I think it's a goddam outrage."

"All I can say is I'm sorry," Powell replied. "If I see anyone with a long pole I'll throw him out."

"If this is supposed to be part of the entertainment, I'm not amused."

"That is one thing I can promise you—it is not part of the entertainment."

Henshaw glared at him and left, just as Dr. Spellick sidled up behind him. Keeping his voice low, Dr. Spellick said, "Do you know there's a woman here who thinks she's Harriet Beecher Stowe?"

"Yes, I know," said Powell. "She is."

Before Dr. Spellick could say anything more, Liz Mc-Cratchney gave a small scream and tried to clutch at the roses covering her left breast. They flew in all directions as though impelled by an explosion, and her husband, who was dressed as the scuba diver, looked at her from across the room. "I told you those damn things wouldn't stick," he said. Then her starboard roses exploded, and she dropped her hands in resignation. "Nobody will believe me," she said, "but this wasn't the way I planned it."

"Come with me," said Kathryn. "I'll get you a blouse."

There was a slight lull after the two women left, but it didn't last long. The guitarists played furiously, and soon the tempo of the party picked up to where it had left off. A glance at the sherry bottle told Powell that the librarian had drunk almost a pint, and he set out to see how she was doing. He came across her talking to the woman dressed as Marie Antoinette, while Dr. Spellick lurked on the fringes of their conversation. The librarian was saying, "You think *you* had a dismal childhood—you should try sometime being brought up by a Calvinist in Connecticut. If it wasn't for my Uncle Sam Foote, I'd have gone out of my mind."

"I don't know about Calvinists," said Marie Antoinette. "I just know it's all hell to be brought up in Sippewissett."

"Well, nothing is as bad as Kentucky," said the librarian. "I got one look at Kentucky, and that was what made me write the book."

"I wish I could write," said Marie Antoinette. "Boy, what a story I could tell."

"Try it sometime," said the librarian. "You never know what may happen."

Muriel Henshaw, perspiring in the heat of her squaw's costume, came up to Powell and said, "How! What's George so worked up about?"

"He thinks somebody's playing practical jokes on him," Powell said. "The only trouble is, he doesn't know who."

"I know a couple I could play," said Muriel. "And come to think of it, I may." She flapped her hand in front of her mouth in a low-decibel war whoop and moved off.

At the bar, Plaskett had been joined by the pirate, and the two men drank in silence for a while, neither one wanting to speak. Then the pirate said, "You went out with that blonde first. What happened?"

Plaskett closed his eyes and shook his head. "I'd rather not think about it," he said.

"I know what you mean," said the pirate. "I just wanted to know if I was crazy."

Plaskett drained his drink, and held the glass out for a refill. "No," he said. "You're not."

Somebody asked Marie Antoinette to dance, and Dr. Spellick moved next to the librarian. He cleared his throat. "How do you do," he said. "I'm Martin Spellick."

The librarian looked at his elaborate fig-leaf costume and nodded. "Pleased, I'm sure," she said.

"I'm sorry; I don't think I caught your name," said Dr. Spellick.

"Stowe," she replied. "Mrs. Calvin Ellis Stowe."

"Ah, yes." He cleared his throat again. "Do you live around here?"

She regarded him speculatively for a moment. "My home is in Maine," she said. "But I've traveled a great deal."

"For business or pleasure?"

"A little of each." She fanned herself with a paper napkin, and looked around the room.

Dr. Spellick edged closer. "Did I hear you say you're a writer?" he asked.

She nodded and smiled.

"Might I have read any of your works?"

Her eyes twinkled. "Silly," she said. "Of course. Have you forgotten 'Sunny Memories of Foreign Lands'?"

"I beg your pardon?"

"About my trip to England in '53. You must have read it."

"Of course, of course." His face took on a glazed, desperate look. "Anything else?" he asked.

"If this is a question game, it's my turn," the librarian said, with a faint edge to her voice. "Why are you wearing that revolting costume?"

Dr. Spellick glanced down at himself. "Actually, I thought it was going to be a lot hotter than—"

"It's not only suggestive, but it's indicative to me of a warped personality. I think you ought to see a psychiatrist." She stood up and made her way to the bar.

Powell went out on the porch for a breath of air, and Kathryn joined him and slipped her arm through his. "I think it's a good party, don't you?" she said.

He hesitated a second, then said, "Yes, I guess so."

"What's the matter?"

"Did Muriel Henshaw tell you the news?"

She tightened her grip on his arm. "Yes, and I think it's wonderful. If that's what's worrying you, forget it. It'll be the best thing in the world."

He took a deep breath. "I hope so," he said.

"You can relax and enjoy yourself, and forget about the ghosts. All that's over now."

"I wish I could believe it."

"It *is!* You haven't seen anything, have you?"

"No, but I've got a feeling."

"Fooey on your feeling. You're so used to worrying you just can't stop. Have you seen Marty Spellick?"

"I talked to him for a moment. Why?"

"I just wondered. He said he wanted to talk to you."

"It couldn't have been very important." Powell glanced inside. "Who's the blonde?" he asked.

"Which one?"

"The one in the smock. She was with Fred Lutchins a little while ago, and before that with Selden Plaskett."

"I didn't see her. Why?"

"I don't recognize her, that's all."

"I'm afraid I can't help you." She disengaged her arm. "Now I've got to be a hostess. Farewell, love, and please try to enjoy yourself."

She went inside, and talked with a few people in the living room, then decided to see how things were in the kitchen. She threaded her way through the guests, stepping over some who were sitting on the floor, and as she approached the kitchen she saw, very distinctly, Uncle George going out the back door. By the time she reached the door he had vanished, and she went outside and looked around, but there was nobody there. She suddenly felt dizzy, and returned inside. Get a grip on yourself, she thought. This is no time for *you* to start seeing things. A small flash of panic hit her stomach, and her heart began to beat faster.

Powell had lingered on the porch, looking at the sea. The moon made a white track on the water, and two or three dark clouds hovered near it, drifting across its face as though in some slow and stately dance. It reminded him of the Navy, and the long hours of the midwatch staring into the blackness, and he was in a reminiscent haze when he saw the figure of a man walking slowly up from the cove. It was tall, and lean, and although at this distance it was impossible to be sure, it looked a great deal like Uncle George. Powell stared in disbelief as the figure approached, and then a large cloud blotted out the moon, and everything was dark. When the moonlight resumed its pale glow, the figure was gone. Very slowly, Powell went down the steps and walked toward where he had last seen it, but there was only the wet grass beneath his feet and the sound of the surf beyond. He went almost to the edge of the cove and he called twice, but there was no answer, and no sign of any living person. He turned and started back, then stopped. Every light in the house had gone out. He began to run, and as he got closer he heard the babble of voices, and saw pinpricks of orange light where people had struck matches and cigarette lighters, and then a figure came rocketing out the back door, gasping and blubbering. It was Gloria Tritt, and before he could speak she had raced down the drive, and disappeared in the darkness.

Inside the house, everything was good-natured confusion. Powell found Kathryn at the fuse box, and with the aid of a flashlight they determined that both master fuses had blown, and there were no replacements. "That's great," he said. "I guess we continue by candlelight then."

"What about the mosquito torches, Pop?" asked Steve, who had been aroused from his bed by the noise.

"I think not," said Powell. "All we'd need would be to knock one over, and the whole place would go up." He paused, and added, "Which might not be a bad idea, at that."

Kathryn got out the candles, of which she had laid in a big supply after the storm, and in short order the house was glittering with their soft light. It had a much more festive air than before, and Kathryn wished she'd thought of them in the first place. The musicians resumed their playing, and three or four couples started to dance, and in one corner a crap game developed, by the light of a high-powered lantern. In the flickering light the people's costumes took on strange new forms, and their shadows jumped and writhed across the ceiling. Muriel Henshaw did an Apache war dance, and received brief but enthusiastic applause. A few people called for Liz Mc-Cratchney, but she had been sobered by her earlier experience, and refused to perform.

Kathryn wondered idly who the blonde was that Powell had mentioned, and she was surveying the room when she saw a man she'd never seen before. He was old, with a weather-beaten face, and he was wearing some sort of seaman's costume, a blue jacket and a peaked cap. He stared directly at her, with eyes that seemed to come from deep in his head. She had the impression he wanted to talk to her, so she started across the room. He moved away, still looking at her, and she followed him out of the living room and into the kitchen, where she was surprised to see him go through the open cellar door, and down the steps. He must have found something down there, she thought, as she descended into the darkness after him.

Powell was on the porch, and although he had never heard Kathryn scream before, he knew the screams were hers. They were high and searing, like those of a wounded horse, and he could faintly distinguish his name in the incoherent shrieks. He leaped through the door, snatched the lantern from the stunned crap players, and raced into the kitchen and down the cellar stairs. The lantern was wrenched from his hand, and it fell and shattered, and he was almost suffocated by the rotting smell of the cellar, but he made his way to where Kathryn was screaming and threw his arms around her waist. "Lights!" he shouted, to the people above. "Somebody bring me lights!" There was the pounding of feet, and several people appeared with flashlights and candles, and Powell dragged the struggling Kathryn up the stairs and into the kitchen. "All right," he said to Steve, who was standing white-faced in the door of his room. "You can get one of those torches now."

Gradually, Kathryn's hysterics subsided, and Powell left her on Steve's bed and, taking the torch that Steve brought him, went down to the cellar and planted it in the ground. Then he took the pickaxe from the corner, and began to attack the wall. He noticed as he did that there was a small bit of seaweed on the ground, and he was aware that the librarian was behind him. "He's in there!" she whispered. "I can feel him!"

"Then let's get him out," said Powell.

The others crowded around, shining their lights on the wall, as Powell swung the pickaxe and chipped away at the mortar. One brick came loose, and then another, and then a hole began to appear, and the cellar was full of rushing wind and noise. Finally, when he had made the hole big enough, he took the torch and climbed into the tunnel, knowing what he was looking for but not sure exactly where to find it. He searched both sides, striking at random with the pickaxe, and then he uncovered a brown, crumbling piece of bone. Scooping the earth away, he found more bones, and then a parchment-like skull with a few hairs adhering to it, and he said, "That's one," and turned to the other side of the tunnel. After a few minutes he found the other skeleton, curled up like a child in sleep and with dark brown crinkled skin clinging to the dusty bones, and he looked up and shouted, "All right, Ebenezer, you bastard, your secret's out! You've got nothing to hide!" His voice echoed down the tunnel, and as he flung the torch like a flaming spear into the darkness there was a searing, rending stab in his back, and he fell to his knees. The pain blinded him for a moment, and then he said, "What a hell of a time to have *that* happen." After that he fainted.

They moved out the next day. Powell went in an ambulance to a Boston hospital, and Steve and Kathryn stayed only long enough to pack their possessions and load their cars. It was a bright, crisp day, and the wind from the sea had a tang of autumn in it. Kathryn was pale and subdued, but she breathed the salt air with pleasure. When the last of the luggage had been loaded, they stood for a moment by their cars and looked back at the house. A limp balloon lay on the porch, the only visible leftover of the party.

"Boy," said Steve quietly. "And to think, I thought this summer was going to be a drag. I thought Pop was handing me a line."

Kathryn smiled. "Never doubt your father," she said. "He knows more than all the rest of us put together." Then she got into the family car, and started down the hill, and Steve climbed into his car and followed her.